HIGHLAND HEROES:

The Adventurer

HIGHLAND HEROES:

The Adventurer

JACLYN REDING

A SIGNET BOOK

FOR CHRISTINE,
A TRUE AND WONDERFUL FRIEND.
Give Zach and Jake a kiss for me.

SIGNET
Published by New American Library, a division of
Penguin Putnam Inc., 375 Hudson Street,
New York, New York 10014, U.S.A.
Penguin Books Ltd, 80 Strand,
London WC2R 0RL, England
Penguin Books Australia Ltd, Ringwood,
Victoria, Australia
Penguin Books Canada Ltd, 10 Alcorn Avenue,
Toronto, Ontario, Canada M4V 3B2
Penguin Books (N.Z.) Ltd, 182–190 Wairau Road,
Auckland 10, New Zealand

Penguin Books Ltd, Registered Offices:
Harmondsworth, Middlesex, England

First published by Signet, an imprint of New American Library,
a division of Penguin Putnam Inc.

ISBN: 0-7394-2967-1

The sportsman now roams o'er the Sutherland hills
And down where the Naver runs clear;
And the land a brave race had for centuries owned
Is now trod by the sheep and the deer.
The halls, where our ancestors first saw the light,
Now blackened in ruins they lie.
And the moss-covered cairns are all that remain
Of the once pleasant homes of Mackay . . .

Unflinching they bore the proud ensign aloft
When their foemen the penalty paid;
And the same noble spirit inspires them to-day
Their poor broken clansmen to aid.
The aged and weak they have sworn to protect
By the "Strong Hand" and kind watchful eye.
For faithful in friendship and valiant in war
Has aye been the Clan of Mackay . . .

Then flock to the standard and join the roll call!
Once more the banner's unfurled,
The slogan's been sounded, and kinship been claimed
By clansmen all over the world.
Exiled or at home, love of country and clan
Are feelings we'll never let die;
Defy and defend, stand true to the end,
And honour the name of Mackay.

—Elizabeth Mackay Bridge of Allan
Scotland, 1889

Prologue

There was a boy, who really thought of himself as a man, sitting on a high bluff, staring out at the waters of the sea.

The wind off the shore rushed across his face, a face that even at the youthful age of twelve already showed the rawboned lines and rigid slant of jaw passed down to him by his Gaelic forefathers.

He was a product of the land as much as of its people. His hair was dark, not quite black, but the color of the rich peaty soil of his Highland home. His skin had been toughened by the harsh north winds that blew across the moors, often with the fierceness of an arctic gale. His eyes, expressive and keen, were a mix of all the shades of green and gold and brown that carpeted the hillsides behind him, his body lean and wiry from having raced across the cragged hills all throughout his short life.

The rock he sat upon was called "Mackay's Stone," and fittingly so, for generations of Mackay men had sat upon that same stoop of granite over the centuries,

watching the twist and tow of this particular stretch of
the Highland sea. His own father, Artair Ros Mackay,
had been one of them.

The sky was fair, the weather warm, and the wind
teasing. The boy narrowed his eyes, shading his brow
with his hand as he tried to focus on a distant bit of
jagged rock poking its head out of the surf like the tooth
of an ancient Gaelic giant.

It was there that he watched . . . and hoped.

Would she come out today?

When the tide was at ebb, he could often see the ship-
wrecked corpses of Spanish galleons, Dutch brigs, and
English men-of-war. The bay was littered with them,
their battered masts sticking out of the water like the
outstretched fingers of the drowning. Through a natural
pull of the sea, they drifted along the sea floor before
coming to their final rest at the bottom of this bay. Some
of the ships, it was rumored, had even taken their treasure cargo down with them, and legend claimed that the
thousands of lost doubloons and pieces of eight that had
been scattered into the depths were the true reason the
sand on the bay's shore was so incredibly golden.

Was she down there, he wondered, *frolicking among
the slumbering hulks? Ducking through yawning port-
holes and gathering up pieces of Spanish gold in the
same way Scottish lasses gathered up bunches of heather
and wildflowers?*

He'd been sitting at that spot for hours, and for days,
and even months before that. Whenever he could manage to steal away to that same spot, and wait for her to
appear.

Just as his father had.

Scarcely a stone's throw off the south shore of the bay

stood a slender cragged sea stack called *Am Buachaille*, The Herdsmen. This high narrow column of sandstone, broken from the mainland by centuries of the tide's pull, was reputed to be the figure of a Mackay ancestor who had stood watching and waiting for her so long, he'd finally turned to stone.

She was myth.

She was fantasy.

She was celebrated clan guardian.

And it was claimed that only a true Mackay could see her, dance with her . . . love her. So he'd always known if he could see her, just once, he would know . . . he would finally be able to say once and for all that he was the one.

The real Mackay.

But it would not, it seemed, be happening this day.

Already the sun was starting to drift lower on the horizon, casting a twilight brush of shadow on the distant isles lurking to the west. Night was closing in quickly on the day, signaling that it was past time for the boy to go.

He got to his feet and began to leave, reluctant as he always was. Somehow he couldn't dismiss the fear that as soon as he went, she would appear, only he wouldn't be there to see her.

He took up the sack he'd left at his feet, a sack he'd filled earlier with the cockles and winkles he'd gathered along the shore and in the beds of the loch that fed inland off the bay. It was a tedious task, but he was always keen to do it, for it gave him yet another reason to come to the spot and watch.

Watch for her.

He walked two steps back toward the hills where he lived. The wind came from the west, a peculiar wind that rushed across the moor grass in a reckless swirl, embracing him, pulling him back. He hesitated, for on that wind he swore he'd heard a song, a siren's song . . .

. . . the song of *an maighdean mhara.*

The boy turned back to face the sea.

And he saw her.

She was even more beautiful than legend had promised she would be. Her dark hair blew on the sea wind like twisting ribbons of black, her slender figure poised upon the stony ridge that had been made for her, so that she might hold court with the fish and the gannets and the puffins.

She sat upon her sea throne, and looked at him.

He could not see her eyes, but he knew they would be bluer than the ocean depths. It was what all the stories of her had promised.

It didn't matter how much time passed, or if any had passed at all. His eyes never left her while his feet carried him forward until he was standing at the shore. So close . . . yet still so far. She held out her hand and beckoned to him. He stood, unable to span the stretch of sea that stood between them.

"Come to the shore, sea maiden . . . come and dance with me."

It was his voice, but he didn't remember having opened his mouth to speak.

She lifted her hands above her head with the grace of a swan—he took a breath and held it, waiting, knowing she would come to him and would bring back the treasured stone of his clan to him. He waited. In a flash of shimmering green, she dove into the depths.

He watched the water, his heart pounding in time to the tumble of the waves on the shore. He walked to the edge so the surf rushed across his toes, splashing against his bare legs, bitingly cold. His feet dug into the soft sand and planted him there.

To wait.

He would wait forever if he had to.

Just like *Am Buachaille*.

He saw the break of water, caught the flash of green that was her tail, and his heart began to pound, clogging in his throat because he knew she was coming . . . coming to him, and only to him—

"Calum! Calum Mackay!"

He blinked. He slowly opened his eyes.

But it wasn't the mystical mermaid who stood blocking the sunlight above him.

It was his foster brother, Fergus Bain.

Four years older and a good six inches taller, the fierce blond towered over Calum with arms akimbo, eyes fixed in a dark and utterly menacing elder-brother stare.

"While ye're aff sleepin' in the grass like a bluidy lamb, Lachlann and I are working our arses off pullin' stones outta tha' scabbert excuse for a field. And look! You hinna gathered a single winkle all the day!"

Calum scuttled to his feet. "Oy, I have! I've got a sack full of . . ."

Fergus snatched up the sack before Calum could reach it. "You've got a sack full o' naethin'." He turned it bottom side up and shook it. "Nae a winkle in it!"

Calum stared at the empty sack, and was utterly mystified.

It had been full just moments before, sitting at his feet as he'd stared out at the . . .

He turned his eyes to the bay.

The sea rock he'd been watching stood empty.

"Da's nae going to be pleased at a' when he comes back from Durness this e'en to find the supper pot filled with nae bit more than tatties and kail."

Fergus was frowning, but the spark in his eyes showed he knew exactly why Calum hadn't gathered any winkles.

"But I saw her, Fergus. I tell you I did this time! She was just swimming in to meet me on the strand when you called out to me."

Fergus looked out onto the bay. "Well, then, where is she now?"

Calum shook his head. "I dinna know. You must have frichted her away."

"Och, lad, you were dreamin' it, you were, like you a'ways are. 'Tis what Da gets for fillin' yer heid with all that clan bletheration when you were a wee laddie. I'm for telling you there is no mermaid in these waters. Nae a thing but dead broken ships and the bones of old sailors."

But Calum knew what he'd seen, and he couldn't bring himself to believe it had only been a dream. How could it have when it had looked so real, when *she* had looked so real?

"She was there, I tell you, Fergus. I know she was. I was standing at the strand just waiting for her . . ."

"But I found you here, lad, lying in the *machair*."

Calum glanced down to where the grass was still flattened from the weight of him. He shook his head. "It canna have been a dream . . ."

Fergus ruffled Calum's dark head with one great hand. "Och, lad, the sound of the sea is a powerful thing. You were sitting 'ere all alone with the sun warming yer face and it tempted you to sleep, 'tis all. 'Tis time to put it ahind you, for we've only anither hour o' daylight to try to gether up some winkles for tha' stew pot. Let's get to it, aye?"

Calum took up his sack in a swipe of pure adolescent frustration as he started down the hill above the loch, behind his brother.

Fergus was probably right. There was likely no more a mermaid in that bay than there was a pot of gold at the end of every rainbow. They were only stories, meant to while away the hours of long winter nights by the glowing light of the peat fire. They nurtured the Scots imagination and filled lads' heads with grand and fanciful thoughts. But Calum was no longer a lad. He was a man. It was time he gave up on grand and fanciful things such as mermaids and magical charmed stones. It was time he came to accept that, much as he wanted, he might never know the answer to the question that had followed him through all his life:

Just who was the true Mackay?

He knew in his heart that he was Mackay through and through, and that was all that should ever matter. So he decided right then he was never going to come back to that stoop and waste foolish hours, waiting and hoping for a glimpse of something that just didn't exist.

Squaring his lean shoulders, he went on in Fergus's wake, kicking at stones and swiping at the tall reedy marram with his fist. Until one last wind swept in off the bay to tease the trailing end of his plaid. Calum hesitated, for on that wind he swore he'd heard a song, a siren's song . . .

. . . the song of the mermaid.

Chapter One

"It is only in adventure that some people succeed in knowing themselves—in finding themselves."
—André Gide, *Journals*

19 May 1747
My last day in Paris.
The sky above the rooftops is bright, perfectly blue, and dappled with tufts of fat white clouds. I close my eyes and the air is soft with the mingling scents I've so come to love, morning breezes, roses in bloom, and baguettes just pulled from hot brick ovens. The birds are nattering beneath the shady boughs of the chestnut trees like ladies gossiping over afternoon tea. And I can hear the children laughing, playing at quoits in an adjacent courtyard, while somewhere, someone is performing a ballad upon the harpsichord . . .

Lady Isabella Drayton lifted her pen from the vellum page of her journal, and sighed. Springtime in Paris. Could there be anything else quite like it in the world?

Sitting in the courtyard garden of the house her father had rented just off Rue Saint Honore, with her morning *chocolat* cooling in a pot on the table beside her, she couldn't think of a single one.

For nearly three months—one-and-eighty days to be precise—Isabella had delighted in the French capital city. Her days had flitted by in a swift succession of late morning strolls through the Jardin de Tuileries, visits to the Louvre Palace to view the royal art collection, and performances of Molière at the Palais Royale.

And that had only been during the first week.

She'd very soon established a routine. On Tuesdays she sipped strong coffee at a window-side table in Café Procope, the quaint coffeehouse she'd discovered just off the Boulevard Saint-Germain where she could watch the incredible bustle of the city pass by. On cobbled streets scarcely wider than a footpath, carriages would careen at breakneck speed—*Regardez!* their drivers would shout, only seconds before narrowly missing pedestrians who would be left waving their fists, shouting a volley of Gallic invective against the retreating noise of the clattering hooves and churning wheels.

On Wednesdays she passed the morning with her letter writing and her sketching—in the garden on sunny days, in the front parlor that faced the street when it rained—filling a constant string of letters back and forth to her parents and sisters at home in England at Drayton Hall. Catherine, not quite nineteen and the eldest of the younger three Drayton daughters, had written faithfully each week, keeping Isabella apprised of the goings-on at home. In her latest letter, received just three days before, she reported that fourteen-year-old Mattie was apparently once again "in love"—Isabella had lost count of how many times it had now been—and that the youngest, nine-year-old Caroline, was simply refusing to accept that she couldn't ride her prized pet hog, Homer, in the sidesaddle races at the fair in Hexham, no matter how showy a step he might have. She'd evidently managed to convince their mother, the duchess, to it through sheer inexorable persistence. The duke, however, wasn't to be swayed.

Most other days Isabella could be found walking along the gay boulevards that followed the curving line of the sleepy River Seine. With its gray-green waters shimmering under the morning sunshine, she would toss chunks of stale bread to the swans and pause to look at the baubles for sale in the stalls of the tradesmen, which she bought as gifts for her sisters back home.

Sometimes she would stand, watching the painters who made their livelihood committing scenes of the famous city to canvas. More often she would sit and sketch them herself. Le Notre Dame, the Pont Neuf at twilight, the magnificent stained-glass windows of Sainte-Chapelle, she'd detailed nearly a dozen of the scenes herself so that she would always have them to remind her of her time in Paris, the most exciting time of her life.

If only Elizabeth could have been there to see it with her.

Isabella's eldest sister would have loved Paris, its sights, its sounds, even its smells. There was a vivacity to the city, that same *joie de vivre* that Elizabeth brought to everything she ever did.

For the whole of Isabella's three-and-twenty years, Elizabeth, now Lady MacKinnon of Dunakin, had been Isabella's closest confidante. She'd been her secret inspiration, doing the things, being the person Isabella could only have ever dreamed of.

When Isabella had been just thirteen years of age, she had fancied herself in love with the seventeen-year-old son of the neighboring Earl of Chilton, Kentigern St. Clive. He'd been everything she'd ever thought a man should be, very blond, very handsome, with a way of looking at her that made her blush to her eyebrows. But what Isabella hadn't known—and Elizabeth apparently had—was that a good many of the young girls across the whole of Northumbria had also fancied themselves in love with him. In fact it was a standing joke the young St. Clive only sought to improve by talking sweetly and smiling handsomely at most any young lass he encountered from milkmaid to noble miss.

Isabella, however, would discover the terrible truth of it on the very day of the same Hexham fair at which Caroline was so set upon riding her hog.

It had been a clear sunny day much like the present one, with the sky stretching as far as the eye could see. Isabella had been picking daisies along the hillside that overlooked the River Tyne, pulling petals one by one, tossing them to the breeze, and asking that same age-old question . . .

Loves me.

Loves me not.

Instead of the result she so very much hoped for, Isabella found herself stumbling upon her beloved wrapped in the arms—and very naked legs—of eighteen-year-old Maggie Flowerdew (more commonly known about the district as Maggie the "Deflowered").

Like most genteel young ladies, Isabella had been duly sheltered from the more unrestrained aspects of human temptation. Thus, she had never seen, would never have conceived such a thing as what lay sprawled before her upon that windswept hillside. She very nearly fainted at the sight of them. Oh, how she wished she had, instead of standing there like some pathetic mute, fighting to catch her breath, staring at them in maidenly horror while they scrambled to their feet, all flashes of white skin and hastily pulled-on clothing.

Maggie had giggled at Isabella's naïveté, thinking it all great fun.

Kentigern St. Clive had merely looked annoyed for having been interrupted.

When Isabella finally did manage to speak several long and terrible moments later, all she could manage was a single, tearful word: *Why?*

"You're just a child, Bella Drayton," St. Clive had said, with the clover into which he'd tumbled Maggie still stuck amidst his sandy-colored hair, and the breeches that had been down around his ankles yanked clumsily into place.

He might well have told her she had horns coming from her head and a nose that looked like Homer's wriggly snout.

Isabella had been humiliated to her thirteen-year-old toes. She had responded by dropping the daisies she had gathered so dreamily as she'd fled to the sanctuary of the Drayton carriage to cry herself numb against the soft velvet squabs while the rest of her family ate berry tarts and watched the races, utterly unaware that her heart had just been devastated.

All except Elizabeth.

She had found Isabella and had held her, smoothing her hair and taking her every youthful sob until after she had quieted and all her tears had dried. And then Elizabeth had done something. Something so reckless and so audacious, it was still talked about each year whenever the Hexham fair came around.

It had been a tradition for as long as anyone could remember that the final contest of the day, before everyone bundled their belongings and children together and headed back for their homes in the village, was the archers' competition. The local gentlemen's sons always entered and for three years running, Kentigern St. Clive had taken the prize. That year, however, more than just a few heads had turned when Elizabeth suddenly announced *her* intention to compete.

Disapproving whispers *hished*, rippling like a restless wind throughout the tiny gathering. To think that a lady, and the daughter of a duke, intended to compete against all those young men?

Shameful had been a word some of them had used.

Scandalous had been another.

But their father, who had doted on Elizabeth, on all of his five daughters really, from the day they'd been born, had given his consent. That was one advantage to having a duke for a father; a certain degree of impropriety could always be overlooked.

The targets were accordingly positioned. The archers, some looking unnerved at the prospect of competing against the daughter of the Duke of Sudeleigh, formed a reluctant line to take aim. And while Elizabeth didn't take the prize that afternoon, she did score her mark rather with a flourish, sinking her arrow dead at the center of a fat old oak—

—the very oak against which Kentigern St. Clive had been leaning.

For as long as she lived, Isabella would never forget the sight of the splendid St. Clive, frozen with shock, with the feathered butt of Elizabeth's arrow sticking at a near-perfect right angle from the tree—quite between his legs and not two inches beneath the perfervid crotch of his grass-stained breeches.

It had always been that way with the two sisters, Elizabeth the dazzling one, with her brilliant red-gold hair and flashing eyes, like a flickering flame, vivid and intense. Dark-haired Isabella had had little choice but to adopt the role of shadow, envying her sister for her spirit and boldness—wishing she could just once be so bold herself.

But Elizabeth was in Scotland now, married to her handsome Highlander husband, and Isabella couldn't think of a man better suited to her sister's fire than the imposing Douglas MacKinnon. He'd brought out a vulnerability in Elizabeth that she had spent the first part of her life trying very hard to deny, while at the same time celebrating her spirit, the headstrong will that made Elizabeth who she was.

They were a perfect complement to one another. And wasn't that always the way of it with love? A chance meeting . . .

Or a slipper in search of the intended foot?

Somehow, incredibly, they always lead to happily-ever-after.

Somehow, magically, Fate finds a way.

For some people anyway.

Not, apparently, for Isabella.

Her Paris holiday was to have been her adventure, her chance for her own encounter with destiny.

Her *last* chance.

It had been agreed before she'd left England that her father and mother would spend the weeks she was away considering a list of prospective bridegrooms for her. It had been Isabella's decision. It was, in essence, her way of giving Fate an ultimatum.

Isabella was a practical girl. She was nearly four-and-twenty, and unlike Elizabeth, who would have happily passed her days living as a spinster had she not met Douglas, Isabella had every intention of one day becoming a wife and, saints willing, a mother, too. She realized that her upbringing at Drayton Hall in the far reaches of Northumbria had sheltered her. Kentigern St. Clive aside, she had only a very limited acquaintanceship with members of the opposite sex. She had been to London once, but had been too young to do anything more than ride in the park in the early morning hours or go along to the modiste's shop with her mother, sitting quietly on a cushioned bench while the duchess had been fitted and fêted and fussed over.

So who better than her own parents to decide who would best suit her? Their own marriage had been arranged, and there couldn't be two people happier to spend their lives together.

It wasn't as if Fate hadn't had ample opportunity. While in Paris, Isabella had attended countless soirées and social gatherings, had been introduced to and flattered and even admired by any number of suitable gentlemen. French and English, viscount to marquis, while they had all of them been gracious and honorable and a few even quite handsome, not one of them had inspired in her so much as the slightest spark of feeling.

Perhaps adventure just didn't come to everyone. Perhaps some people were simply destined to lead quiet, comfortable, rather *ordinary* lives, without chance encounters, without the unexpected . . .

. . . without a mysterious gallant bearing that fated slipper.

Her parents certainly had. They'd had over five-and-twenty years of an arranged and *ordinary* life.

And now, it seemed, Isabella was to as well.

She let go a deep, slow sigh. "It isn't too late, you know," she whispered to the clouds, giving them a small frown. "If you've anything planned, dearest Fate, anything at all, there is still this one last day, this one last night before I must leave my chance for adventure behind."

On the morrow, Isabella would turn back to England, with a stop on the way at the French royal palace of Versailles. The duke and duchess had received a royal invite some months before, but her father and mother had been unable to make the crossing with her. So the duke had sent Isabella in his place, with his widowed sister, Isabella's aunt, Idonia Fenwycke, as her companion, to pay the family's respects to Louis XV and his queen. Isabella had been enjoying Paris so much, had been reluctant to leave it for the pomp and ceremony of the Court, she had put off the visit until she'd nearly run out of time altogether.

So she would stop now, briefly, as she made her way to the Calais coast, where the ship awaited to take her back to England. And then after tomorrow? It would be time for Isabella to return to her life, to her future in England—a future that would very soon include marriage and children, with a husband Isabella had yet to meet.

While the idea of a marriage did possess its own excitement, Isabella couldn't ignore a niggling sense of apprehension at the prospect of becoming a wife to an utter stranger. She certainly knew well the intimacies that took place between a man and woman. She had, after all, seen it sprawled vividly upon that hillside at the fair and had overheard enough cryptic comments made by her mother's acquaintances at tea. It had been Elizabeth, however, who had explained everything to her, answering her sister's questions honestly and with a candor that had left Isabella dumbfounded.

It had been just before Isabella had left for France. The two women had been sitting in Elizabeth's bedchamber at the MacKinnon's town house in Edinburgh. Elizabeth had come to see her sister off with the happy news of her expected child, due later that year. The announcement of it had tugged at something in Isabella, giving root to a new and unfamiliar longing. Isabella had always known she'd wanted children, but it wasn't until that moment, while watching the quiet joy of it in Elizabeth's eyes, that the *need* to be a mother had made itself known.

It was a yearning that had only grown since.

"It just seems so very *personal*," Isabella had said. "Doing *that* with a man."

"It *is* personal, Bella. Good gracious, can there be anything more personal than that? But believe me when I say it isn't just what you saw when you found that wretch St. Clive at the fair. It is much, much more than that. When it is with the man you are meant to spend your life with, it is natural and right and the most beautiful, most liberating thing a woman can experience."

"But how do you know, Bess? How do you know when you've met the man you really, truly are meant to be with? It's not as if there are scores of happy husbands and wives running about, all joined by fate and happy for it. Just look at our parents' acquaintances. There are just as many who are miserable as there are those who are contented. Even when you first met Douglas you had no idea he was *the one*. As I remember it, you thought him naught but some poor dim-witted farmer . . ."

"Bella, please, don't remind me. I was the one who was dim-witted."

"But you found him, Bess. Through circumstances that were almost unbelievable, you found the one you were meant to be with. You were one of the lucky ones. You always have been."

Elizabeth had taken Isabella's hand and squeezed it. "And so will you be, Bella. So will you . . ."

So will you . . .

"Bella? Bella, dear?"

A voice called from inside the house, breaking Isabella from her thoughts.

"Bella, are you there?"

Isabella turned toward the door. Only then did she realize that her eyes were wet with tears.

She quickly swept a hand over her face, blinking them away. She straightened her shoulders. "Yes, Aunt. I'm here. In the garden."

There came the responding swish of a heavily brocaded skirt. "Ah, there you are."

Lady Idonia Fenwycke was the elder sister of Isabella's father, although they looked nothing at all alike, except perhaps in the roundness of their faces and a slight squaring of their chins. On her father, this feature only lent to the overall impression of ducal strength. On her aunt, however, it gave an appearance that was unfortunately mannish, contrasting with her small stature and the soft tuft of white hair that frizzed from beneath her linen cap like the tail of a rabbit.

Somewhat empty-headed (Elizabeth often referred to her as "dim"), Lady Idonia had passed her time in Paris accompanying her niece and reminiscing about the days when she had been to the French capital city before, back when her husband, Lord Fenwycke, had still been alive, during the splendid reign of Louis XIV, the Sun King.

At times, she even convinced herself she was back in that time.

"Here you are, dear," she said, handing Isabella a folded and sealed parchment. "'Tis a letter just arrived for you."

Isabella took the letter, noticing immediately that it was addressed to her in her mother's hand.

Her heart gave a little jump as she stared at it in the light of the morning sun. "It comes from Drayton Hall."

The duchess had promised she would write to Isabella before she left Paris to tell her their decision of a husband for her. She would detail his name, rank, and any other pertinent information she could offer, allowing Isabella to spend the few days it would take to make the crossing considering their choice.

When the letter hadn't come during the previous weeks, and when Catherine had made no mention of it in any of her letters, Isabella had begun to wonder that the duke and duchess hadn't been able to settle on anyone suitable at all.

Until now.

Even as she turned the letter over to break the wax seal, Isabella knew that as soon as she opened the page and read its contents, her life would never again be the same.

So she hesitated, staring at that seal, the impression of her father's ducal crest, as if it had taken on the form of a Pandora's Box.

"Aren't you going to open it, dear?"

Isabella looked up. "Hmm?"

"The letter, dear. Are you going to read it?"

Giving it a last glance, Isabella tucked the letter inside the pages of her journal to mark her place. Then she turned to her aunt with a small shake of her head. "Not just yet, Aunt. Perhaps later. It is our last day in Paris and I wouldn't wish to waste the daylight. Besides, isn't it time for our stroll along the river?"

Isabella wasn't ready to give up on Paris just yet.

Chapter Two

There is a corner of Scotland far beyond the Highland line, some ninety miles as the gannet flies northwest from Inverness. It is a restless, lonely place, the sort where the ghosts of the past seem a handsbreadth closer to earth than to heaven. The winds of the north and the west and the east converge upon this spot in a swirling contest of wills, and the sun rarely succeeds in shining through the heavy shroud of murk and mist that seems ever intent upon cloaking it.

To the fleet of the Norse king Haco who came to this land back in 1263, it was called simply the *Hvarf*; to the ancient Gael it was known as *Am Parbh*. Both names, translated from different lands, designated the "turning point" at which seafarers for centuries had marked their way along Scotland's northern coast, to the south in one direction and to the east in the other. It was the Sassenach, however, whose unschooled tongue so often corrupted the languages of others, who was to give this place its present and more widely known name. In this particular instance, it was surprisingly fitting.

The place was called Cape Wrath.

Calum Mackay stood on that spot, at the very edge of the ancient land of Caledonia, on a red rock promontory that jutted out above an untamed sea. Cormorants circled far below him like leaves swirling on the breeze for he stood some four hundred feet above the level of the sea. He was alone on the windswept cliff, watching the sails of a retreating ship through the lens of his spyglass. The wind changed, pulling at the ends of his plaid and whipping his hair wildly about his face and neck. But he did not move, did not so much as shift his weight until the sails had disappeared into the mists of the east.

Were he to see himself reflected in the lens of that glass, Calum almost wouldn't recognize himself. He looked a good deal more like some ancient Gaelic warrior than the gentleman's son who'd attended university in Edinburgh little more than a decade before. His dark hair was long, longer than even he would have preferred to wear it, and the lower half of his face was covered by the scruff of a beard he used to conceal himself. His face around his eyes and nose was tanned from the sun and burned from the harsh sea wind against his hazel eyes. His mouth, set in a firm line, bridged a stern jaw beneath its bearded cover, a jaw that marked him as stubborn most of the time—and utterly uncompromising others.

This was a man who didn't often relent. Once decided, he could almost never be swayed from his course. This inherent defiance showed even in the clothing he wore for beneath his coat, he wore the kilt in shades of dark green, black, and blue, and he carried his father's broadsword, its basket hilt strapped around his waist alongside a brace of flintlock pistols that he kept loaded and primed should he be called upon to fire.

The English hadn't yet outlawed them, although it was said they soon would. But Calum wasn't concerned. For as long as he had a breath left in his body, the skirl of the bagpipe would be free to wail upon the wild wind, and the blade of the broadsword would forever flash and sweep to determine the line between right and wrong.

The laws of the Sassenach simply did not extend to Cape Wrath.

"They've gone?"

The winds had blown in so fiercely off the sea, Calum hadn't heard the other man's approach on the path behind him.

He turned, nodded, then checked the spyglass one last time to reassure himself the ship had truly gone. "Aye, just past Whiten Head. With a sturdy wind they'll be ready to meet Belcourt's ship afore it is in sight of the firth."

Malcolm Mór MacCuick stood like a venerable Highland oak, reaching a height that approached seven feet. His hair was a mixture of dark and silver and long enough to just brush his great shoulders. His face was obscured by the bristly growth of a beard beneath eyes that had seen more misery than anyone should ever have to endure.

In the muscles of his arms alone M'Cuick held a strength that could crush the breath of life from a man. Calum knew this because he'd seen the man do it. Couple that with the steely swing of a broadsword and the man was a veritable weapon of war.

Calum first came across M'Cuick on the deck of an English frigate out on the English Channel. He'd been in the midst of taking on a half dozen Hanoverian soldiers who were of a mind to clap the man in irons. He'd pitched the first of them overboard, the second through the door of the hold. Before Calum had been able to blink, M'Cuick was through the next three and was dispensing with the sixth by way of a head butt that surely had cracked the poor man's skull through.

It was only later that Calum would discover M'Cuick should never have been there at all. The ship had been a prison frigate transporting Jacobite prisoners to the Colonies. And M'Cuick had been no more a Jacobite rebel than that fat Hanoverian sitting on his stolen throne in St. James.

Malcolm MacCuick was a farmer, a father and a husband, who had made his simple living on a croft just outside Inverness. His crime had been nothing more than his proximity to the battlefield of Culloden, and a turn of events he could never have avoided.

It had been a frostbitten morning that sixteenth day of April the year before. M'Cuick had been with his son working the fields of his farm, struggling to force the plow through a sleety rain, preparing for the growing season not far ahead. He'd heard the report of the cannon echoing across the moor, caught the distant shouts of charging men. But M'Cuick had been determined to stay clear of any involvement in the troubles. The Crown, after all, had promised to spare those of its Highland subjects who refrained from joining the rebellion. No matter his political leanings, M'Cuick had a wife and young daughter at home, and his son not yet thirteen. His family needed him far more than the intrepid but wholly outnumbered Bonnie Prince.

The conflict, however, hadn't been content to leave Malcolm M'Cuick in peace.

The first wounded had begun arriving shortly afore mid-afternoon, hobbling on legs that had been splattered with grapeshot, some carrying, others dragging those who'd been too weak or injured to walk on their own. M'Cuick had always been what one would call a kind-hearted giant, and he could no more turn away the injured rebels than he could resist the beseeching eyes of his six-year-old daughter, named Mary for her mother, when she'd asked, "We're going t' help them, aren't we, Da?"

By the time the company of pursuing government troops had arrived, M'Cuick and his wife had nearly twenty rebel wounded lying on beds of soft straw in their byre. The English captain, mad from the massacre he'd just left, didn't hesitate long enough to listen to M'Cuick's explanations. They simply peppered them all, he and his wife and children, with a volley of musket fire before setting the byre aflame, burning the wounded alive.

But musket fire hadn't been enough to fell Malcolm Mór MacCuick.

He'd lain there, bleeding from a wound in his side, and listening to the screams of the rebels as they burned, listening, too, to the last struggling breaths of his son and his daughter, and then finally his wife who lay fallen beside him. He heard the laughter of the English soldiers as they'd looted his meager home, killing his small stock of sheep and cattle while smashing the dishes one by one that had been his wife's most precious belongings.

He'd been found two days later by a band of rebel soldiers who had tended his wounds and fed him from what few provisions they had. A week later, as they'd tried to cross the River Ness, they'd been overtaken by a government detachment who were out scouting for Jacobite stragglers, taken and thrown in a prison to await their sentencing and transport as criminals.

But M'Cuick's ship had never made it to the Colonies. As it had rounded Rattray Head on Scotland's eastern coast, it was overtaken by another ship, a ship the English crew later swore had to be a ghost ship, painted a ghastly gray and parting the mist with the call of the pipes echoing on the wind like the wail of a *bean sidhe.*

That ship, the *Adventurer*, was the same ship Calum had just stood to watch vanish into the east.

"Once they've got Belcourt's 'bibles,' we'll have that last piece we need," Calum said to M'Cuick as he turned from his vantage and started back down the path.

"All we can do now is wait."

The Palace of Versailles

Isabella stood at one end of the *Salon de l'Oeil-de-Bœuf* amid a mélange of posing courtiers—ducs, vicomtes, and painted comtesses, emissaries, liveried footmen, and palace guards. They all postured about trying very hard to be noticed, some voices droning in a cacophony of French and English, others in Italian, and still others in Portuguese.

Broad panniered skirts in colorful silks and satins caromed one into the other. Elbows, dripping lace, prodded unsuspecting backsides. Even the air was congested by a miscellany of scents—human perspiration at battle with bergamot, neroli, and ambergris—while hair powder drifted about velvet-clad shoulders like the first dusting of a winter's snow.

With each turn of the clock, the mob seemed to swell, until very soon Isabella found it difficult to simply breathe.

"I do hope it doesn't take much longer," she murmured more to herself than to anyone else, as she struggled with the cumbersome box she held. It was a gift for the king from her father, and it had been no easy task carrying it there.

She caught a glimpse of the palace gardens out a nearby window and found herself longing to step out for some air, even as she knew she daren't risk missing her name when it was finally called.

They had arrived at the palace some three hours earlier, handing the guardsman who met their coach the letter that would hopefully grant them an audience with the king. They'd been shown to the salon to wait . . .

. . . and wait . . .

. . . and wait some more while the crowd had only swelled, to the point that Isabella seriously questioned whether another person could possibly fit inside the room.

Just then she noticed the imposing figure of a lady, her skirts at least five feet in breadth, pushing her way through the overcrowded doorway like a beribboned battleship.

Apparently another person *could* fit into the room after all.

"Do you see him, dear?" said Aunt Idonia beside her. The woman stood barely four feet and ten, so Isabella could scarcely see her head even though she was standing on her toes and craning her pudgy neck above her lace neckerchief to try to see. "Do you see *le Roi Soleil?*"

Isabella turned, smiling in apology to a young courtier whose elbow she'd brushed. "Aunt, that Louis isn't the king any longer. 'Tis his great-grandson now, Louis the *Fifteenth*."

She decided not to mention that if by some stretch of divine providence the previous Louis were still king, he would by then be the rather ripe old age of one hundred and nine.

"Goodness," was all Idonia could say before a trumpeter's blast sounded out, signaling that the captain of the guard was readying to summon the next name on his list.

Isabella looked around the room. There was no possible way the king would be able to see them all. She began to wonder if her errand would prove a colossal waste of time as the door leading to the king's private apartments opened and closed.

Voices hushed. Necks craned. The room fell so silent Isabella could hear the grumble of someone's hungry stomach who was standing nearby. Suddenly, a voice bellowed out in French from the opposite side of the room.

"Lady Isabella Drayton and Lady Idonia Fenwycke of Drayton Hall in Northumbria!"

Isabella's heart gave a nervous lurch.

Heads began turning left and then right, searching the crowd for the stranger who'd been called. Some whispered. Others muttered, grumbling that they hadn't yet been chosen. Isabella quickly arranged the gift box under one arm, took her aunt by the hand, and headed off for the door, struggling to weave her way past the scores of others standing in her way.

Pardon . . .

Excusez-moi . . .

S'il vous plaît, monsieur . . .

It took several minutes and a great deal of effort, and by the time they arrived, the captain was readying to call the next name on his list.

"Non!" she cried out.

He gaped at Isabella as she shoved through the crowd. *"Oui, mademoiselle?"*

"You just called for me. I am Lady Isabella Drayton," she answered in practiced French. "And this is Lady Idonia Fenwycke."

The captain frowned blandly. "The king does not much like to be kept waiting, mademoiselle."

"Yes, I'm certain but I—"

He spun on his heel and marched through the door.

"Oh, no." Isabella looked at her aunt. "We were too late getting through the crowd. Now we'll never get to see—"

"Mademoiselle," whispered a palace guardsman who stood like a statue to one side of the door. He motioned with a quick shake of with his periwigged head. "You are to follow the captain inside."

Isabella smiled at him. "Oh, thank you so very—"

"Mademoiselle Drayton."

The captain had reappeared, looking quite annoyed with her. "Do you or do you not wish to see the King of France this morning?"

"I do. I do," she said again and hastened to meet him, quickly dragging Idonia behind her.

The captain didn't say a word as he ushered them through a series of at least a half dozen different chambers, each more elegant than the last. Walls were papered in rich red silk beneath gleaming gold and sparkling chandeliers. Their footsteps echoed on floors tiled in gleaming black and white marble. It was quite like entering the gates of Olympus and leaving the mortal world behind; indeed the rooms reflected that same notion as they passed through chambers named for Venus, Diana, Mars, and Mercury, each with scenes of their divine namesake emblazoned across the lofty ceilings.

They arrived at the most magnificent chamber of them all, the Apollo Salon, which served as the king's throne room. As she came through the doorway, Isabella found herself pausing to stare; it was impossible not to. What lay before her quite literally took her breath away.

The walls were covered with gold and silver silk that shimmered beneath the lights of the chandeliers. Gilded candelabras in the figures of life-sized goddesses surrounded the room beneath the image of Apollo racing his chariot across the ceiling above them. A portrait of Louis XIV dressed in royal ermine regalia hung on one wall. Directly across hung another, similar portrait, with the subject wearing the same robes and striking much the same pose. It was the image of the boy-king, Louis XV, and it looked to have been painted some two decades earlier. The king couldn't have been any older than nineteen, perhaps twenty.

Several guards and ministers stood about the room, chatting quietly together and watching her entrance. The throne stood at the opposite end of the room, on a dais that was covered with a rich golden carpet beneath a large red and gold canopy.

The captain who had shown her there stopped before the dais, bowed his head, and announced, "Lady Isabella Drayton and Lady Idonia Fenwycke of Drayton Hall in Northumbria, Your Majesty."

There was a pregnant moment before a voice finally summoned, "Come. Come forward, mademoiselle."

Isabella walked cautiously forward.

She had heard tell amidst the drawing rooms in Paris that Louis was a handsome man, and indeed he was, from his perfectly coiffed and powdered wig to the high red heels of his jeweled and buckled shoes. His was a stately beauty, his mouth slightly pursed, and dark heavy eyes above a prominent Bourbon nose. He appeared to be of a middling height, yet somehow, even sitting, everyone else in the room seemed to shrink in comparison.

Isabella stopped before the dais and swept into a low and graceful curtsy. Beside her, Idonia did the same though not so low and not so graceful.

"It is an honor to meet you, Your Majesty," Isabella said upon rising. "My parents, the duke and duchess, send their warmest regards to you and Her Majesty, the queen."

The king regarded her with a pleasant smile, his fingers steepled before him. "We have been anticipating your arrival, mademoiselle." He sat forward on the throne. "I understand from your father's letter that you have been to Paris these many weeks?"

"Yes, Your Majesty. This was my first visit to France."

"Tell us, did you find our fair city to your liking?"

"Oh, indeed. I think it the most beautiful place I have ever been."

Her answer seemed to please the king. His smile deepened and he nodded in agreement. "Well, then, may this not be your last visit to us, eh?"

Isabella looked down and noticed the gift box she'd set at her feet. She bent to retrieve it, holding up the round, brightly wrapped parcel. "May I present a token from my father?"

The king moved to take the box from her. "This looks like a hatbox, mademoiselle? Tell me, does my friend the duke send me *un chapeau Anglais* to take the place of my French crown?"

He chuckled as his own jest as he took hold of the box. Just then a sound came from inside of it, a highly pitched, mewling sort of noise that seemed doubly loud in the quiet of the room.

"What is this?" Louis said, obviously puzzled. "A hat . . . that whimpers?"

He pulled the ribbon bow that held the lid in place and opened the box to reveal a small white kitten tucked away inside on a tasseled pillow. It was a rare angora Persian that had taken her father some trouble to acquire, and the kitten had spent the past weeks in Paris with Isabella, skulking about the town house. He would now have an entire palace to explore.

The kitten lifted its sleepy head from the pillow, blinked at the king, and mewed.

"*La!* It isn't a hatbox at all. It is a *cat* box!"

As the others in the room laughed at the king's jest, Louis lifted the kitten out of the box, cradled him in his silk-clad arm, and scratched him behind his pointed ears.

The kitten responded with a happy purr.

"Your father, he knows how much I love *les chats*." He held up the kitten before him, very close to his nose. "But what shall we call you, *petit*?"

"If I may be so bold, Your Majesty. I had taken to calling him Étoile while we were in Paris."

"*La! C'est parfait!* Because he is so brilliant and so bright . . ."

"And he is quite a happy traveler, too. He sat curled upon the back of the coach seat all the way here, watching the scenery pass through the windows."

Louis glanced to where a young woman, uncommonly beautiful with large eyes and an elegant mouth, had come forward to stand beside him. She stood poised like a delicate dove. "Look, *ma chère*? Is not *le petit chat* beautiful?"

The lady smiled and inclined her head, stroking the kitten softly. There was an ease and informality in the touch of her slim fingers as she stood beside the king, their heads bowed together. She could not be the queen, this woman, Isabella knew, for Queen Marie was some seven years older than Louis and it was quite known that since the birth of their tenth child, they did not much associate with one another. These two whispered together and when the woman laughed and reached up to touch Louis softly on the side of his face, Isabella realized she must be none other than the king's inimitable mistress, the Marquise de Pompadour.

It was a thought confirmed not a moment later by the king himself.

"The marquise would be honored if you would grace us with your company this evening at a small supper in her apartments here at the palace."

Supper? Her father hadn't said anything about her staying at the palace any longer than to exchange a few pleasant words and curtsies.

"Oh, I do thank you, Your Majesty. It would indeed be a great honor, but I'm afraid I must decline."

Isabella heard a soft gasp behind her. She noticed several of the courtiers standing nearby open their mouths in astonishment. One of them even shook his head at her in disapproval. Apparently the king and his mistress were not customarily refused.

She quickly explained. "I am traveling with my aunt, you see, on our way back to England. We had not planned to stay the night at Versailles, but were going to continue onward for the coast. I'm afraid we did not engage rooms for the evening."

"That can be easily remedied by *mon secrétaire,* Pitou. We shall find an apartment for you and *ta chère tante* here, at the palace, for the night."

He glanced to his right, apparently to Pitou, who stepped forward, nodded, bowed, and immediately set off.

"There. You see, it is already settled. Now you may spend the day enjoying the pleasures of Versailles instead of stuffed away inside some creaking carriage. Then you may depart for Calais on the morrow refreshed and rested. *Oui?* And I can even provide you with company for your journey." He waved to a man who stood across the room. The man walked quickly forward, an older gentleman who wore a rather large periwig.

"Lord Belcourt here has been visiting us from England and departs on the morrow from Calais as well. I'm certain he would welcome the company of two ladies in his coach."

"Oh, indeed, Your Majesty," the man said. "In fact, as it seems we are on the same ship, and since I am personally acquainted with Lady Isabella's father, the duke, it would be an honor to see the ladies safely delivered all the way to Edinburgh."

Isabella could see no polite way of refusing. "Thank

you very much, my lord. Your Majesty." She dipped into another curtsy. "We would be honored."

Louis took her hand and pressed a light kiss to it.

"Until tonight then, Mademoiselle Drayton."

Chapter Three

The palace gardens were every bit as grandiose and fantastic as the château itself.

Mythical fountains in gold and bronze shimmered beneath the summer sun. The roses and wisteria bloomed brighter, smelled sweeter than any Isabella had ever before seen. There were boxwood hedges, clipped and shaped in symmetrical elegance. Even the birds flitting about the cherry trees seemed to sing with an airier song, all lending to the illusion of a flawless unspoiled paradise.

With the help of one of the palace pages assigned by the king to act as their guide, Isabella and Idonia spent the afternoon taking in every wonder—the glorious fountains of Apollo and Neptune, the perfectly formed parterres lined with exotic trees. They enjoyed a gondola ride on the elegant Grand Canal, and sampled succulent fruit fresh from the trees in the *Orangerie*. They climbed each and every one of the famed Hundred Steps and then paused to catch their breath against the tightness of their stays on the Terrace overlooking the long stretch of *le Tapis Vert.*

It was amazing, really, that not a century before that same magnificent panorama had been naught but a modest hunting lodge amidst miles of barren marshland, with no woods, no water, and no view. Within the space of an age it had been magically transformed into a collection of fourteen different groves, brilliant chambers in an outdoor garden palace, separated by grand arbors of chestnut and elm. Fountains powered by hydraulics that made streams of water dance and bubble were hidden all throughout, complemented by marble statuary reminiscent of an ancient Grecian grotto.

It was impossible to see it all in that one short afternoon, but they took in the highlights, ending their tour at the famed Pall Mall lawn. There, while Idonia stopped to watch some of the courtiers at play, Isabella slipped away for a stroll through the Topiary Maze to reflect privately on the evening ahead.

Just the idea of being surrounded by strangers, on display, having to actually *talk* about herself, was enough to make her stomach turn a reel. She was only supposed to have stopped at the palace *briefly,* to make a momentary gesture of goodwill on her father's behalf. She was to have been announced to the king, present him with the gift her father had sent, and then she was to be off.

But, now, somehow suddenly, she was staying on for the night, and more so than that, she was supping with the king in the private apartments of his most notorious mistress!

How had this happened?

Anyone else would be turning cartwheels at such a boon opportunity.

Anyone, that is, except Isabella.

Unlike her older sister, who sparkled amongst company with whom she could exchange ideas and impart her many thoughts and opinions, Isabella was happiest as the quiet observer. She was content simply to record her thoughts in the private pages of her journal and sketching book, thoughts she would never dare dream of sharing with anyone else.

As she walked through the *labyrinthe,* along the hedge-lined *allées* and past covert hidey-holes perfect for a lover's tryst, Isabella tried to convince herself she had nothing to be anxious about. If there was one thing she had perfected over her three-and-twenty years as a duke's second daughter, it was a talent for making herself invisible in a crowded room. She would sit quietly and smile when called upon, pick over her plate, and stand back to watch the other players perform their parts. And then, as soon as propriety allowed, she would slip away, just as she had done at the countless country suppers hosted by her parents at Drayton Hall. Then come the morning, she would be on her way to England, and Versailles would be naught but a pleasant reminiscence to one day tell her children about before bedtime.

In the name of St. George, who did she think she was fooling?

A simple supper, indeed! There was nothing at all simple about the palace of Versailles. Even as she tried so very hard to say the opposite to it, a dozen different dilemmas buzzed through her head.

What would she say?

What was she going to wear?

How should she arrange her hair?

How would she manage to arrange her hair at all without her maid there to attend her?

Since they hadn't anticipated staying the night at Versailles, Isabella had sent Sofia ahead with their trunks and parcels to be loaded onto the ship at Calais. Thus she had nothing with her but the elegant yet simple day gown she had chosen that morning, and the traveling clothes tucked away in her portmanteau that she had intended to wear while she made the crossing to England.

The coiffure Sofia had arranged for Isabella, a simple coil pinned at the back of her head, had been acceptable for visiting, and easily able to accommodate a smart straw hat for traveling. But supper was an entirely different circumstance, with an entirely different set of standards. And supper at Versailles with the King of France? The standard hadn't yet been written for so eminent an occasion.

She could ask her aunt to help her, she knew, but the thought of the woman's own usual coiffure, a style popular at least four decades past, was enough to give her pause. She had little choice. She would simply have to manage on her own. She had watched her own maid nearly every day of the past two decades, and had even attempted the occasional *tête de mouton* on her sisters. Surely she could accomplish the semblance of a style, albeit informal, if only—

Isabella didn't see the gentleman standing on the path before her until the moment when she walked right into him.

"Oh, goodness! I am so sorry. I . . ."

The collision sent the brim of her straw *bergère* hat to collapsing over one eye.

Setting the hat to rights, Isabella looked up into eyes that were a soft gray-blue—on a face that was almost . . .

. . . familiar.

"*Pardon, monsieur,*" she said quickly. "I'm afraid I was so caught up in my thoughts, I did not see you standing there."

He was a younger gentleman, very close to her in age. His hair was light, although he wore it powdered so she couldn't quite tell its natural color. He was dressed in a coat of beautiful silver-gray silk that matched his eyes with shining silver buttons and a brocaded waistcoat in shades of pale yellow and blue. He wore a sword at his side and had a tricorne tucked *à la chapeau bras* under his arm, and he was looking at her oddly as he said, "It was my doing, Mademoiselle Drayton. I should not have stepped out onto the path unannounced like that."

He knew her name?

He spoke to her in French, but his voice carried the slight timbre of an accent—Italian perhaps?

"You know who I am?"

"*Oui, mademoiselle.* I missed seeing you earlier in the salon. A palace guard told me I might find you here in the *labyrinthe,* so I came to seek you out."

He had seen her with the king in the salon? Isabella was only growing more bewildered.

"I am afraid you have the advantage, monsieur, for while you already know my name, I am not in possession of yours. We have been acquainted before today?"

"*Non, mademoiselle.* Not directly, though perhaps it

would help if I told you I am acquainted with your sister . . ."

"I have four sisters, monsieur."

"Oh." He was clearly surprised. "I speak of Lady MacKinnon, of course. She did me a great service once. In fact, if not for her assistance, I would not likely be standing here speaking with you now."

Isabella peered at him, realization suddenly dawning. "You . . . you are Charles Stuart," she said softly. "The young Chevalier."

Grandson of the deposed James II of England, Charles Edward Stuart—the Bonnie Prince—had arrived on Scotland's coast two summers before to raise his father's standard as the rightful holder of the united crowns of England and Scotland. Isabella and Elizabeth both had followed the reports of the rebellion closely. Isabella realized the reason he had looked familiar to her was because she had recognized him from the many engravings that had been published of him during those turbulent months.

It had been a very mixed rebellion. There were those who believed the Stuarts should rule simply by virtue of their place as most direct descendents of Charles II. Others would not countenance another Catholic ruler, and so had looked to the nearest Protestant cousin, George of Hanover, who spoke not a word of English and made no effort to disguise the fact that he preferred his native Hanover to this new realm. The Duke of Sudeleigh, Isabella's own father, had held a tenuous position, both political and familial, caught by a blood tie to both sides that stretched all the way back to Henry the VIII.

"My sister has told me much about you." Isabella

dropped her eyes to her skirts and swept into an elegant curtsy. "It is an honor to make your acquaintance, Your Highness."

"Come." The prince took her hand and urged her to stand. We are cousins, no? However remote the relation, such formality is not necessary among family." He frowned deeply. "Nor, I daresay, is it required before a prince who is without his palace."

The prince's handsome face, Isabella noticed, had darkened with a cloud of melancholy at the memory of his defeat in the rebellion. She quickly sought to lighten the mood.

"It is a good thing you came to find me when you did, sir, for I fear I had gotten myself quite lost in this maze. I've been walking past that same statue for at least a quarter hour hoping someone might chance by who could rescue me from this impasse."

"Well, let us see if we can remedy that." The young Chevalier gave a soft smile and offered Isabella his arm. Together they walked along the hedge-lined pathway.

As they went, they passed a curious array of bronze and stone fountains concealed among the dense shrubbery. Nine-and-thirty in number—each one depicted a different Aesopian fable and its consequent moral. The prince told Isabella that Louis XIV had had the labyrinth built for his son, le Grand Dauphin, late the previous century, as a grand example of life's twisting and turning journey—and the lessons to be learned along the way.

"It really is quite an innovation," the prince went on as they came upon the figures of "The Fox and the Monkey King" frolicking amidst a shower of dancing water. "You see in the labyrinth, just as in the natural world, one can easily take the wrong path, or meet with an impasse that necessitates a retreat and often a different course altogether. But with fortitude and determination, he"—he looked at her—"or *she* will always find their way through, wiser for having made the journey."

From the way he spoke, and the glint of determination in his eyes, it seemed to Isabella that the prince had not accepted any notion of defeat in his bid to regain his father's crown, but fully intended to one day return to Scotland, to try again to take back the throne.

They had come to the labyrinth's exit, with the windows of the palace glittering before them in the ebbing afternoon sunlight. Isabella had enjoyed her time in the prince's company. He was pleasant to talk to, and had never pressed her to declare any loyalty, either to his cause or that of the rival Hanoverians. He simply seemed happy to have shared those few brief moments with her.

"I am afraid I must take my leave of you now and start back for Paris." The prince gave a bow of his head. "I've plans to attend l'Opéra tonight, and it is my understanding that you are to sup with the king and the Marquise de Pompadour?"

For the brief time she'd been with him, Isabella had been able to forget about her anxiety of the evening to come. Now, however, she sighed. "Yes, though I fear I will make quite the fool of myself. I hadn't expected to stay at the palace and I am without fitting attire or even a maid to help me dress my hair."

The prince took her hand and kissed it. "Mademoiselle, you are a vision as you are. I've little doubt that you will sparkle amidst the rest of that swarm of buzzing courtiers." He bowed his head again. "*Au revoir, ma chère cousine.* And may you have a safe journey on the morrow. Please send my compliments to your fair sister when next you see her."

Isabella nodded, then stood and watched as he walked away. She didn't turn until he had vanished around the flowering hedge line.

Idonia appeared at her side. "I was beginning to fear I'd have to send in the palace guard after you." She had been waiting for Isabella at the maze's exit. "But I see you found a gentleman to help you. And quite a handsome one, at that. Who was he, dear?"

Isabella, who knew that few were aware of her sister's part in helping the prince escape that previous summer, simply answered, "I've never met him before, Aunt. He was nice enough to help me find my way out."

"He did not try to take any liberties with you, did he?" For all her eccentricities, Idonia took her role of chaperone quite seriously. "The French are never proper when it comes to matters of passion. Believe me, dear. I know this well."

Isabella fought back a smile. "No, Aunt, he was a perfect gentleman. In fact, I would venture to say he had the manners of a *prince*." She turned. "Now shall we go and see if we can come up with a proper coiffure in time for this evening's supper?"

For their stay, the ladies had been given a courtier's apartments in the north wing of the main palace that looked out onto the gardens. Though spare in size, the two rooms were richly decorated with brocades and gilding, and high carved ceilings. To make the most efficient use of the minimal floor space, the bed had been built nichelike into the wall, with a rolled pillow and heavy bedcovers of rich ruby damask. There was a corner washstand, a small dressing table, and an armchair near the small marble-framed hearth. The only other furnishing was a tall mahogany armoire that took up the better part of one wall.

Isabella was sitting at the dressing table, twisting and pinning her hair into a succession of different coiffures, each equally disastrous, when she heard a knocking at the door. She glanced to the ormolu clock on the mantel, which read half past five, then at the reclining figure of Idonia who was napping on the bed in the adjacent chamber.

"That cannot be the footman come to fetch us already . . ."

She was right. It wasn't a footman at all, but a maid, who smiled sweetly when Isabella opened the door and bobbed a polite curtsy.

"*Bonjour, mademoiselle.* I have been sent to bring this to you."

A swathe of deep green was draped over her arms.

"Oh, 'tis lovely, but I think you must have the wrong room. Much as I wish differently, I'm afraid that does not belong to me."

But the maid only stepped around her and came into the room. "*Mais oui, mademoiselle.* This is the room. And you are the very lady the gentleman described."

"Gentleman?"

"*Oui, mademoiselle.* He asked that I give you this note."

Isabella took the folded parchment from the girl and turned to read it in the light of the wall sconce.

My Dear Mademoiselle,
Minette is at your disposal to assist you with your
coiffure and your gown. Though time would not
permit me to procure you a fitting court gown, this

*jupe gown and Minette's expertise with the needle and
thread should do the trick for supper this evening. She
is in the employ of one of the palace's most respected
modistes. Please accept this small gesture. It is the
least I can do in return for the kindnesses shown me
by your sister when I, too, was in desperate need.*
                                            Yours, C. E. S.

When she looked up again, Isabella saw that the maid,
Minette, had draped the skirt over the back of the chair
for Isabella to see.

It really was beautiful. Made of a rich emerald green
satin, the full petticoat skirt was figured with designs of
seashells and dolphins in fine threads of gold and silver.
It had been woven in such a way that when the candlelight shone just right, the fabric rippled, as if it had been
magically crafted of seawater. Isabella could but stare at
it in silence. It was the most thoughtful gift she'd ever
received.

"Should you wish to try it on?"

Isabella spent the next two hours being coiffed and
primped and fitted for the impending evening. Minette
was indeed a mistress of her craft. In minutes, it seemed,
she had taken in the skirt to fit it to Isabella's narrow
waist, setting it off with an ivory lustring robe embroidered with blue and green flowers. The sleeves of the
robe fitted tightly to Isabella's arms, ending at her elbows in a triple row of flounces, each wider than the
last, edged with a cascade of lace that fluttered elegantly
whenever Isabella moved her arms. She replaced Isabella's own smaller traveling skirt hoops with the much
wider *panier à coudes* worn by the ladies of the court.

They were so wide, Isabella could quite rest her arms upon them when she walked.

Minette took the overskirt of the gown's robe and looped it up in back in a manner that she called *à la polonaise,* setting each gather with a silk rosette. But the finishing touch was the gown's stomacher. Made of emerald green silk, it was chased and figured in silver and gold threads with sequins and tiny seed pearls in a design similar to that on the skirt. The effect was so stunning Isabella had to stifle a gasp when she turned to look at herself in the pier glass.

She almost didn't recognize herself.

"Oh, Minette. It is lovely. Truly, truly lovely."

Like any artisan, the maid smiled proudly. "Now let us see about your coiffure, mademoiselle."

At the appointed hour, a palace footman came to knock upon the door, conveying Isabella and Idonia by candlelight through the palace hallways, into the king's own apartments, and on up a narrow flight of stairs to the private apartments of the Marquise de Pompadour.

"Mademoiselle Drayton. Madame Fenwycke. So happy you could come."

Louis XV's mistress greeted them both warmly, drawing them into a generous room peopled with what must have been at least a dozen others.

As soon as they arrived, the conversations that had been buzzing fell silent and every powdered and rouged face turned to look at them.

The marquise's apartments were resplendent both in size and décor. Plasterwork ceilings carved in elaborate relief stretched above pristine parquet floors. There was a carved marble fireplace and tall arched windows that looked out onto the gardens and surrounding countryside. Carved fruitwood furnishings and portraits framed in gilt only added to the air of elegance and grace.

And the players on this grand stage were no less impressive.

There were powdered coiffures set with feathers and pearls, velvet coats trimmed in gold braiding, and gowns cut provocatively low over creamy bosoms bedecked with glittering jewels. Isabella crossed the room and immediately recognized the king, Louis, sitting in a chair near the fire. He was engaged in conversation with a gentleman whose face she couldn't quite see. His clothing, however, was very rich, deep-colored velvets and shimmering silks.

"My ladies, come, allow me to introduce you to the others."

The marquise was herself dressed to the height of fashion in a gown of rose-colored satin with a strand of pale pearls the size of Caroline's play marbles. She ushered Isabella and Idonia about the room, introducing them to each of the other guests, an intriguing mix of personalities, noblemen and women, foreign dignitaries, and artists, including the author Voltaire. Lord Belcourt, her escort for their journey the next day, was also present.

It took nearly an hour to make the introductions and by the time they had finished, a footman had appeared to announce that it was time to go in to supper.

At once, the others took to their feet, crowding after their hostess as she led them into another chamber, where a table had been set with porcelain and fine sparkling crystal. Candles burned from chandeliers and tall silver candle stands. A team of footmen stood against the far wall, waiting to serve. The table filled quickly as chairs were spoken for. Being a stranger to the scene,

Isabella had thought to simply find herself any seat that might be left. She was more than a little surprised when she was directed instead to the seat next to the marquise and across from the king.

"Bonsoir, mademoiselle."

The gentleman with whom the king had been speaking earlier appeared at her other side.

As he bowed to her, Isabella saw he was a man of advancing years, in his sixties, she guessed, of a medium height, a slender, graceful figure, and a captivating smile. His eyes, however, were his most stunning feature. They were dark and compelling as he took her hand and pressed a kiss to it.

"Bonsoir, monsieur . . . ?"

"Oh, do forgive me," Madame de Pompadour quickly broke in. "We missed you earlier, monsieur, when you were chatting with the king. Mademoiselle Drayton, allow me to introduce to you our good friend le Comte de St. Germain. Monsieur le comte, this is Lady Isabella Drayton of Northumbria in England. She is the daughter of the king's good friend, the Duke of Sudeleigh."

"Ah, Lady Isabella Drayton," he repeated, and she noticed then his voice carried a slight accent. It was one she couldn't readily identify. "I do not recall having seen you about the palace before tonight. Have you been at Versailles very long?"

"Lady Isabella is only visiting us for the evening, Comte," answered the marquise for her. "She leaves for Scotland on the morrow."

"Scotland?" St. Germain bowed his head. *"Enchantez, mademoiselle.* Your hasty departure, however, is certainly France's loss."

Something about the way he looked at her made

Isabella nervous, though not in a frightening way. It seemed almost as if just by looking at her, touching her hand, the comte could uncover her most cherished secrets.

St. Germain lowered into his chair and the marquise signaled the footmen to begin serving.

Isabella noticed that while everybody else received generous portions of roast fowl, buttered *haricots*, and *cuissot de chevreuil*, the comte's supper plate was left conspicuously empty. He was given only a small pot of tea that when he poured looked a peculiar greenish yellow in color and gave of an unfamiliar aroma, like exotic spices.

"You are not eating supper, monsieur le comte?"

"*Non,* I do not partake of wine or meat, mademoiselle. I find it muddles my thoughts. I will have my supper later in my own apartments. For now, I take tea made from a mixture of herbs that I discovered while traveling in the east. Would you care to try it?"

He poured a splash of the stuff into her cup even before she could offer a response.

Knowing it would be rude of her to refuse, Isabella took up her cup. The scent of the tea struck her, intense and earthy. She took a tentative sip.

"It is tasty," she said. "Not bitter, but—" she hesitated, "—familiar somehow. I can't quite think of what it reminds me of."

Madame de Pompadour agreed. "I said the very same thing, mademoiselle. It is wondrously soothing when I am suffering from an upset stomach. I have begged Monsieur to tell me what it is, but despite my pleas, he has refused to reveal it." She slanted the comte a coy glance. "Just as he has refused to reveal the place and date of his birth. He is a most elusive man, our comte. Some say he is even *ageless*."

The marquise lowered her voice then, ducking her head closer to Isabella. "You see, I have it from the Countess de Gergy, who was ambassadress at Vienna some fifty years ago, that when she first met le Comte de St. Germain, even then he appeared exactly the same as he does now."

St. Germain gave a small chuckle. "Ah, madame, the good countess is too kind."

The marquise lifted her head. "So you admit you know the countess?"

"It is true, I knew Madame de Gergy many years ago."

"Ah, *oui*, but how many years ago, sir?"

St. Germain lifted a brow. "Many, *many* years ago."

"If this is true then you must be more than a hundred years old, monsieur!"

Isabella noticed that the conversation had begun to draw the attention of some of the others sitting at the table.

"That is not impossible, my dear marquise," St. Germain said blandly, "although I confess, it is also possible that Madame de Gergy, for whom I have the greatest respect, is simply mistaken."

"Oh, *la!* Monsieur," Madame de Pompadour chided, "you always respond in riddles. Perhaps you will answer this. The countess also tells me that you gave her a strange elixir that enabled her to preserve her appearance for some five-and-twenty years without there appearing even the smallest change, as if you had distilled it from the very waters of the Fountain of Youth."

St. Germain merely smiled, glancing at Isabella. He did not, however, respond.

"One cannot argue that the countess is a woman of uncommon beauty at her age," the marquise persisted.

Still the comte offered nothing.

"If this is true, why do you not give this same elixir to the king? So that our beloved sire may rule France forever?"

The marquise's comment had succeeded in drawing the king's attention, as well as that of everyone else sitting at the table. The room was silent, forks hovered before open mouths as everyone awaited St. Germain's reply.

When it came, however, he spoke it in Russian, leaving everyone to peer at him quizzically.

Everyone, that is, except Isabella.

She laughed out loud, the only one at the table to do so, drawing stares from the others. She felt her face flush in embarrassment.

"Ah, the mademoiselle from England speaks Russian?" asked the comte.

"A little," she responded. "My father encouraged his children to study various languages. I was fascinated by the story of Csarina Elizaveta Petrovna, and so chose the Russian tongue."

"Ah, then you must tell us, Mademoiselle Drayton," said the king. "What did le Comte de St. Germain just say in response to the marquise's questioning why he does not offer his strange youth-preserving elixir to his sire?"

Isabella glanced at the comte.

St. Germain inclined his head, smiling. "By all means, mademoiselle. Do tell His Majesty what I said."

She looked across the table at Louis, who sat waiting for her answer. Isabella could feel the eyes of the entire room watching her. Finally, she said, "Monsieur le comte said that the royal physicians would have him tortured and broken on the wheel were he to think of drugging Your Majesty."

The king erupted with laughter, with the others immediately following suit, both at the comte's jest and at Isabella's delivery of it. Isabella felt herself relax. Wine was poured. The comte took up his empty wineglass, holding it aloft to her in a silent congratulatory toast.

The rest of the supper passed pleasantly enough, and afterward some of the guests parted, slipping away through shadowed corridors, while others stayed on for coffee and conversation. Still others withdrew to an antechamber for cards.

Never having been one inclined to the stakes of gambling, Isabella strolled to the opposite side of the room to more closely admire a painting that graced the far wall. It was an unusual piece, a still life of a necklace draped over a woman's slender fingers set with diamonds, rubies, and pearls. A seemingly simple subject, it had been painted in such a way as to show each stone's own sparkle and brilliance. Isabella found herself wondering that she might just reach out and lift the piece right off the canvas.

"You like the painting, mademoiselle?"

Isabella turned to see that le Comte de St. Germain had joined her, moving so quietly, she hadn't noticed him until he was standing right beside her.

"Indeed, monsieur. I have never seen such a talent for effecting the quality of light onto a canvas. Look at the ruby. See how it reflects every shade of red. I should like to know how the artist portrayed the nuance of the light so flawlessly."

The king, holding a cup of *café*, had come to join them.

"Then you must ask him, Mademoiselle Drayton."

"Ask him, Your Majesty?"

"*Oui,* for the artist stands here beside you, none other than monsieur le comte himself."

Isabella looked at St. Germain. "Indeed, monsieur?"

He inclined his head modestly.

"However did you make the jewels sparkle so brilliantly? They look so very real, as if through some magic you melted them down just so that you could brush them upon the canvas."

The comte looked at her with a smile on his lips and a glimmer in his dark eyes. "I am glad to know you admire the painting, mademoiselle. I should be delighted to paint one for you if it would persuade you to forgo your return to England but a while longer, so that we might continue to enjoy your company."

Isabella thought of the letter her mother had sent to her and her eminent return to England. "I'm afraid that is impossible, sir. I am expected by my family. But I thank you for the offer of it."

"Isabella, dear," Aunt Idonia broke in then. "We really should retire. We've a long journey on the morrow and you must get your rest. Lord Belcourt tells me we'll need to depart rather early if we're to make Calais on time."

"Of course, Aunt." Isabella smiled in apology to the others. She curtsied to the king. "*Bonsoir,* Your Majesty." She turned to St. Germain and offered her hand.

"Monsieur le comte. It was an honor and a privilege to meet you both."

The comte bowed to her. "*Enchantez*, Mademoiselle Drayton. I can only hope our meeting this evening will not be our last."

Isabella would learn no less than an hour later just what the comte had meant by his last words.

Chapter Four

Isabella was curled against an armchair, enjoying the warmth of the hearth fire and putting the finishing touches to a sketch by candlelight when a soft scratching sounded at the door.

She glanced at the clock. The hour was late, far too late for visiting. Idonia had long since retired, but Isabella had found herself restless after the events of the day and the prospect of the morrow's journey, so she'd taken out her sketching book in hopes of settling her thoughts.

Setting her chalks and pencils aside, Isabella crossed the room on slippered feet and opened the door onto the shadowed face of one of the palace footmen.

He looked as if he'd been awakened. His wig was askew and his shirt was hanging half in and half out of his breeches. In his hands he bore a small silver tray, atop which lay a folded note.

"Pour vous, mademoiselle."

Isabella took the note and quietly thanked the footman. He bowed his head as she turned from the door to read it.

> *Mademoiselle,*
> *There is a matter about which I find I must speak to*
> *you afore your departure on the morrow. My request*
> *might seem peculiar, since we have only just this*
> *night met, but I beg your indulgence in this. Please*
> *meet me in the Galerie de Glaces precisely at*
> *midnight. I give you my word as a gentleman I intend*
> *nothing dishonorable.*
> > *Yours, le Comte de St. Germain*

Isabella glanced at the clock. It read a quarter hour before midnight.

She knew very well she should not be meeting a man alone, let alone meeting a man she'd only just met alone and at midnight. Still, something about the comte intrigued her and she found herself glancing across the room to where Idonia lay snoring softly in the shadows of the bed. A sound sleeper, she would never notice if Isabella slipped from the room for a brief stroll through the palace. And she wasn't going all that far. Only to the *Galerie*, a floor below and in the wing adjoining their apartment. She would be back long before her aunt ever took notice.

Isabella skimmed the note a second time, then folded it and started quickly to get dressed.

She wouldn't have the time to lace into her stays, so she simply slipped on her skirts and the jacket of her traveling habit that she had already laid out for the following day. Her hair was down, freshly brushed for the night, and she left it that way, spilling over her shoulders

in a twist of dark curls that wound its way nearly to her
waist. She slipped her feet into a pair of shoes with a soft
sole and a low heel that would allow her to move quietly
across the palace's marble floors. Then, with a last
glance behind, she headed for the door.

Isabella gathered the bulk of her skirts in her hand as
she made her way along the quiet corridor. There was
no one about, not even the footman who had brought
her the message. Only darkness, shadows, and the pale,
pale moonlight shining through arched and mullioned
windows.

Her feet scuffed softly on the steps as she descended
the marble staircase. Somewhere, from behind the cover
of a closed door, she heard a woman giggle seductively.

Isabella passed through a door at the end of the hall-
way, descending into a curving stairwell. Then through
another door and along another corridor. Within minutes, she was standing at one end of the lengthy and elegant *Galerie des Glaces*—Versailles's renowned Hall of
Mirrors.

The sight that met her eyes had her stopping, standing,
and staring.

The moonlight glittered on myriad crystals that
danced like fairy lights along the twenty or so chandeliers that hung from the ceiling overhead. The lights reflected in the seventeen arched windows, and the equal
number of magnificent mirrors that lined the wall across
for which the room was named. Looking at it all at once
made her feel quite as if she were standing in the midst
of a star shower.

The room itself was empty.

Isabella walked quietly along the polished parquet
floor, studying the various works of art in the moonlight.

There were ceilings painted by Le Brun celebrating the reign of the Sun King, and LeMoyne sculptures carved in the figures of the gods. When she had arrived at the palace earlier that day, the room had been so crowded with courtiers, she hadn't been able to truly appreciate the elegant gilding and rich marble that graced the celebrated room. Standing there now, alone in the near darkness, the vast chamber was resplendent in the moonlight, whispering with the ghosts of masked balls and stately processions from an earlier era.

There was a bust of Louis XIV, the man whose vision had created the palace. She could just close her eyes and picture him, all that glorious majesty, holding court in that same room. Although they had called him the Sun King, she found the moon suited him more, cloaking his regal face in mystery and shadow.

When the comte stepped suddenly from those same cloaked shadows, Isabella gasped out loud.

"I didn't see you there."

Isabella took a slow breath to steady her pounding heart. He had been standing so still, she had thought him just another of the Roman statuary that stood tucked in the shadowed alcoves.

"Mademoiselle," he said softly. "I am pleased you decided to come."

He was dressed as she'd left him hours earlier, in his suit of rich silk and velvet.

"*Oui, monsieur.* Your message seemed quite urgent."

"Indeed, it is. Come, mademoiselle. Let us walk together."

The comte took her hand and led Isabella away from the light of the windows, drawing her farther into the shadows. "You see, I have been waiting for you for some time, mademoiselle. Many, many years."

Isabella's skin prickled at his touch, still, somehow, she wasn't afraid of this man. He was mesmerizing, like the flickering of a flame to the moth.

"But how can that be possible, monsieur? You did not know me before today."

"This is true. I did, however, know *of* you. I have always known of you, Isabella."

Isabella . . .

When he said her name, his voice was smooth like warm cream. It gave her gooseflesh.

"I'm afraid I do not understand."

"Perchance this will help to explain it."

Isabella watched, afraid to blink, as the comte reached inside his coat, removing something, something that hung from the length of a silver chain.

It was a stone, a crystal encased in crisscrossing bands of engraved silver. It was uncut, in its natural state, yet deep within, it glowed with a milky fire that even the darkness of the night could not subdue. When Isabella looked at the stone more closely, she felt the oddest sensation, as if it were familiar, as if she'd seen it sometime, somewhere before.

But that wasn't possible.

"Do you know what this is?"

"No," she said, even as she took it, feeling the weight of it against her hand. It was cool, as ice, to the touch.

"This stone was once the property of the kings of the Gaels, more ancient than anyone can accurately trace. It was given to the MacAoidh, to the Sons of Fire, centuries ago by *an maighdean mhara*."

Isabella had an ear for most languages when spoken,

could usually identify them. This one, however, wasn't one of them.

"Mahj-een . . ." she attempted.

"It is Gaelic, mademoiselle. Man's most ancient tongue. It means 'mermaid.' It was the mermaid who enchanted the stone."

"Enchanted it?"

"Aye. Its powers are many, both healing and mystical. As such it is sought after by many who would abuse it. It has been missing from the MacAoidh for some time. And since then, all has not been right. A great unrest has descended, and continues to seethe even now. The stone, it must be returned, very soon, else all hope will be lost forever."

Legends.

Enchantments.

It was just the sort of story that Isabella could get lost in.

"It is a fascinating tale, monsieur, indeed, but what does any of this have to do with me?"

"In each age, mademoiselle, there are powers at work, powers higher than anything we of this earth can command. Some credit them as God, others the work of a darker entity. Still others believe they are the forces of nature. Whatever your belief, you must know this. For each transgression, there is a virtue. For each evil, there is good. It is the natural order of things which keeps the balance between the elements—wind, water, earth, and fire. All four of these elements came together to create this mystical stone. A terrible transgression was committed when it was taken. As such there must be a virtue to restore it. And I believe *you* are that virtue, Mademoiselle Drayton."

"Me? But, how . . ."

"You must take this stone, and you must return it. You must restore the balance. The rightful MacAoidh awaits." He looked at her closely. "There is, however, a complication."

"Isn't there always?" Isabella asked, at once fascinated and frightened of the comte's ominous words.

"There are two of the Sons of Fire, very much alike, yet very different, too. It is your task to choose between them. Choose rightly, and all will be as it should. Choose wrongly, and you shall shift the very course of history."

Isabella had been so engrossed in the comte's evocative words, she hadn't even noticed when he slipped the chain around her neck.

Now, suddenly, the stone weighed upon her.

"Wait . . . no . . . this is not— I don't even know who—"

Her words fell silent as she lifted the stone up by its chain, staring at it in the moonlight. It was mesmerizing, as if it were filled with thousands of sparks of brilliant light. As soon as she touched it, wrapped the weight of it in her fingers, the stone began to glow, lit by a fire deep inside. First blue, then a pale, pale red. It was no trick of the light, no sleight of hand. It was real, for the stone had grown warm, almost hot against her skin.

It was as he had said. The stone was enchanted.

"You see, even the stone tells you. Heed the stone, mademoiselle. It will lead you to where you must go. It will lead you to Caledonia. Once you are there, all will come to you. Until then—and please heed me well—you must not let loose the stone. Guard it with your life, with your last breath, until you have found the real MacAoidh. Only then must you release it. And only unto him."

"So it is a man . . . ?"

And then, as if he'd been a trick of the moonlight, the comte turned, and vanished.

"Monsieur? Monsieur le comte? Where have you—?"

But she was speaking to the shadows.

Isabella stood there, alone in that brilliant room, trying for some time to decide whether the past several moments had truly happened.

Had it been a dream?

Had she walked in her sleep to find herself there in the *Galerie* alone?

But, she couldn't have because the weight of the stone was heavy around her neck and her heart was pounding even now.

The comte was right. It was no ordinary stone. As she climbed the dark stairwell leading back to her room, it held a glow that couldn't be explained, lighting her way.

Heed the stone . . . it will lead you to where you must go . . .

Who was this MacAoidh he had charged her with finding? And why had he chosen her?

As she made her way slowly back to the apartment, Isabella wondered if she should just take the chain from around her neck, give the stone to a palace footman to return to the comte the next morning after she'd gone. She could forget all about this meeting and this night. She could go back to her life, to her future in England.

But something he'd said, the subtle danger in the comte's mystical words, gave her pause.

It must be returned, else all hope will be lost forever.

Forever.

Isabella had wanted an adventure.

Little did she know, the adventure had only begun.

*   *   *

Captain Jeremiah Grange scanned the northern horizon with the keen eye of a lifelong sailing man.

It was a dreary day, the skies dull and gray, the wind brisk, slapping at the sails on his sleek new sloop as they cut through the restless churn of the North Sea.

It was the sort of day that kept sailors sharp about their wits. At any moment, a sea squall could burst from behind the sagging clouds and buffet them off their course. But Grange had been traversing these waters between England and the Continent for nigh on thirty years. He knew every stretch, every stream, and every pull. It was how he made his living, and he was proud to say he'd weathered more than his fair share of sea gale with ne'er a man of his crew lost.

It was that sort of success that gave a man his confidence, a sense of ease in the way his gnarled hands rested upon the spokes of the ship's polished wheel. But it also served to give him another sense, the *sailor's wisdom* they called it, that mysterious gift that allowed him to look out at the empty expanse of water and wind and sky stretching before him and know, just know something was brewing.

"Ahoy!" he called to Davy who sat high in the crow's nest on the foremast. Davy had the best eyes of his crew, like a hawk, that lad, and he took to his duties with a true sailor's pride. "Eyes wide, lad!"

"Aye, Cap'n!" a voice called from above. "She's thicker'n coal smoke, she is, today."

"Bloody fog . . ." Grange muttered to himself, and pulled the collar of his coat closer against his ears to stave off the biting wind.

He'd be easier, he knew, if he were only making the short crossing from Calais to Dover. It would be five, six hours at most and he'd have sight of land at most all times, not this changeable, inscrutable enigma of the open North Sea.

Had he his choice, he'd like to turn the ship along shore of England, particularly in such a fog, but knew his timetable required the open sea, away from the fishing trawlers and other smaller craft that peppered the shallower waters of the coast. He'd be forced to slow, likely doubling his sailing time, and he rather doubted his passengers were of a mind for a pleasure cruise. And he'd promised his wife, Hester Mary, for whom his ship was named, that he'd be back at home in Harwich in time for their wedding anniversary.

It would be five-and-twenty years this year, and Hester set great store by that sort of thing. For weeks, she'd been planning a big supper with their daughters, Anne and Jane, and all the little ones, and had even splurged to buy the ingredients for an iced cake. The thought of the cake reminded Grange that he had yet to stop at the haberdashery to buy her a pretty bonnet for her gift. Hester would like that. She was a good woman, patient and understanding when it came to most things—and it certainly wasn't easy being the wife of a sailing man—but if he had any intention of celebrating six-and-twenty years with her, he had better keep to sailing out on the open sea . . .

Where anything, or anyone, could be lurking.

"Good morning, Captain Grange."

The arrival of the lady Isabella chased thoughts of foggy seas and pretty bonnets straight from the captain's thoughts. Aye, he'd been faithful to his Hester for all of those five-and-twenty years, and would carry on that same course, but it certainly didn't mean he couldn't appreciate a pretty face when he saw one.

Grange turned, tipped his hat. "Mornin' to you, Lady Isabella. A mite bit early in the day t' be about, no?"

She smiled and just the sight of that smile seemed to warm the brisk sea air.

"I don't mind the wind. I just couldn't stay belowdecks with all this to behold."

"Naught much more than the mist and the water today, I'm afraid, my lady. Even the sea terns stayed at home."

It wasn't until the moment he'd said it that Grange realized the truth of his words. There were no birds. Anywhere. The superstitious sailor in him had him tightening his fingers on the wheel.

"Perhaps it is nothing out of the ordinary to you, sir, for you see it most every day. But to me it is glorious."

She pulled back the hood of her cloak and turned her face to the wind, eyes closed, arms wide as she embraced the day. Her dark hair, only loosely tethered with a blue ribbon, fluttered in the breeze, caressing her chin, a pale cheek, the tip of her graceful nose. Her lips were curved in a smile of pure, innocent pleasure.

Oh, to be thirty years younger . . .

Grange reined back the thought when he happened to notice his crew. Up in the rigging, standing about the deck, they were all of them poised like eager panting puppies, watching the lass instead of seeing to their duties.

"Davy!" he shouted, effectively drawing the attentions of all. He glared at them one and all while calling, "Eyes wide?"

"Aye, Cap'n!"

The crew broke from their collective daze. They turned, resuming their work about the decks and masts. The wind seemed to soften. Grange relaxed his hold just a bit on the wheel, filling his lungs with a deep breath of salt air until . . .

Davy's voice sounded again, this time a degree less assuredly.

"Cap'n?"

"Aye? What is it, lad?"

"I'm . . . not quite sure, sir. I think I might see something. Behind the fog . . ."

"Where?"

"Afore . . . dead ahead . . . it looks like . . ."

Grange craned his neck, trying to see above the foredeck. At first it looked like just a simple shifting of the mist, the ripple of the sea against shadow and light. Until another few moments passed. He looked closer, and what he saw made the lines around his eyes, the result of squinting too many years against the wind, crinkle into deeper, uneasy crevices.

That shifting shadow was looking very much like the figure of another ship.

Grange's pulse tripped. *You've nothing to fear,* he told himself even as his hands tightened against the ship's wheel. *The French would ne'er dare attempt any mischief this far to the north . . . not with a treaty of peace all but signed betwixt the two crowns . . .*

"Davy, use your glass. D'you see any guns, lad?"

"Aye, sir. Fifteen, maybe twenty."

"Gun ports?"

"Open, sir." A moment passed, and then, "Sir?"

"Aye, Davy?"

"She's an odd craft. Ne'er seen one like it. She's

painted gray, even her sails, like she belongs to the fog somehow . . ."

"Captain Grange." It was Lady Isabella's voice. "Is there any cause for alarm, sir?"

He scarcely heard her. He certainly didn't answer her. He was too caught up trying to decide whether he should slow up to draw alongside the other ship, or call for more sail, turn to starboard, and make a run for it.

"Davy!" he shouted.

"Aye, Cap'n?"

"Is she flying colors?"

A pause. "Aye, sir. She's wearing the red Meteor . . ."

The British nautical flag. Grange let go a breath of relief.

"It's union down, sir. And it looks like there's a fire on deck . . ."

"Hold!" Grange shouted without another moment's hesitation. "Heave to, lads! She's in distress!"

The crew jumped to order, scrambling up the rigging like spiders on a web, pulling up lines and repositioning the sails with clockwork precision. It was a maneuver they'd practiced time and again, and which they executed this time to perfection. In minutes, the ship was no longer pulling on the water's current, but drifting, losing speed. Grange held to the wheel, steering a flagging course for the other ship through the shadows, parting the fog with a pendulous, almost eerie silence. It seemed as if the very wind had paused to hold its breath.

Very soon the other ship came into view.

She was a sleek-looking brig with two masts, square-rigged. As Davy had said, she was painted a milky gray that made her difficult to see in the fog. Grange could see no one on deck or up in the rigging through the cloud of black smoke that plumed up from the deck. Her sails were furled, and she bobbed sluggishly on the sea current, seemingly deserted.

Grange steered to port, preparing to come alongside.

"Davy, d'you see anyone?"

"Nay, Cap'n There's too much smoke. But I think I can make out her name." A moment passed. "She's called *Adventurer*."

It wasn't a familiar craft, but she could be out of one of the northern ports, Newcastle or Aberdeen.

"You there, Simmons," Grange called to one of the deckhands. "Take some of the men with you down into the hold and bring up buckets and rope so we can board her and put out that fire before she's lost for good. The rest of you, keep a watch o'er the bulwark for sign of anyone who might be in the water."

Grange didn't even want to think about the possibility of hauling in corpses.

He steered the *Hester Mary* until she was nearly abreast of the other craft. He locked the wheel and started toward the bow. It was then he noticed the other flag, a second one fluttering in the breeze from the ship's jackstaff. It was a flag he'd never before seen, a white background with a shielded blue lion rampant. Above and slightly off center was what looked like a hand clutching something—a dagger? He couldn't clearly see.

But he did clearly hear, a moment later, when the eerie silence was ripped by a raucous cry.

Bratach Bhan Clann Aoidh!

Grappling hooks hurtled over the side of the sloop, catching on the bulwarks and effectively tethering the two ships shoulder to shoulder. *Hester Mary* groaned against the additional weight, and came to a sudden, jarring halt.

Pandemonium followed.

The figures of some thirty men, maybe more, appeared on the deck of the *Adventurer*. They had wild hair and bearded faces and were screaming the most fearsome noise Grange had ever heard. They began spilling onto the foredeck of the *Hester Mary,* yelling, shrieking, brandishing broadswords, flintlocks, and studded targes.

And then Grange realized it wasn't screaming he heard. It was the bagpipes, and a single man stood on the foredeck of the *Adventurer*, blaring out an infernal noise.

Good God, they were pirates . . . Scottish pirates!

The next minutes flashed before Grange like the sequence of a nightmare. Before he could so much as begin to bark any orders to his crew, the raiders had surrounded them, forcing them into a tight clump in the middle of the quarterdeck. They were the fiercest lot of rabble he'd e'er seen, with their wild faces and fierce eyes that seemed to glow with fire.

"See here," Grange shouted for want of anything better to say. He didn't even know if they could understand the king's tongue. "We've nothing for you to take. We are not a merchant ship. I am a simple transport sloop. My cargo is my passengers."

His heart was pounding in the back of his throat as they stood and glared at him and his crew.

"Easy, mon. We know wha' you're carrying."

Tall, blond, and with the clear blue eyes that revealed the blood of the Norseman, the self-proclaimed leader of the unlawful bunch came forward to face Grange.

He was a veritable mountain of a man wearing the Scottish plaid and three pistols strapped across his chest.

A broadsword with a blade that could fell a small tree stretched from his brawny arm.

He glowered at Grange. "How many passengers?"

When Grange didn't answer quickly enough, he repeated, this time on a growl, "How many!"

"We've just five besides the crew," he admitted, knowing if he tried to deceive the man, he'd only be found out in the end. "I swear it to you."

"Get them out here."

Grange shifted his gaze to his first mate, Burgess. He gave him a single nod, and the man turned, heading for the lower deck.

"Go wit' him," the Scotsman said to one of his men. Then he turned to a jumble of others. "You three. To the hold."

They nodded and were off. The Scot turned to Grange again.

"Any o' your crew tries to stop us or interferes in any way, they'll be shot."

Grange tried to swallow back the lump that was clotting his throat. He'd heard about this sort of thing on the open sea, but never, *never* on the Channel. It was why he'd chosen transport rather than the merchant trade. It was supposed to have been safer.

They stood and waited, and Grange found his gaze straying unwittingly to the blade of the Scotsman's sword. It was pitted and scarred from past use. He'd little doubt the man wouldn't hesitate in using it again.

The sounds of clang and clatter started coming from the hold belowdecks as the pirates rummaged and searched through their cargo. Grange didn't know what they hoped to find. He had only their food supplies and the luggage of his passengers. This wasn't to have been a lengthy crossing.

Lord Belcourt, and the lady Isabella's aunt were led onto the deck, along with the only other passengers, two elder French spinsters who were meeting their recently widowed brother in Edinburgh. They were all of them dressed in their nightclothes, having been roused from their beds.

"Whatever has happened, Captain?" asked Lady Fenwycke. She looked very near to a swoon, her bosom heaving beneath the lace of her nightgown. "I was napping below and these ruffians came tearing into my cabin!"

"Yes, what is the meaning of this, Grange?" echoed Lord Belcourt, clearly agitated. His periwig was slightly crooked on his head, as if it had been hastily donned. He looked sternly at the giant Scotsman. "Now see here. What is this all about? I demand an explanation."

The Scotsman advanced on him, pulling a flintlock from his belt and placing the nose of it right against the man's chin to silence him. "Here's yer explanation, Sassenach."

Everybody froze. Lord Belcourt's eyes went as wide as saucers. He was trembling. Having spent his life, no doubt from the moment of his birth, intimidating others, he wasn't at all accustomed to being on the receiving end. Grange wouldn't have been surprised to see the man wet himself.

Standing on the opposite side of the gathering, Isabella gasped when Idonia suddenly crumbled to the deck. Thankfully Isabella succeeded in catching her just before she hit the deck.

"Please, don't do this."

Isabella's words, softly spoken, had the effect of a thunderous roar, drawing the Scotsman's attention away from the sniveling Lord Belcourt. While the two French sisters tried to bring Idonia round, fanning her face, loosening the ties of her night rail, Isabella stepped forward. Though inside her heart was pounding, she managed to lift her chin to stare at him. The Scotsman regarded her with a menacing stare. Then she spoke, and it took every effort just to keep her voice from quivering.

"Take whatever it is you've come for, but please do not spill blood over it. Surely a man's life is worth far more than a few possessions."

The Scotsman simply continued to stare, but his expression did soften. For a moment, Isabella thought she might actually have gotten through to him . . . until the foolish Lord Belcourt opened his mouth again.

"You'd best listen to her, Highlander. You've no idea the gravity of your error in waylaying us in this manner. Have you any idea who I am? I am a noble lord. I am a member of the Privy Council. The king will have your head on a pike above Tower Hill just like the rest of those filthy Jacob—ack!"

Whatever Belcourt had intended to say was choked off when the Scotsman took him by the laces of his nightshirt and hefted him bodily from the deck. The man's wig slid from his head, exposing his bald head as he danced about like a thief at the end of the hangman's rope, his feet dangling and his eyes bulging from his quickly reddening face. The Scotsman forced the nose of his pistol past Lord Belcourt's trembling lips.

"Threaten me with yer charlatan of a king again, Sassenach, and you'll find yerself wit' a mouthful of black powder instead of teeth . . ."

He cocked his pistol.

The two French sisters screamed.

Idonia, who had momentarily revived, fainted once again.

Isabella took a step forward, holding out her hands in a gesture of surrender. "Please, I beseech you . . ."

"Fergus!" interrupted one of the other pirates. "The lass! Look! She wears the—"

"Wheesht!"

The Scotsman—who was apparently named Fergus— dropped Lord Belcourt, dropped him hard so that he landed on his rump with a thump. Belcourt started yanking on his nightshirt, gasping for air as he fought to loosen the ties. Then the two, Fergus and the other, started arguing in Gaelic—Isabella recognized the rich throatiness of the words from her interlude with the Comte de St. Germain at Versailles. She couldn't understand them, of course, but whatever the one was saying to Fergus, it had something to do with her, because they both turned to look at her more than once.

Finally, Fergus stepped before her.

"That stone you wear," he said. "Where did you get it?"

Her fingers went instantly to the chain around her neck. Isabella scolded herself for not having hidden it inside the jacket of her habit when she'd had the chance. They apparently intended to take it.

You must not let loose the stone. Guard it with your life, with your last breath . . .

Isabella took courage in the echo of St. Germain's words. "You may not have it."

"Oh, really?" He folded his arms across his chest. "And why is that, lassie?"

"Because . . . it doesn't belong to you."

She realized the ridiculousness of what she'd said the very moment after she'd said it. Good grief! The man was a pirate!

He merely smiled. "Aye? And why should that concern me?"

"Because . . . it is enchanted, and if you take it, misfortune will befall you."

She had no idea where that had come from and a part of her fully expected the Scotsman to laugh, double over and clutch his belly while his comrades saw to the task of depriving her of the stone.

Astonishingly, though, he didn't. He just looked at her, as if weighing the truth of her words against his desire to take the stone.

Isabella took up the chain and cupped the stone in the palm of her hand. She took a deep breath, closed her eyes, and willed the stone to respond the way it had the first time she'd held it at Versailles. She opened her eyes. A moment later, the stone began to glow.

"Och, Fergus . . . d'you see tha'? It's just like—"

"Of course I see it, you bluidy eediot. I'm not blind."

The men who had gone belowdecks had returned. They were hauling crates and trunks, taking them from the *Hester Mary* onto their own ship.

One of them, Isabella noticed, was carrying her portmanteau.

"Wait! What are you doing? That is my satchel."

Fergus, who was looking at her strangely, simply smiled. "Well, then, that is grand, lassie. You'll be needin' it. I've decided that you're to be coming with us."

Chapter Five

Cape Wrath, Scotland

A sea wind keened softly through the room, fluttering the frayed edge of a worn tapestry that hung over the arrow slit cut into the castle's stone wall.

The air was cool for summer, and the breeze chilled the slumbering figure lying on the shadowed bed. Outside, dawn was just breaking, and the echoing call of the kittiwake, carried on the wind, slowly roused the man from sleep.

Calum rolled onto his back amidst the rustling of the heather and bracken that stuffed his bed's mattress. He lay still for several moments, his legs twisted in the bedclothes as he listened to the sound of the surf pounding its unrelenting rhythm upon the shore far below the castle walls. He blinked, focusing on the oaken beams that crisscrossed the ceiling above his head. His sleep had not been at all a restful one, and he waited for his senses to come fully awake, sluggish as the break of day after a night that had been filled with visions . . .

A dark-haired merlass . . .

. . . and a stone that swirled with the misty colors of the sea.

It was a dream he'd not had since he'd been a lad.

At one point he'd woken, certain he was no longer alone, had even risen from his bed to check the shadowed hall outside his chamber before he'd told himself he was imagining things, that this sleeplessness was due more to the peculiar "savory" sauce M'Cuick had given him with supper the night before than any ridiculous vision. Those "spices" they'd gotten off the galley they'd boarded near Berwick Point had probably been some Far Eastern form of morphia.

Yes, that was it. That had to be it.

Throwing off the bed woolens, Calum stood and stretched on bare feet against a cold stone floor. The chill air blew across his bare body as he pulled on his loose shirt and then wrapped and belted himself in the thick folds of his plaid. He walked to the corner washbasin, pausing to stare at the reflection that met him—

—and wondered at the stranger who he found staring back.

With his long hair tangled about his bearded face, a face that was weathered by the sea, all he needed was an eye patch to make the masquerade complete. He'd been playing the part of the outlawed pirate so long he'd begun to lose sight of the Calum Mackay of old, the Calum who had once believed in clan legend, who had watched that quiet stretch of shore, day after day, secure in the knowledge that a mermaid would one day appear to him.

Where was that lad now?

Blinking away his weariness, Calum poured chill

water into the basin, cupped it in his hands, and doused the remnants of sleep from the foggy corners of his brain. His skin tingled from the cold as he finger-combed his hair into some semblance of order, then bound it with a slender strip of leather at his nape.

He left the room, making his way along the shadowed corridor and down the dim, derelict stairs, crossing floors that had once sported rich woven carpets, but were now cracked and sprouting naught but weeds. He walked through a chamber whose roof had collapsed some years before, leaving it open to the morning sky. The stone walls were green and slick with sea moss, and a family of storm petrels had taken to nesting on the window ledge that had once served as vantage for hope-ful Mackay maidens. There were no tapestries to grace the stone walls, no warm and welcoming hearth, only ruin and neglect, and the echo of what had once been one of the great Highland fortresses.

Castle Wrath was the place of legend, where the kings of Scotland had once come for protection, and where Highland warriors had fought, often to the death. An an-cient Mackay stronghold, the castle had been abandoned by the clan and its chief some centuries before for more civilized ground some miles to the east. Since then no one came any longer to Castle Wrath. Neglect and the harsh sea winds were its only occupant.

Surrounded on three sides by a dozen miles of empty moor, the castle stood on a rocky promontory that faced the mighty waters of the Minch. There were no lights ever lit at night that might be discerned by a passing ship, and any who looked upon the place would only see the same decaying ruin that Calum had found when he'd returned there a year before.

It was the perfect hideaway for a pirate.

Calum knew every stone, every underground passage-way, for he had played amongst the derelict chambers as a child. There was a rabbit warren of tunnels that stretched all throughout the battered cliffside. With his foster brothers, Fergus and Lachlann, Calum had spent his youth conquering the world at Castle Wrath, using branches of driftwood for broadswords and anything else they could find for targes, muskets, and the occasional lochaber ax. Lachlann, being the youngest, was rele-gated to the role of the English, and thus was always de-feated by the mightier Scots. Calum always played the role of his father, only in his imaginary kingdom, Artair Ros Mackay never died.

He conquered.

And he lived forever.

By all accounts, there hadn't been a Scotsman truer than Artair Ros Mackay. He'd been in line for the clan chiefship when he'd made the decision to come out with the Jacobites back in 1715. He'd intended to lead his clan to glory, to restore Scotland's stolen independence. Instead he'd fallen on the field of battle, leaving behind a young wife whose belly was already swollen with the next generation of Mackay warrior.

Reared on Jacobite tales of righteousness and honor, Calum had always known that the day would come when he, like his father, would be called to defend that which must be held most dear. That day had come late the sum-mer of 1745 when news had reached them of the Stuart prince's landing.

Calum hadn't hesitated a moment in joining the rebel-lion, despite knowing that his clan, acting on the orders of his uncle the chief, had refused to come out officially for the prince. It was with an unfathomable shame that in the space of just three decades a clan that had for centuries been proudly, fiercely loyal to the royal Stuarts, even earning a peerage for it, had cartwheeled completely to the opposite side.

Now the Mackays claimed support for the Hanoverian usurper. And Calum stood alone. But he wasn't fighting for his clan. He was fighting for Scotland, just as William Wallace, just as the Bruce, just as his father had done before him.

For seven legendary months Calum had marched with the Jacobite rebels, proudly wearing the white cockade in his bonnet. They'd been on the very brink of victory, taking first Prestonpans and then Falkirk in a routing of the Hanoverian forces. They'd marched all the way to Derby, within one hundred twenty miles of London. The Elector who styled himself George II had ordered his household readied for a swift evacuation.

Then had come Culloden.

For a battle that had lasted less than an hour, it shouldn't have turned the very tide of the rebellion. But it had. It had left the rebels stunned, with little choice but to scatter to the hills with the government troops pursuing on their heels. For over a fortnight Calum and his kinsmen managed to elude capture, camping out in caves, hiding away in the heather, fully expecting to rejoin their regiment.

Fully expecting to fight again.

They had been near to Loch Carron on Scotland's western coast, on their way to the isles where they had heard the Bonnie Prince was in hiding. Tired, hungry, and with little else but the clothes on their bodies to protect them from the harsh Highland conditions, they'd scarcely put up any fight when they were set upon by a company of English soldiers.

Calum had been away from the camp, foraging for anything he could find for them to eat. He'd bagged a hare, caught a salmon with his bare hands, and he'd returned just as the soldiers were dragging his brethren off, tied one to the other like beasts in the field.

He'd trailed them to Inverness, helpless to do anything as they were beaten and taunted, denied any but the barest minimum of dry meal on which to survive. A couple were killed. Others died from the severe conditions before they were ordered to Edinburgh, held in the hulk of a prison ship where they were to draw the lots that would determine when they would be put on trial for their lives.

But Calum had no intention of waiting that long.

He'd scoured the city taverns, the dark alleys, and the out-of-the-way wynds, gathering a crew of loyal countrymen. Then, in the name of the prince, Charles Edward Stuart, they stormed the government brig, HMS *Osprey*, where the Jacobite prisoners—where his brothers—were being held. Under cover of a moonless night, they overpowered the guard, and set them adrift in a small skiff on the sluggish waters of the Firth of Forth. It would have taken them till morning to reach the shore. By then, Calum and his men and the English *Osprey* had vanished into the mists.

Many regarded Culloden as the end of the rebellion. While the *battle* had indeed been lost, for Calum and a good many of the Jacobites who'd survived, it had never meant that the *war* had been lost as well. The rebels simply needed to regroup, to assemble their troops and plan their next strategy. They had beaten the English before and they could surely do it again. But they needed their men, who'd been scattered to the four winds, taken prisoner by the Hanoverians.

It was for this reason Calum had decided to take to the seas. To find them, those Highland heroes, and to bring them back to fight again. He'd started with the very man who had set them all on the road to rebellion that fateful summer before.

He'd gone to see the Bonnie Prince, Charles Edward Stuart.

It had been late autumn the year before when Calum had sailed the *Osprey*, now renamed *Adventurer,* for the coast of Calais. Leaving his crew to attend her, he went on to Paris where he found the prince, along with various Jacobite officers who'd fled Scotland, Lords Ogilvy and Elcho, Glenbucket, and the Lochiel heirs. As hoped, they were already preparing for a return to the Highlands. All they needed was the funds and the men to fight. When Calum told them his intentions, and offered himself and his crew in their service, they very swiftly awarded him a commission as a Jacobite privateer.

Calum's mission was twofold. He was to hunt down and attempt to overtake any Hanoverian vessel. He was to free any prisoners, take on those who might want to join his crew, and seize any vessel that could then be put into service for the prince. English captives were to be set free, preferably in a place that would take some effort to return from. And a portion of the spoils were to be divided up amongst the crew, the rest held in reserve for the sovereignty. Thus, the *Adventurer* and any ships they seized became an unofficial fleet as part of the Jacobite navy.

The Elector George, however, hadn't agreed.

He had declared the crew of the *Adventurer* naught but a "true and wicked scourge of the seas."

Pirates.

Marauders.

Traitors to the Crown.

Though the authorities didn't know Calum's true identity, in absence of a name, they had begun calling him simply "The Adventurer." Because of his success in slipping in virtually unchallenged, the reward for his capture had climbed to a prize of some twenty thousand pounds, second only to the Bonnie Prince himself.

Calum read the reports of his exploits, both real and imagined, with a mixture of amusement and utter disbelief. Somehow he had never likened himself to the lawless, godless brigands who had pillaged and plundered their way through the stories of his childhood. True, they raided ships and did indeed rob them. Yet, to their credit, they had never taken another life unwarranted and they always adhered to the honor and the code of the rules of war.

The Hanoverian forces could ne'er make that same claim.

In an attempt to quash the Scots into complete submission, a writ of "no quarter" had been issued by the government against any who had taken part in the rebellion. They unleashed the Elector's own son, William, Duke of Cumberland, upon the Highlands in a mission that would earn him his nickname of "The Butcher."

Homes were ravaged, castles that had stood since the days of William Wallace were pillaged and burned with nothing left behind to attest to their history but crumbling blackened shells. Innocent lives were put to the sword without benefit of trial, and any who dared to speak out against these injustices was immediately silenced, taken prisoner, and banished from their homeland.

It was those helpless thousands for whom Calum had taken up his cause, sailing the *Adventurer* to overtake the prison ships and liberate the condemned. If he died doing it then he would die with honor. During the past year, he had saved more lives than he could count, delivering some to safety in France, others back to their homes in the Highlands.

There was, however, a more personal motive for Calum as well.

When he had been born some six months after the death of his father, Calum's uncle, who had been named clan chief in the interim, had ordered Calum given in fosterage to a Mackay clansman. It was a tradition deeply seated among the Scots. A lad, after all, needed a father, and since Calum's own had been taken from him, Uilliam Bain had been appointed to take on the role.

Uilliam was a good man, a hardworking crofter, and a stalwart Scot. He had raised Calum as a brother to his own two sons, Fergus and Lachlann, and had instilled in him such qualities as Highland honor and Scottish virtue. They were traits that Uilliam Bain had worn proudly that April morning in 1746.

Despite being of an age far older than most who had marched onto that battlefield, Uilliam Bain had stood beside his three sons, ready to fight to the death for the honor of his nation. They'd been among the front lines and had proudly shouted out the Mackay war cry—*Bratach Bhan Clann Aoidh!*—as they'd rushed at the redcoats with broadswords and targes at ready. Uilliam had fallen in the second charge, his ankle shattered by grapeshot. The lads had lifted him from the field to the safety of a drystone dike, leaving him while they went back to take up the fight again.

It was the last any of them had seen of him.

Word reached Calum months later that Uilliam had been put aboard a prison hulk. It had sailed about the isles, picking up other rebel prisoners, then on to Carlisle on England's northwesterly shore, where the captives would be tried by the Privy Council. Calum and his brothers, Fergus and Lachlann, knew that when the time came, they would have just one opportunity to save him. To do so with success, they would need to determine just where and when would be the best time to strike.

So Calum had turned his sights on Lord Henry Belcourt.

As a secondary councilor of the Privy Council, Lord Henry had been given the task of managing the records of the Jacobite prisoners. He had traveled across the Continent in the name of the Crown to negotiate the exchange of the foreign prisoners. While at home, he had stood by to watch as many a Scottish nobleman lost their head, calmly ticking a mark beside each name as rebel after rebel swung from the gallows.

Lord Belcourt was known for his meticulous record-keeping. He knew the names, the alleged crimes, and the locations of every rebel prisoner, and he had recorded them all for posterity's sake into a collection of journals that had come to be known as Belcourt's "bibles." It was said he intended one day to publish them as a glorious record of the Scots' final fall.

Calum, however, had another idea.

With the information contained on those pages, Calum and his crew would know how to find Uilliam. When news had reached them that Lord Belcourt was to be crossing the Channel from France, Calum had decided to send his crew to intercept them.

It would be the first step in the most important mission of their lives.

"Good morrow to you, M'Cuick," Calum said as he came into the castle kitchen then.

In contrast to the bleak neglect of the chambers above it, the kitchen looked as fresh and new as it had in its heyday. Copper cooking pans and cast-iron kettles hung from freshly whitewashed walls. Casks of wine from the finest French vineyards stood beneath joints of smoked meats by the fire. Fruits and vegetables from faraway lands, bananas and pineapple fruit, awaited in wire baskets. And the goliath of a man who made this place his domain stood with his back to the room before the light of the kitchen hearth.

He said nothing as Calum entered the room, just continued to stir his porridge pot with an attention and precision that would not be interrupted. Unlike the others, M'Cuick had no interest in taking to the sea. He'd never wanted the fight, had been pulled into it unwillingly— and had paid the ultimate price. When he'd gained his freedom from the prison ship where Calum had found him, M'Cuick had had nothing to go home to. Nothing but the memories of the family he'd lost. Knowing the horror he'd faced, having watched his family butchered before his eyes, Calum could only imagine that the man had seen his fill of killing and violence.

So M'Cuick stayed on at Castle Wrath, cooking for the men, cleaning their laundry, and growing herbs and flowers in tiny clay pots. Instead of a sporran to hang around his waist, he now sported an apron cloth. And in place of the broadsword, he was found brandishing a basting spoon.

"Have you anything in that pot of yours this morning that might soothe my empty belly?" Calum asked.

M'Cuick turned from his cooking fire to regard Calum with a lazy nod. "Aye, there's porridge, and bannocks baking on the fire."

"Porridge is good. You've none of your curious spices in it, aye? Whatever you fed me last night must have addled my senses. I didn't sleep an easy wink all night."

M'Cuick scratched his grizzled head. " 'Twas naught more than some ginger and a pinch of saffron. 'Tis good for the digestion, it is, and it'll keep you from having a gas in your belly."

Calum chuckled. "Aye, well, it wasn't any belly gas that kept me awake through the night last night. 'Twas dreams. Odd dreams . . ."

Clearly concerned, M'Cuick took up his book and started leafing through the pages. It was called *The Boke of Goode Cookery,* and in it were recipes, household hints, and miscellaneous lore examining most every aspect of the kitchen and its environs. It was a book they'd discovered among the other plunder after one of their more profitable raids and the man lived and breathed by what he read in the pages of that tome.

"Says here the saffron is a revitalizer of the blood and an aphrodisiac . . ."

An aphrodisiac?

"Good God, man, are you trying to kill me?"

M'Cuick looked at him. "Nae a thing wrong with trying to give you a wee push in the direction of the lasses, Mackay. I've not seen you so much as glance at one since . . ."

"Since never," Calum finished. "In case it's escaped your notice there are no lasses here. 'Tis a rule, and we have it that way specifically because they muddle the thinking."

"Och, aye, that they do. But 'tis a fine muddling, it is."

"Aye, well I've no need for such muddling."

M'Cuick frowned. " 'Tisn't healthy for a braw lad such as yourself to be living no better than a monk. Take yerself aff to Durness for a wee bit. I hear tell of a lass named Jenny Sinclair there who will make you glad you were born a man when she—"

"Enough!" Calum didn't want to discuss the subject of his sexual appetite, or lack thereof, any further. "I'm a simple man, M'Cuick, from simple origins. I'm thinking plainer fare is more to my liking. Agreed?"

M'Cuick looked at him, frowned, and then shook his head, muttering all the way to his cooking pot where he heaped a spoonful of oats into Calum's bowl.

Calum took up a cup from the sideboard and started pouring tea from the kettle simmering on a hook over the fire, thinking quietly to himself until M'Cuick spoke again.

"Fergus has been by asking after you."

"Fergus?" This was unexpected news. Calum turned. "They're back a'ready?"

"Aye. Returned late last nicht, but winna tell o' it to anyone but you."

"Why didn't you say something afore now?"

"You dinna ask!"

Calum took a deep breath, waiting. When the man didn't say anything more, he said, "So? Where are they?"

"In the hall, waiting for you."

Completely forgetting his breakfast, Calum took up his tea and headed out the door, trying hard to ignore the niggling sense that something, somehow, had gone terribly wrong.

Chapter Six

Fergus was the first to greet Calum when he came into the hall. He stood from his chair and embraced his foster brother with a single, welcoming clap on the back that left Calum blinking from the sheer force of it.

Fergus was Uilliam's eldest son and four years Calum's elder. More brother than blood, he was the friend Calum had been able to count on for as long as he could remember. There wasn't anything Calum wouldn't trust him with.

Fergus's younger brother, Lachlann, sat at one end of the table, five years shy of Calum's own one-and-thirty. He was a near-perfect copy of his older brother, but for the six inches that separated them in height, eyes that were more gray than blue, and the unnatural angle of his hooked nose that had been broken in a brawl with his brother six years before. The lass who had been the cause of the scuffle was now long gone, wed to an island man who'd turned her head even more quickly than Fergus had vowed it would. The misshapen nose, however, would remain, a reminder of the fickleness of a lass's fancy—and testament to the devotion of a brother who'd had to hurt the brother he loved in order to keep him from the far greater hurt of a broken heart.

Next to Lachlann, Mungo MacLeod rested his bulk on a spindly legged chair that looked as if it might splinter beneath his weight. He was uncle to the two Bain brothers on their mother's side, a barrel-bellied Scot with hair the color of a dying flame, more red than blond, and streaked now with the white that marked a man who'd passed his fiftieth year. With him sat his only son, Hugh. Although the youngest of them all at three-and-twenty, Hugh MacLeod nonetheless had a head that thought with the shrewdness and wisdom of a man twice his age, a trait passed down to him from his father.

They sat around a stretch of table with a bottle of whisky set betwixt them. Just the very presence of that bottle told Calum that the mission had been a success.

Why then did he feel so wary?

He lowered into a chair, and had his tea while he listened to Fergus's account of the voyage. Fergus told Calum of the *Hester Mary*, and how the ploy of a fire on the deck of a seemingly deserted ship had gone off without a hitch. They described Lord Belcourt's indignation all the way down to the crooked tilt of his hastily donned periwig. The crew, taken unawares, hadn't put up any fight. They'd essentially drifted in and then sailed right off with Lord Belcourt's trunks all within the space of an hour.

It wasn't until the very end of the story that Calum nearly choked on his tea.

"You did what!?"

He hoped, prayed he'd heard Fergus wrong.

Unfortunately, he hadn't.

"We took the lass. The one I told you about."

"What do you mean you *took* her? Are you saying you brought her here? To the castle? Are you completely daft?"

Fergus had to raise his voice to be heard above Calum's outrage. "We had to bring her with us, Calum. We had no choice."

In that instant Calum's day had gone from not so nice to very, very bad.

"We're not real pirates, you bluidy idiots! What next? Will you burn a village? Torture a small child perhaps?"

"Calum, will you listen t' me? We had to take her. She has the stone."

Stone.

Just the word had Calum's mouth shutting with an audible snap. He looked at Fergus. "The . . . ?" His voice fell to a near whisper. "You are certain? You are certain it is *Clach na Bratach*?"

"As certain as any of us can be since we've ne'er seen the stone for ourselves, only heard tell of it in stories. 'Twould be our da who could tell us true but he wasna there to ask. It looks just as we were always told, and there it was, hanging from the neck of this lass like a tinker's bauble. What were we supposed t' do? We cudna just let her go aff with it and have it disappear for anither age."

M'Cuick had come into the room then, bringing Calum's porridge and a fresh pot of tea. He sat at the table to join them, and it was quiet for a few minutes while he ministered to his tea, adding sugar, a touch of cream, stirring it.

Finally Calum spoke.

"Who is she?"

"We dinna know."

"Who is who?" asked M'Cuick, having missed the first part of the conversation.

Calum didn't answer him. He was too busy trying to figure out what could have made men he'd always thought of as canny do something so utterly muckle-headed. Now, suddenly, he had a captive to deal with. Beyond being a considerable inconvenience, it went against the very articles of the letter of marque that governed their deeds on the sea, the letter of marque that had been signed by the prince himself.

In essence, Calum had just become the pirate he'd been accused of being. They'd be lucky if it didn't lead the whole of the Hanoverian army straight to their door.

"She was with Belcourt, you say?" he asked absently, trying to put some semblance of legitimacy to the thing. "Perhaps she is a daughter, or a niece . . ."

"We could ransom her," suggested Mungo. " 'Twould be interesting to see how much of a ransom Belcourt would be willing to pay for his own kin when the value of ours is so apparently worthless."

Hugh was of another mind. "I say we send her back home t' him, but with a Scotsman's bairn growin' in her belly. I heard tell of it among the French in our regiment at Falkirk. They called it the *droit du seigneur* or something like that."

Lachlann looked at Calum. "What the bluidy hell is he talkin' aboot?"

"It's an old medieval custom. It allowed the lord of the land rights to a new bride's body, and thus her virginity, on the night of her wedding. A way of improving the blood, they called it."

"Aye," said Hugh. "Auld Edward Longshanks gave his men the right back in the days of Wallace and the Bruce. They used to take our lasses and pass them around to their lords like playthings, thinking they could breed the Scots blood right out of us. So I say why shouldna we return the favor with this lass? We can all have a go at her."

Calum was just about to tear into Hugh for the vulgar suggestion when M'Cuick took one hammy fist and banged it down upon the table. "I refuse to be left out of this conversation any longer. What the de'il are you talking about, ransoming lasses and breedin' bairns . . . ?"

Calum looked at him. "They've brought a lass back with them."

The man's face lit up like a bloody spark. "A lass? Brilliant! We were just discussin' tha', weren't we, Calum? You won't be needin' Jenny Sinclair after all, eh? And I can certainly use the help in the kitchens, wha' with the laundering and the housekeepin' . . ."

"She's not that sort of lass, M'Cuick."

He thought about it a moment. "Well, then what sort of lass is she?"

Calum frowned. "She's the 'captive' sort of lass."

M'Cuick's mouth formed a silent "oh," but the expression on his face showed he clearly didn't understand. A moment later, however, he turned to Fergus, shaking his head dolefully. "I ken a man's needs and all, Fergus Bain, but yer a braw-lookin' lad. Could you no' find yerself a willing lass? Jenny Sinclair in Durness wouldna have turned you out. Probably wouldna e'en have charged you . . ."

"You daft ouf!" Fergus shook his head. "We took the lass because she has the stone."

"The stone?"

"Aye. *Clach na Bratach.* The Mackay charm stone."

M'Cuick only looked further confused.

"'Tis an old clan legend," Mungo broke in, seizing any opportunity to justify their witless actions. "'Tis the legend of *an maighdean mhara nan MacAoidh.*"

M'Cuick translated what he'd said from the Gaelic. "The Mermaid of Mackay?"

"Aye, the verra one. It was centuries ago," Mungo said, falling into the lyrical voice of the *seanchaidh,* those ancient Gaelic storytellers of yore. "Longer ago than any o' the living could e'er remember. The Mackay chief was for fishing out on Sandwood Bay when he spotted a bonnie maiden sitting atop a sea boulder. Och, she was a vision, she was, combing her long dark hair with a seashell and singing the loveliest song he'd ever before heard. He was captivated, he was, as much by her beauty as by her enchanting song. He sat upon the shore and listened to her, hour after hour, until the sun began to dip o'er the isles to the west. He was afraid if he left, even so much as turned his head away, he might ne'er see her again."

Mungo paused, as any great storyteller would, for added effect. The pause worked. The others, excepting Calum, were staring at him, rapt as they awaited his next words.

Calum, on the other hand, was staring into his tea.

"Now," Mungo went on, "when it seemed the mermaid might have finished with her singing, Mackay called out to her, beckoning her to the shore. But the mermaid, she only shook her head and beckoned him back to her, to the sea. She was so beautiful and the smile that she gave him stole Mackay's heart. He knew in that moment he had to have her for his wife."

"A mermaid for a wife," M'Cuick snorted. "What'd he do? Offer her a nice herring from his fishing net as bait?"

"Nae, you lump," Mungo went on, cutting the huge Scotsman a glittery stare. Mungo had no patience for a man who didn't appreciate the telling of a good tale. "Our Mackay was much more canny than tha'. He promised the lass if she'd come to the shore, he would dance with her. Ah, what a heady temptation for the lass it was, for dancing was a thing she cudna do in the sea. And Mackay knew she would have to shed her shimmery tail skin to do it, knew, too, that if he could snatch up the tail and hide it, she would be unable to return to the sea. She would have no choice but to remain his forever."

"And tha's exactly wha' happened," Hugh piped in, stealing the glory of the story from his father. "She came ashore and she shed her tail skin so that she could dance with the Mackay. They danced and they danced until the moon was shining high in the night sky, glimmering on the waters of the bay like diamonds. After a spell, Mackay let go of the mermaid and stood back to watch as she continued to dance alone, twirling about the shore on her land legs. She was so caught up in this new experience, she ne'er noticed when Mackay took up her tail skin from where she'd left it on the shore and hid it in the bottom of his fishing sack."

"Oy, the wily Jock!"

M'Cuick, it seemed, had grown interested in the tale. He was leaning forward on the table with his chin in his hand, eyes fixed on Hugh and Mungo.

Mungo went on.

"Without her tail skin, the merlass cudna return to her home in the sea. So she wed the Mackay and they had seven bairns—four lasses, three lads. Years passed and the merlass and her Mackay were happy, aye, but she ne'er forgot her true home. She a'ways felt a longing for the sea. Then one day, when the Mackay was out stalking about his estate, the bairns came a'running to their mither all in excitement, bringing her a strange green cloth they had found in their father's old bothy. They thought it a present for their mammie, but she recognized it at once as her long-lost tail skin, and knew she could finally return to her home in the sea."

"Losh!" M'Cuick threw up his arms. "So the man tends to her, gives her a home and a family, loves her, and she just thinks to up and leave?"

"'Tis the way of the merfolk, M'Cuick," Mungo sighed. "There's naught can be done for it."

He took a deep breath, and continued with the story. "That night, afore Mackay had returned, she took up her tail skin. Tucking the bairns into their beds for the night, she kissed them each good-bye and headed for the shore. Just as she slipped into the water, Mackay happened by on his way home. He spied his wife and knew she must have found the tail, knew too that his worst fear had just come true. He shouted to her, begging her not to leave him, but she only shook her head. She loved him, aye, but she cudna change what she was. Even without her tail skin, she would always be of the merfolk. But afore she vanished into the dark sea, she threw to him a stone, a marvelous merstone on which she had cast a spell to protect the clan for so long as her bairn's bairn's bairns carried on."

M'Cuick actually had the beginnings of a tear glistening in the corner of his eye when he turned to look at Calum. "And this lass they've brought to you. She has this merstone?"

"So they tell me. The stone disappeared some thirty years ago and hasn't been seen since." His voice softened. "My father died for that stone, died carrying it into battle for King James, our rightful king."

This last statement brought a chorus of "ayes" from the others. Glasses were filled and whisky was toasted to the king over the water.

The group fell silent, savoring the whisky's sting.

"So why did you no' just take the stone from the lass?" M'Cuick asked a few moments later. "Why did you hae to take the lass along wit' it?"

"A'cause there is a curse on the stone."

"A curse? Then why the de'il do you want it?"

It was Calum who answered this time. "The curse is only on those who take it by force."

M'Cuick scoffed. "Och, come on wit' you now . . ."

"'Tis no' a laughing matter, M'Cuick. Back in the days of the Bruce, a rival Sutherland once stole into Castle Wrath, and snatched the stone, killing the old chief's son and grandson for villainous measure. A fortnight later, the fiend's wife awoke to find him dead in their bed, marked several places over by the bite of an adder. She, however, had been left curiously untouched. Others who dared to steal the stone met with freak deaths, hideous disfigurements, or some just suddenly vanished. Eventually the stone was returned to the Mackays, usually by the perpetrator's next of kin who were desperate just to pacify the stone's ominous wrath."

Which only made Calum wonder just how the lass had come by the stone.

"So all you need do is convince the lass to give the stone to you," M'Cuick said.

"So it would seem." Calum turned to Fergus. "Where is she now, this lass?"

"Up in the seaward chamber."

"You left her alone?"

"Nae. I've set Dermid and Graeme t' guarding the door. Not tha' it's needed. She'll no' be going anywhere, Calum. We're in the midst of nowhere, and besides, she's no idea where we are. We could be in China for all she kens of it. She dinna e'en know why we took her in the first place."

Oh, but she did.

Though Fergus didn't realize it, the chamber into which he'd locked Isabella was in the very same tower, only two floors above the hall where he now sat. He didn't realize that cut into the thickness of the wall behind him was a narrow shaft that ran the full height of the tower. In the castle's heyday, it had been used for the dumping of wash water and other waste. Now, however, it provided the perfect device for her to listen to their conversation, to their plans for what they intended to do with her.

And, now that she'd heard them, Isabella knew just what she needed to do.

Chapter Seven

Calum took the stairs to the lass's chamber with a particular slowness, stopping once, and then twice to reflect along the way.

He had, after all, absolutely no idea what he was going to find when he got there.

So they'd taken a hostage. He'd come to accept that. It wasn't as if he had any real choice in the matter. What was done, was done. Now he just had to decide what to do about her.

He could simply let her go, and at first he'd considered doing just that. He would make Fergus do it, put her right back on that ship, and drop her at the nearest inconspicuous landing point near Edinburgh. They could forget any of it had ever happened. After all, it was Fergus's doing that had brought her to the castle to begin with. Calum need not see her at all.

But there was one thing that had him changing his mind:

The stone.

Other than to have known his father, it was the one thing he'd wanted all his life. And now it was here, somehow, inexplicably within reach.

Who was she? How had she gotten the stone? Was she older or young? Fergus hadn't said, but somehow Calum had gotten the impression that she was some years shy of matronly, yet old enough to have at least graduated the schoolroom. If she was quite young, she must at this point be frightened half to death. She'd been taken captive by a mob of pirates and brought to she-had-no-idea-where. What if when he went into that room she were hysterical? What if, two seconds after he opened the door, she took one look at him, screamed her face blue, and then fainted at his feet?

Or what if she wasn't there at all?

For all anyone knew she could have escaped and was even now wandering the *parbh,* those endless miles of wind-lashed moorland that stretched beyond the castle's walls? Men had been known to vanish out there, never to be seen again.

What if the stone was lost with her?

What if?

What if Fergus and the others had injured her when they had spirited her away? And just how exactly *had* they spirited her away? Had she fought them? Had they had to subdue her, bind her hands and mouth, threaten her with any number of injustices?

Fergus had never said and so, obviously, Calum's imagination took over.

Calum shook his head. Oh, the scene it must have been, for while his people had certainly been reiving and thieving for centuries, the notion of his men attempting what they had made Calum cringe. Any number of misfortunes could have befallen the lass. She could have taken ill during the journey north. She could be in that room, alone, burning up with a fever and with no one being the wiser.

They didn't even know who she was, or where she'd come from.

They didn't even know her name.

Dia, just the thinking of it was giving him a pain in his head, right between his eyes. And he had reached the top of the stairs. The door to her chamber stood right before him.

He could put if off no longer.

Calum approached the door with no small amount of unease. The two men Fergus had stationed outside were slumped against the wall. They appeared to be dozing, until he quietly and deliberately coughed. They shot to their feet, ready for his orders.

"Laird?"

"Has she said anything?"

"Nae. Been quiet as a dormouse, tha' one."

Calum didn't even bother asking them if they were sure she was still inside the room. Letting go a breath of resignation, he reached for the latch on the door.

The creak its hinges gave off sounded like a mournful moan.

He pushed it open. The room inside was dark. There were no windows and there was only a single candle burning. It threw a fluttering mix of shadows across the pitted stone walls, making the place look more like a dungeon than a bedchamber. It was quiet except for the echoing sound of the surf breaking on the rocks beneath the castle cliffs. She didn't scream. She didn't make a sound. Calum stood there for a long moment, leaving the door open behind him to allow in the light.

"Lass?"

Silence.

And then he saw her.

She was sitting in a chair in the far corner, her feet tucked up beneath her, half in, half out of the shadows. She was wrapped in a length of faded woolen. She wasn't screaming. She wasn't even blinking, it seemed. Yet as he drew nearer, peering at her in the darkness, he could see her shoulders were trembling.

"You are cold," he said softly.

Or scared to death, he thought to himself.

She barely looked at him. "A little."

A little of both, he decided.

Her voice was quiet, nearly a whisper, and smoky rich, the sort of voice well suited to a darkened room. He moved in closer and her scent immediately took hold of him, a scent that was everything that is woman—herbs, sweetness, and that something else that draws a man in just as seductively as the flickering warmth of a hearth fire on a chill winter night.

Calum took a step back. His vision had adjusted to the darkness well enough for him to make out the shape of her face, the sweep of her nose, the elegant tilt of her chin. What he saw when he finally took her in was enough to make him blink.

Twice.

Hers was a face that could have been carved from alabaster, uncommonly, otherworldly beautiful. Thick lashes swept against a cheek that was pale as the moonlight, that looked smooth as the finest pearl. Her hair was dark, how dark he couldn't quite tell, but it fell in untidy tendrils about the curve of her ear. He found himself taken with the urge to brush it away with his fingertips so that he could better see her.

She was simply exquisite.

Her brow arched in a soft curve above her eyes and her mouth revealed lips that were slightly parted, full and finely shaped. He knew just looking at it that her mouth would be soft. What he didn't know was how it would taste, how it would fit to the shape of his own, how its kiss would . . .

Calum blinked, startled at himself.

What the devil had made him think that? It was almost as if he'd been—

—*enchanted.*

He shook his head to clear it.

"Who are you?" She stared at him. "Why have you brought me here?"

Hers was a cultured voice, smooth and with words precisely pronounced. Moreover, it was unmistakably the voice of a Sassenach.

"I am Mackay." He was almost afraid to ask. "And you are?"

"I am"—her brow drew close, confused—"did you say you were MacAoidh?"

She had pronounced the name in the ancient way, with the Gaelic inflection—*Mack'uy*—which was odd. Most Sassenachs seemed determined it should be *Mac-kay.*

Who was this woman?

"Aye. I am Calum Mackay of Wrath."

She looked startled, her brow wrinkled in confusion. But then, after a moment, she simply nodded and said, "Yes. Yes, of course you are."

It seemed as if she was speaking more to herself than to him.

Calum watched as she sat forward on the chair, looking at him with a peculiar expression, as if she were trying very hard to be brave, while at the same time a little frightened, too. It was interesting to watch the conflict of emotions that flashed across her face, like the flipping pages of a book where the story changes one chapter to the next.

The woolen that had covered her slipped from one shoulder, revealing that she wore a traveling gown, the sort with a flared jacket that had been fashioned after a man's and that buttoned up the front to her chin. It was a fine garment, silk adorned with braiding and many buttons, indicating she came from a background of some affluence.

Was she Lord Belcourt's daughter?

God help them if she were.

"You won't need that," he said when he noticed that she was clutching a candlestick, blunt end up, underneath the woolen, just in case, he realized, she should need to cosh him. "I've no intention of harming you."

She nodded. She didn't, however, set the candlestick aside.

She slid her legs forward from where they had been curled beneath her and he saw the skirts, layers of them. He caught a glimpse, just a hint of white stocking and delicate, arched foot. She stood and faced him at a height that barely reached his chin, even with the cocked heels of her shoes. The light from the hall behind him shone on her face and he saw her hair, dark as midnight, against eyes that were startlingly blue.

Blue as the depths of the Hebridean sea . . .

Calum found himself getting lost in those eyes, mesmerized by them, until she moved, and the chain she wore around her neck sparked in the light.

He'd almost forgotten the stone altogether.

He felt himself suck in his breath as he looked at it settled softly against her breasts.

Calum had never seen the MacAoidh charm stone, had only heard it described around the light of the peat fire on chill winter nights. But the moment he saw it hanging on that silver chain, he knew. It was as if every drop of Mackay blood within him sang with it. *This is the one.* Even in the near-darkness, it held a mysterious, inexplicable light, speaking to the very origin of his name.

MacAoidh—the Sons of Fire.

Calum reached out his hand as if to take the stone, but his fingers stopped inches away, hovering just out of reach.

"This stone you wear," he said softly. "Where did you get it?"

Her fingers lifted to the chain as if to shield it from him. "Why do you ask?"

"Because it belongs to my family."

She nodded. "Yes, I know."

"It was taken many years ago."

"Yes . . ."

Calum stood back and looked at her. "Did you steal it?"

It was a senseless question, he knew, because she wasn't nearly old enough to have taken the stone—in fact, she couldn't be any older than two-and-twenty, perhaps three. But that didn't mean the stone hadn't been left to her by someone, a relative perhaps—

Perhaps even his father's murderer.

"Did I steal it?" She looked startled at the question. "No. I only intend to return it." And then she repeated. "I only intend to return it to its rightful holder."

Those words, *rightful holder,* sparked at something, a lifelong shadow of insecurity that lay deep inside of Calum. He took a breath, held it, and asked, "And who is the rightful holder?"

"I do not yet know."

He frowned. "Where did you get it?"

She stared into his eyes, deeply. "I think you already know that."

She wasn't providing any answers. Only questions. More questions.

Calum took a step toward her, leaning in close, his voice like the rasp of sand against stone. "Who the devil are you?"

If he had hoped to intimidate her into spilling the truth, he was sorely disappointed. She merely looked back at him and blinked.

"I think you already know the answer to that, as well. I think you've known it all your life."

Calum took a step back. And then another. He stared at her. And he scowled.

"I don't know what sort of trickery you seek to practice, lass, but you've no notion what you're about. I will have your name. And I will have it now."

She swallowed, betraying the nervousness she was trying so hard to hide.

"My name"—she hesitated—"my name is Maris."

Maris?

"I do not know any Maris, lass."

"You're certain of it?"

"Aye. Quite certain. I have been all across this land and I have never encountered anyone with that name."

She lifted her chin. "Who said anything about it being on the land?"

Calum stared at her.

Maris.

It was Latin for "of the sea."

Had that been her name? The one he'd seen in his dreams?

He pushed the thought away just as soon as it had come, trying to ignore his drumming heartbeat. "What are you saying? You're not . . ." He shook his head against the very thought of it. "You're not trying to tell me that you're a . . ."

Mermaid.

Though he hadn't spoken the word out loud, his thoughts had all but bellowed it. Could it be? Could *she* be?

The saner side of him dismissed the notion out of hand as nothing more than stuff and nonsense, and childhood dreams. But there was a part of him, the part that had been reared on tales of superstition and legend—in particular, *that* legend—that couldn't help but wonder, just a little, if it might be even the slightest bit possible.

How many hours, days, months even, had he spent sitting on that bluff above that bay, waiting and watching those brilliant blue waters for that legendary lass to appear? Could it be that the lass he'd been calling to in his dreams was suddenly, inexplicably standing before him, wearing the very stone he'd been seeking all his life?

But how could she be?

"You're lying," he said.

"That is possible," she said softly. "But it is also possible that I was sent here, to return the stone. To restore the balance." She looked deep into his eyes. "To choose between the two."

Calum felt a chill all the way to the bottom of his belly.

How? How could she have possibly known, when even most of his crew didn't?

"I don't believe you," he said, more to himself than to her. Only to his thoughts, it sounded more like "I don't believe *in* you."

"Do you believe in this?"

Calum watched as she lifted the stone into her hands before him.

It was as if he stopped breathing. He opened his mouth to speak, but the words fell silent when he noticed that the stone had suddenly begun to glow. First it turned a dull, dark red, then lighter, pink to orange to vibrant yellow, as if the lass held a secret, mystical flame right in the cup of her hands.

In the light from the stone, Calum could see her eyes, wide with wonder, her face radiant as the summer sun.

All his life, he'd heard the tales of the stone, and of the merlass who'd brought it to his people. He'd watched for her, waited for her, believing that someday she would return, believing, too, that she would return the stone.

Believing she would return the stone to him.

But as he'd grown older, more practical, Calum had begun to abandon those boyhood dreams as fairy-tale nonsense, the yearning for days that were long since past.

But the dream itself would not be denied. For when he'd banished it from his thoughts by day, it had only stolen into his sleep at night.

And now?

Now she was here.

There was no denying this. And there was no denying this lass.

She looked at him above the light of the stone, which had cooled to a milky blue-green, and said, "Do you think this a bit of trickery, too, Mr. Mackay?"

Calum wondered if she meant the stone . . .

. . . or her.

He never had the chance to answer her.

"Laird?"

The voice came from behind him. As soon as it did, the light inside the stone went out like the flame of a candle to a gust of wind.

Calum drew a slow breath. He didn't so much as shift his eyes away from the lass to answer Lachlann who stood at the door.

"What is it?"

"There is"—Lachlann hesitated—"an urgent message just arrived for you."

A message. That could only mean one thing.

"I'll be down shortly."

"The, uh, *messenger* who brought it awaits your response."

Damn!

Calum nodded to Lachlann. "Have him await me in the lower hall. I'll be there in a moment." He turned to look at the girl again. She had not moved nor had she said a word. "Lachlann?"

"Aye, Laird?"

"Send down to M'Cuick to see what he can do about offering our guest something to eat."

He stared at the lass. A part of him didn't want to go,

didn't want to turn away lest she somehow magically vanish.

Just like the Mackay and the mermaid . . .

"I must go. There is"—he hesitated—"a matter which requires my immediate attention." He stared at her. "This conversation, however, is far from over, madam."

She simply nodded, and Calum turned to leave the room.

Isabella finished the last sip of her tea and set the cup in its saucer with a tiny porcelain *chink*. She pushed back her chair and stood to walk about the room with the sound of her footsteps scuffing on the floor around her.

After her encounter with Calum Mackay, she had been shown to what had once been the great hall, where the castle populace would have gathered in another age to hear the latest news, plan battle strategies, and celebrate great victories. The ceiling rose high above her head, and banners would have once hung from the rafters, fluttering a swirl of colors whenever the wind whisked through the ramparts off the sea.

Weddings would have been witnessed there, births announced, and families would have made memories that would last for generations. And perhaps, just once, a duel might have been fought, with claymores sparking against the very stones she stood upon. She could almost imagine it, the desperation of thrust and parry, the stumble of the weaker warrior, and then the victor towering, breath fogging from the cold as he listened to the dying rush of his foe's last drawn breath.

Now, however, the room was just a lonely, dispirited shell of a place lost deep in the bowels of a seemingly deserted castle. Veins of cracked mortar spidered the stone walls like aged leafless ivy. At one end stood a cavernous stone hearth that looked as if it hadn't been used in more than an age. The floors were scuffed, the plaster that covered the walls pitted and cracked.

Outside the window, she could see now in the daylight that much of the castle compound lay in similar ruin. Whole sections had buckled, and outbuildings were naught but stone skeletons perched high above the cliffside.

Nothing but sea and endless sky stretched in the distance. It looked quite as if they stood at the very edge of the earth.

Isabella paused for a moment at the window. Apart from the fact that they were obviously somewhere in Scotland, she had no idea where they'd brought her. She had tried to keep watch from the ship's deck as they'd sailed, but had gotten lost in the swirl of the mist and murk that had surrounded them. From the bite in the wind and the direction of the daylight, however, she could only imagine that they were somewhere far to the north. Unfortunately her knowledge of that vast unknown part of Scotland was scarce. Anytime she'd looked at it on maps, it seemed as if the mapmaker had stopped recording the names of towns at Inverness, leaving the section above it as blank as a painter's canvas.

She'd endeavored just to keep track of the days that had passed since she'd been taken. The *Hester Mary* would have reached Leith by now where Elizabeth and Douglas, her father and mother and sisters, would have been waiting to greet her. What had Idonia told them? Her mother would be beside herself with worry. Douglas and the duke, and Elizabeth, too, would want to come immediately after her. But how could they possibly do that? They would have no idea of where to find her.

How could it be that less than a fortnight before she had been in Paris, where the most exciting thing she'd seen had been the man with the trained monkey at the Place Royale? And to think she'd been lamenting the fact that she'd never had an adventure, had resigned herself to the belief that it just wasn't meant for her.

Now, in just a handful of days, she had visited the French king, had had supper with his famous mistress, and had been given an enchanted stone by a mysterious comte. And then, she had been carried off by a band of Scottish pirates to a clifftop castle somewhere in the wilds of the Highlands.

Was Fate making up for lost time all at once?

But while it didn't seem as if the Scots had waylaid the *Hester Mary* by coincidence, Isabella didn't believe she, or the stone for that matter, had been their primary objective. Their reasons for intercepting them had had something to do with Lord Belcourt. She'd gathered that much from the conversation she'd overheard through the soil chute. The fact that they were Mackay pirates and had recognized the stone she wore could have been nothing short of—

What was the word the author Mr. Walpole had coined?
—serendipity.

And what of the man Fate had brought her to, what of this Calum Mackay?

When he had come into that room to confront her, Isabella hadn't known what to expect. With his dark eyes and long hair, and the beard that covered his face, he had the appearance of an utter brigand.

And he was a brigand, a highwayman of the sea. Hadn't

he and his men suggested ransoming her? Hadn't they suggested doing far, far worse than that? She shuddered as she remembered the Scotsmen's conversation about the archaic and utterly horrific custom of the *droit du seigneur.* They suspected she was somehow related to Lord Belcourt, and they sought revenge against him just for the fact that he was an English lord. What would they do if they discovered her father was a duke, and not just any duke, but the English Duke of Sudeleigh?

In order to keep herself safe, Isabella knew that she'd need to keep her identity a secret from them. At the moment, they weren't at all sure who she was. So she had led Mackay to believe that she was a mermaid, this "Maris" come to bring the stone back to the clan. It was the only thing she could think to do.

He didn't want to believe her, she knew. In fact if pressed, she had little doubt that he would deny having considered it even for a moment. But much as he might deny it, there was a part of him—however small—that wasn't totally convinced that she *wasn't* a mermaid.

And as long as he wondered, even that little bit, she knew she would be safe.

Chapter Eight

Isabella stood just inside the low doorway, taking in the castle kitchen, taking in, too, the man who had obviously made the place his lair.

He was as tall, if not taller, than a good many of the trees in her father's knot garden, but where they were elegant and shaped with a gardener's topiary precision, this man was broad across the shoulders beneath the linen of his shirt, naturally imperfect, and without the slightest hint of ornamentation.

His hair was long, thick, and peppered with gray. He kept it tied back with a bit of leather, yet even then it escaped about his bearded face, falling over his dark eyes. His shirtsleeves were rolled back over huge forearms that at that moment were kneading a ball of dough in a wooden bowl. A kettle simmered happily over the fire behind him, and various trenchers of chopped ingredients were set about the top of the center table.

In contrast to the rest of the castle, the kitchen was surprisingly clean and outfitted with most everything a kitchen would need. The aroma coming from the room was positively divine. It was all the best of baking and simmering and stewing mixed together, and it wrapped itself around her like the warmth of a soft cloak.

"Whatever it is that you're making, it smells wonderful," she said.

The man turned, startled by the sudden sound of her voice. Wrist deep in floured dough, he stared at her. He didn't say a word.

"I was . . ." Isabella chanced a step farther into the room, into his lair. "I finished with the breakfast you gave me and thought I'd bring my dishes down from the hall."

He just continued to stare at her. Finally, he tossed his head in the direction of the corner basin. "You can leave them in there."

His voice was gruff, but not loud. It put her in mind of a bear's growl.

Isabella crossed the room and set the dishes in a washbasin that was already nearly filled with other dishes and pots that needed washing.

"The food was very good," she said, again attempting conversation with him, hoping to appeal to his pride as a cook. "The tea was especially tasty. I wonder . . . would you have any more?"

His hands worked the dough for a few silent moments, kneading, turning, pressing. "I'm for fixin' a fresh pot soon as I get these bannocks on the fire."

Isabella watched him a few moments more. "Could I . . . perhaps . . . help you with them?"

He looked at her and the answer in his eyes said he wanted to refuse. But a moment later, something changed in his expression. It was the slightest softening of his dark eyes, an easing in the lined angles of his face. He took up the ball of dough in his hands and slapped it onto a floured bit of space on the center table. Then he took up a wooden rolling pin that had obviously been well used, and held it out to her. "D'you ken how to roll?"

"Indeed."

She hadn't lied. Throughout her childhood, Isabella had spent hours in the kitchens at Drayton Hall. She would pick berries in the gardens to bring to the cook, Dora, for her cakes and sweet pies. And she would sit and take tea while the workings of the place went on with an almost mechanical precision. And as she'd grown older, Isabella had become intrigued by the workings of the place, and had found herself inventing excuses just to go and watch as Dora would toss handfuls of ingredients into her great wooden bowl, seemingly effortlessly, that somehow, magically, were transformed into delectable culinary creations.

Eventually, Bella had dared to ask if she could help. At first, Dora had refused. Isabella soon learned how territorial cooks could become about their kitchens. Also, as the daughter of a duke, there was a very definite line between those who performed the work and those for whom the work was performed.

But Bella had gone to her parents and expressed her interest to them. The duke, always one who held great store by learning, had agreed for purely educational reasons. A future wife, after all, could only benefit from a thorough study of the kitchen she would one day govern in her own home.

Bella had taken to the task with a natural enthusiasm.

To her, it had been like another form of artistic expression.

While her sisters had found pleasure in other things—Elizabeth in books, Catherine playing the spinet, Mattie in the garden, and Caroline, well, Caroline in anything that could get her into trouble—in cooking, Isabella found a new and different outlet for creating. She loved the idea of taking that which was grown from the earth and combining different aspects, such as the sweetness of strawberries or the tart of a lemon, to create something new and unique. Her first real attempt had been a treacle sponge pudding and lemon custard that had put quite a smile upon her father's face when he'd tasted it. She had been fourteen, and the sense of accomplishment that first endeavor had given her hadn't diminished since.

Isabella started rolling out the bannock dough into the shape of a large flat round, glancing at the cook for an approving nod. He showed her how to shape each bannock with her hands, and then place them on the flat iron *gridheal* that he then hung on a hook at the side of the fire. She stood and watched it bake, rising, browning. Then she took it from the fire and set it on the table to cool.

When she'd finished, Isabella turned. "Is there anything else, Mr. . . . ?"

" 'Tis M'Cuick," he said, cutting some potatoes into a large pot.

"M'Cuick," she repeated with a half smile. "Is that your Christian name, or your family name?"

"My family name, but everybody calls me by it."

"What is your Christian name?"

He looked at her. " 'Tis Malcolm."

"I much prefer that." Isabella smiled. "It suits you."

" 'Tis what my wife called me." He blinked and his expression shifted, softening. "Afore she died."

Isabella recognized the sadness that had crept into his eyes, clouding them. "I'm sorry."

He shook his head, but his voice was heavy. "Nae, 'tis naught to be sorry for in the telling of my name. Truth be told, I miss hearing it."

"Would you mind if"—she hesitated—"perhaps I were to call you 'Malcolm,' Malcolm?"

His hands went still, one holding a potato, the other the knife he'd been using to slice them. Finally he said, "That would be just fine, miss."

Isabella smiled. "And you may call me Bel—" She faltered. "Maris. My name is Maris."

Malcolm looked at her. She knew he didn't for one moment believe that was her name. Still, he said, "Maris it is then, miss."

He looked about the cabinets and shelves that lined the whitewashed walls. "I've all different sorts of things, spices and herbs and such, for flavoring, but I'm not quite certain what to make of them. I've a book, but it doesna do much for Scottish dishes . . ."

Isabella rummaged through the nearest shelf, pulling out some of the herbs she had seen Dora use.

"For instance," he went on, "wha' would you add to better flavor the powsowdie?"

Isabella absently opened an earthenware jar of thyme and gave it a quick sniff. "Powsowdie? I'm afraid I don't quite know what that is."

Malcolm had moved on from the potatoes and was fixing the pot of tea he had promised. "Oh, 'tis there in the pot."

Isabella looked to see the huge black pot sitting in the washbasin. She reached for the lid, pulled it away, and had a look inside.

The "powsowdie" looked back.

She shrieked, clanging the cover back down. "What is that?"

M'Cuick looked up from the teapot, with an expression that could only be called blasé. "I tol' you, lass. 'Tis the powsowdie."

"It is a head, Malcolm!"

He nodded. "Aye, a sheep's heid. Hae you ne'er had the powsowdie afore?"

Isabella closed her eyes, trying to banish the image of that glassy-eyed stare from her mind as she swallowed back the wave of distaste that was sweeping through her stomach. "No, I have not."

"Och, lass, 'tis good. An auld Scots tradition. We a'ways hae it when the lads come back from a successful mission on the seas. And tha' heid is a fine one, indeed. Singed the wool off it myself afore I soaked it in tha' pot through the night to make it tender. No' all you need do is tweak out the eyes and split it down atween its ears so we can . . ."

He glanced at her. "What's troubling you, lass? You're looking a wee bit green. Dinna the cheese I gae you wit' breakfast agree wit' you? It can be a wee bit strong, I'm told."

Isabella took a deep breath. Then another. "Please," she said, her voice shaky as a twig, "may I please have some tea?"

"Certainly, lass. Just finished brewing it. Here you are."

Isabella took the cup, breathed in the tea's scent, and readied to tip the cup to her lips when—

"What is in this tea?" she asked, thinking if they kept a sheep's head in a pot for supper, there was no telling what they passed off as tea.

M'Cuick looked at her, confused. "'Tis tea, lass."

She glanced at him. "Just tea? No special ingredients? Entrails? A hoof perhaps that went into the brewing of it?"

Malcolm chuckled softly and shook his head. "Nae, lass. Jus' the tea. A fine gunpowder sort, too. All the way from China."

Isabella lowered into a chair and sipped tentatively at the stuff, praying it would settle her churning stomach. She glanced up once, caught sight of the pot once more, then turned her chair so that her back was to it.

For the better part of the day, Bella and M'Cuick prepared a feast together. Keeping a good ten feet between herself and the powsowdie pot, Bella showed him how to stir the custard so it wouldn't burn over the fire, while he taught her the trick of shelling winkles.

They chatted while they worked, first about casual topics, but then Isabella began to turn the conversation toward her captor, and his reasons for bringing her there, hoping to glean some sense of just who Calum Mackay of Wrath really was.

"Malcolm, how did a man like you end up with a band of lawless pirates?"

"Och, but they're no' pirates, lass. Not in the sense you're thinking."

"But look around you," she said, referring to the bounty that surrounded them. There were valuable, highly taxed coffees and teas, exotic pineapple fruits, and platters of silver on which to serve them. "Everything here belongs to someone else."

Malcolm shook his head. "Och, but Mackay, he's got verra good reasons for what he does, Miss Maris. Honorable reasons, too. Aye, if it weren't for him, I'd be on the other side of the ocean right now, slave to another man."

Isabella considered his words. "You were one of the Jacobites?"

"Nae, lass. Tha's just it. I ne'er came out for either side in the rebellion because it was said if I dinna fight, I winna be punished later. I had a family to protect."

His voice was growing heavy again. Isabella sensed a need in him to talk about it. "What happened, Malcolm?"

"I lived close by to Drummossie Moor."

"Where the battle of Culloden was fought?"

"Aye. I could hear the cannon fire from my field, but I ne'er went near the place. I had to keep the bairns and my Mary safe. After the battle the wounded started coming, looking for help. They were in a fearsome way, all cut by bayonets and shocked from the cannon shelling. My Mary and I, we ne'er asked them whose side they'd fought on. We only sought to treat their injuries and ease their pain."

"Of course," Isabella said. She would have done the same.

"The government soldiers soon arrived. Some of the men we'd treated were Jacobites. They said we were all rebels. They killed all the wounded, and then they . . ."

His words dropped off as his eyes grew red, glossy with tears. He pressed his lips tightly together, biting back the emotion that had seized him. Isabella reached out and took his hand.

He looked up at her. She had never seen such anguish,

such obvious heartbreak, as she saw in his eyes at that moment.

"They killed my Mary, and then my daughter and our son. They shot us all, only I wasn't given the chance to go with them. I lived. I lived hearing them die. It is a sound I can never forget."

Isabella covered her mouth with her hand.

"I went after them," M'Cuick went on. "I went after them to kill them, but they caught me first and threw me into a prison hulk as a rebel. Nae matter how I tried to explain, that I hadna taken a part in the fighting, I were sentenced to transportation to the Colonies. I dinna care. My life was o'er. Without Mary and the bairns, I dinna care what happened to me. I prayed I'd die in that stinking ship's hold, begged the dear Lord to give me some disease, the typhus, so I could join my Mary in heaven. We were on the seas, just rounding Peterhead, when I heard a commotion above us on the deck." He looked at her. "'Twas Calum Mackay. He'd come to free us. I thought I had wanted to die, lass. But the moment I saw him, saw him standing on that deck with his sword gleaming in the sunlight, I knew I wanted to live. I wanted to live because that is what Mary would have wanted."

Isabella was silent, trying to understand. "So Mackay only raids to free prisoners from transportation ships?"

"Aye, lass. King George, he thinks that by ridding himself of every last Scot, he'll no' have to wirra about another rebellion. They call it 'the cleansing o' the glens,' miss."

Isabella had heard of this from her sister Elizabeth's letters, but now, hearing it thus, she recognized the injustice of it.

It was an injustice that Calum Mackay apparently intended to rectify.

"What about all this then?" she said, referring to the spices, the silver, the casks of French brandy, all of it stolen. "If he's not a pirate, then where has all this come from?"

"'Tis the spoils of war, miss. Calum, he's got a letter of marque from the Bonnie Prince himsel', designating him a privateer in the Jacobite navy. 'Tis sure, we get to enjoy some of it, but most of it is kept here for the day when the Bonnie Prince will return as the rightful holder of the Crown of Scotland. And he only takes from the same men who are molesting the Scottish countryside. Look there." He pointed to two paintings that hung from the kitchen wall. They were framed in gilt and looked completely out of place amongst the pots and pans that lined the wall beside them. "Those were to be delivered to a Lord William Blakely, a decorated Hanoverian commander who had given his troops free rein to plunder their way across the glens around Fort William. He bought those paintings with the money he made selling off Scottish cattle and sheep that he stole from innocent crofters like mysel'."

He turned her attention to an elegant rosewood sideboard that stood against the far wall. "That pretty piece there was making its way to Monkston Hall."

Isabella recognized the name. "The Earl of Monkston?"

"Aye. The same Earl of Monkston who begged, bribed, and outright threatened to ensure the passing of the Act of Union forty years ago, thereby stripping Scotland of its independence. There are brandies imported for the Duke of Hartley; spices and teas and chocolates from Holland bound for St. James Palace." M'Cuick's eyes lit up then. "Aye, but the true gem isna to be found in this kitchen."

Isabella looked at him. "It isn't?"

"'Tis a bonnie Trakehner stallion that had been given as a congratulatory gift to the Duke of Cumberland, from his cousin, Frederick II of Prussia. He's seventeen hands of pure elegance and strength he is, black as the devil with a blaze of white slashed from forelock to nostril."

"I read about that horse," Isabella said, remembering the headlines in her father's copy of the *London Evening Post.* "Some even accused Louis of France of having masterminded the theft of the horse when it was reported he had been riding a new mount very similar in color in the Bois de Boulogne."

M'Cuick chuckled. "Aye. Wonder wha' that butcher Cumberland would say if he knew that his prized Prussian pony is now grazing on Highland pastures, wandering brae and burn, and enjoying the company of a rather appreciative troop of pretty Highland mares, eh?"

Isabella fell silent as she tried to take in everything she'd just learned. It was not at all what she'd expected when she'd first set out to question Malcolm about Calum Mackay. In fact, it was just the opposite.

"So tha's it, eh?" Malcolm said several moments later, pulling her thoughts back. "Tha's the stone they're all talkin' about?"

Isabella simply nodded.

"'Tis a wee bit smaller than I expected. A pretty thing it is, though." He paused, then added, "They say 'tis enchanted." Malcolm took a sip of his tea. "They also say that you're a mermaid come to bring the stone back."

He was testing her, she knew. Isabella looked at him. She didn't reply.

"Are you a mermaid, lass?"

In the short amount of time Isabella had spent with him, she'd found she liked the man immensely. It made it difficult for her to lie to him. So instead she said, "What do you think, Malcolm?"

M'Cuick looked at her, searching her eyes. Then he simply smiled. "I think"—he took another sip of tea—"I think that I've seen naething yet to suggest that you cudna be a mermaid. And until I do, I'm for thinkin' who am I to say tha' you aren't?"

Chapter Nine

Night was falling fast as Calum made his way back to Castle Wrath.

The rendezvous that had called him away that morning had taken longer than he'd expected. There had been details to go over, plans to make. Though the weather had held fair throughout the day, the skies had thickened steadily along the ten miles he had crossed along the journey back, threatening rain.

Even now the wind off the North Sea bullied the empty stretch of moorland he traveled, brisk and biting against the cover of the belted plaid he had drawn up around his shoulders. His hair had been harassed from the tie that held it and was now blowing about his face and shoulders. Deer-hide *cuarans* wrapped around his feet and lower legs, lacing from toe to just below his knees. They, and the plaid, would be his only protection should the skies above him suddenly decide to break with the downpour that so often buffeted this part of the Highlands. There were no trees, not a one, beneath which he might take cover, only empty moorland and rolling hills that in the coming months would be splashed red and violet with the sweetly scented carpet of Highland heather.

Calum paused for a moment on the last rise, called Dunan Mor, to take in the landscape that stretched out before him. It was a breathtaking country. He had traveled to lands afar, had sailed the seas, and had himself stood in the presence of a prince among the most palatial surroundings. Yet to him no place had ever approached his homeland in comparison.

To the north there were stark awesome cliff sides that plummeted to the sea as if cleaved by a giant claymore. To the east, mountains watched over valleys boggy with rainfall, cut through by rushing burns whose waters ran clear as glass. The ancient Reay forest lay to the south, where clan chiefs for centuries had hunted for deer and other game, and where legends of witches and otherworldly folk abounded.

But it was at its farthest point, to the north and to the west, that Cape Wrath awaited—ancestral fortress, birthplace of warriors past . . .

. . . Calum's home.

It had been his father's legacy, left to him by his father, who'd been given it by his father before him, the former clan chief. It was the place Artair Ros Mackay had always intended to revive. It had been his dream, Calum had been told by those who had known him, to return the castle to the glory it had held generations before.

It was a dream that had never been realized.

Artair Ros Mackay had not been born with a warring spirit. He'd had a scholar's heart and had spent his childhood years poring through the pages of his country's history, reading of the great patriots like Robert the Bruce, William Wallace, and Andrew de Moray. It was in those very studies that a rebellious seed had first been planted.

He'd fallen, Calum had been told, in 1715 at the battle of Sheriffmuir, leaving his wife with her belly swollen with his heir. He'd never returned to Cape Wrath. Artair's body had been thrown into an unmarked grave with all the other Jacobite casualties that day. And from then on, the Mackay stone had simply vanished.

Until now.

As Calum stood on that windswept bluff, he couldn't detect so much as the flickering of a candle coming from the shadowy, almost imperceptible silhouette of the castle . . .

. . . the castle where *she* waited.

The one who'd returned the stone.

The lass who called herself a mermaid.

In truth, Calum had thought of little else but her all the day.

He refused to acknowledge any truth to her tale of who she was and where she'd come from. She was no more a mermaid than that Hanoverian usurper sitting in London was his rightful sovereign. It was naught but a fabrication—how could it not be? Even if she did seem to know things she shouldn't, Calum was reasonably certain that if his ancestors ever were going to send him a mermaid, it would not be in the form of a Sassenach, no matter how lovely a lass she might be.

Och, and lovely she was.

In fact, if he was ever to envision his mythical mermaid, the one he used to dream of as a lad, *she* would be it.

It was the contrasts he saw just in looking at her, her hair, black as night, wild as the north wind, and thick against fair, fair skin that looked untouched as the newest snow. Even in those few short moments he'd spent with her, looked at her, her image had been burned into his memory. He was unable to deny the suggestion of the mysterious that seemed to surround her. It was her eyes, he decided along that lonely stretch of a peat cutter's path he walked, more so than anything else about her. For they were indeed a mermaid's eyes, blue as the sea depths, and turned just slightly aslant, giving her the look of the faerie folk.

But she wasn't any faerie.

She was a Sassenach, and she was playing at some sort of game.

Somehow, Calum couldn't quite say how, the lass had known who he was without his even saying. Thus she could identify him, could identify all of them. He couldn't allow her to leave. Were they to set her free, she could have the whole of the Hanoverian army beating at his doorstop within weeks, days even. The best reason for their success thus far in raiding the English's ships had been due to the fact that they were all of them unknown. Without a name to give the enemy, the Crown was hard-pressed to pursue them. And as far as the rest of the world was concerned, Calum and the other members of his crew had either been left for dead on a battlefield or banished from the kingdom . . .

Forgotten.

Ghosts.

And Calum meant to keep it that way, even if it meant

holding the lass against her will. She had the stone. And now that it was back among the Mackays, he had no intention of allowing it to vanish again.

For as long as he could remember, Calum had been fascinated by the *Clach na MacAoidh*. Legend had it that the charm had foretold the fortunes, both good and bad, of the clan chiefs, and that just the dipping of it into water would cure any sickness. It was said to change color to predict the outcome of an impending battle, and Calum often wondered if his father had consulted it that final fateful day. Throughout his childhood he had imagined himself one day bringing the stone back to the clan, in honor of his father. It was as if he'd always known deep down that the day would come.

Which only made Calum wonder just how the lass had come by the stone.

It was a question he intended to find an answer for that night.

Calum slipped easily along the crumbling stone wall that had once stood as the castle's curtain wall, where guards had walked the parapets many a long-ago night. The entrance to the castle was along a narrow stretching pathway that wound its way up a rise on its southern side. In days of yore, access to the castle compound had been through a single opening that was defended by both portcullis and numerous gun ports. Over the past half century since the castle had been abandoned, the original guardhouse had fallen to neglect, the portcullis gate long removed and taken elsewhere.

Surrounding the courtyard, inside, there was a scattering of smaller buildings set about the two central towers. In its heyday, Castle Wrath had been more a separate walled city than a castle. Its remoteness had made it nec-

essary for self-sufficiency. There had been gardens, stables with a blacksmith's forge where tools and pots for
the kitchen had been cast along with great Scottish claymores, even shoes for the chief's horses. In the middle
of the courtyard, ringed in stone, was the cistern that
provided the castle with its fresh water by way of a well
dug deep into the cliff side. There were storehouses, a
brewery, a mill for grinding meal, and a chapel whose
arch yet stood in sacred defiance of the north winds.

Calum crossed to the main tower where he took the
small tin lamp that awaited. They used smuggler's lamps
to light their way, enclosed on all but one side, to shield
the light from being seen outside. Ahead, in the hall, he
could already hear the others, conversations droning,
disagreements breaking out and then fizzling just as
quickly. A fire would be blazing in the great stone hearth
and ale would be flowing from wooden kegs as swiftly
as the waters of the River Naver.

When he reached the doorway, Calum saw that a company of some fifty of his men, of all ages and from all
across the Highlands, had gathered. They were there to
collect their portions of the spoils.

After that first mission when Calum had comman-
deered the HMS *Osprey,* he had set about establishing a
network of operatives in both London and Edinburgh. It
was how he was informed when a ship carrying the con-
victed was preparing to set sail for the Colonies. A messenger would arrive, like earlier that day, and they would
prepare for another mission. They certainly couldn't
save them all, but those they did save would often ask to
join Calum's crew. They had so little left at home to return to.

If they didn't take a place on board the *Adventurer* or

one of the other ships they'd turned to the prince's service, the men would return to various posts throughout the countryside to work as clandestine scouts or informants. For those who sought to join the crew of his ship, Calum had imposed a foremost rule. They could have no wife, and no children. There would be no exceptions.

It was not that he had anything against a man having a family. What they undertook was a dangerous mission. They could, any of them, be overtaken at any moment, and Calum could not bear the possibility of having to tell any child that his father had been killed because of their association with him.

Thus far they'd been fortunate. In the past ten months, they'd lost just one, and that had been due more to the lad's own rash stupidity than anything else. He'd been young. He'd been priming for the fight, not fighting for the cause. And because of it he'd ended up with an English soldier's musket ball imbedded in his temple. Yet, even though he knew there was no way he could have prevented it, the lad's death had not sat easily with Calum.

"Laird!"

M'Cuick called out to Calum from across the room when he saw him standing in the doorway. From the tenor of his voice and the spark in his eye, it appeared he'd been imbibing from the wine kegs for some time.

"Come, join us! There's French wine and tobacco weed from the Colonies. And you should see the silver pissing pot our boys got! Engraved and everything . . . can you believe tha'? They have made a fine haul this time, they have!"

As Calum came into the room, nodding in greeting to the men just returned from *The Adventurer*'s latest foray, he saw that indeed they had made rather an impressive haul. In addition to the ship carrying Belcourt's belongings, they had raided two other English vessels. There were furnishings in elegant mahogany, imported silks and laces, expensive cellars of salt, and casks of highly taxed teas. The men would divide most of it amongst themselves, and sell whatever they didn't wish to keep. Calum rarely took any of the pieces for himself, unless they came across something that was of particular value either to him or to the cause, such as Cumberland's stallion—or the personal traveling trunks of Lord Henry Belcourt.

"We took the trunks up to the study," said Fergus, as if reading Calum's thoughts.

Calum nodded, thinking he'd stay just a wee while in the hall, to oversee the divvying of the goods, then he'd slip off to spend the rest of the night poring through Belcourt's books in search of Uilliam's whereabouts.

" 'Ave a drink o' ale with us, Laird?"

Calum turned to the beaming face of Hamish Beaton. It appeared from the redness in his cheeks, and the spark in his eyes, he'd been nipping at the ale cask himself. He was a young lad, no more than sixteen, who before the rebellion had passed his days working alongside his father on a farm of some two hundred acres near Glen Moriston. His nights had been spent vying for space on the small box bed he shared with three of his eleven brothers and sisters. Now, little more than a year later, they were all of them gone, his father killed on the battlefield at Culloden, his mother lost to the harshness of winter without the shelter of their home, only after watching each of his brothers and sisters succumb to illness, starvation, or both.

Hamish himself had been at the nearest point of starvation when Calum had first found him, locked deep in the stinking, rat-infested hold of a government prison ship. It had taken a sennight of M'Cuick's barley bree and milk-and-whisky possets to even bring the lad to his feet again, shakily as it was. Though he looked little more than a bag of bones now, it was a far cry better than he'd been all those months ago.

"My thanks, Hamish," Calum said, and patted one bony shoulder as he took the tankard and swallowed down a healthy swig of it. The ale slipped easily down his throat and the tankard emptied quickly, only to be re-filled twice over.

Calum felt the tensions of the day start to ease. As he sat watching the others, he let the ale and the brandy they'd begun using to toast their success melt away his disquietude. He ate a little, some cheese and a bite or two of M'Cuick's haggis. He made his way among the others, exchanging nods, listening to stories, until he finally reached the far corner of the room where M'Cuick and a handful of others stood, huddled around something.

"Laird," said M'Cuick upon noticing his arrival. "Will you look at tha'? Have you e'er afore seen such a peculiar-looking apparatus in your life?"

The group parted to reveal a chair of sorts made of finely carved and gilded wood and upholstered in rich red velvet. It was actually two seats joined together at a center armrest, but instead of standing side by side like a bench or a settee, these two had been joined with each facing the opposite direction from the other, a sort of Z-shaped double chair.

"Wha' do you suppose it could be?" asked Hamish, his eyes alight with adolescent wonder.

"D'you suppose it's some sort of Sassenach instru-
ment of torture?" someone else suggested.

Calum circled the chair to get a better view. "Nae, it is
too ornately carved and its wood too dear for such an
elementary purpose."

"I know!" called out another, Hugh perhaps. "I'll bet
it's used for someone who's reading and who doesn't
want someone else reading over their shoulder . . ."

"Och, you *eediot*," said M'Cuick. "Wha' would you
ever know about reading?"

This started a volley of comments and suggestions
from the others as to what, exactly, the furniture maker
could have been thinking when he'd created such a
unique and bizarre-looking chair. The crowd around the
chair swelled as everyone pressed forward to see it and
offer their opinion of what could be its use, until finally
M'Cuick stepped upon the hearthstone so that he towered over the heads of the others. There he stood, simply
stood, and waited for the others to fall silent so that he
might be heard by all.

"I know what it is," he proclaimed with all the fanfare
of a trumpet blare.

Everyone turned, watched, waited. The fire crackled
in the hearth behind him.

"'Tis for the poor mon who weds himsel' to a trollie-
bags of a wife, so as to keep him from having t' look at
her a'day!"

A roar of manly laughter erupted, rocking the room,
only to be silenced in the very next moment by the
sound of an unfamiliar and all-too-feminine voice.

"Actually, Malcolm, its purpose is just the opposite of
that."

Calum swore he could hear every jaw in the place

drop and every head turn to where the lass, his alleged mermaid, stood suddenly framed in the doorway.

The room had fallen so silent, one could have heard a pebble bounce along the length of the stone floor.

Apparently undaunted at having the attention of some fifty or more gruff-looking men trained upon her, the lass walked calmly into the room. She parted the sea of male bodies with but a lift of her brow and tilt of her rose-tinted lips.

Calum stood and watched her. The firelight from the hearth glowed on her pale skin, setting her dark hair aflame with shades of rich red and bronze against silky endless black. She had changed from the traveling habit she'd worn earlier that day, into a gown that was cut low over her breasts, revealing a lovely expanse of skin that only set off the brilliance of the stone she wore more to advantage. Beneath the elegant cut of the gown, she wore a shimmery green skirt that was set with brilliants and glassy beads. It sparkled in the firelight with every movement of her body, swishing around her legs. Calum caught the whispers of the others rippling around the room.

She's the mermaid . . .

'Tis legend . . .

Clach na MacAoidh . . .

So her fabrication had already reached the others, Calum thought, and from the looks on their faces— wonder, awe, reverence even—a good many of them appeared to have fallen for it, too.

Every man who stood in that room was feasting on her with his eyes, feasting, too, on the size and brilliance of that stone. Calum found himself taken with an imme- diate and overwhelming unease. Though they were his men and he had instilled a code of honor among them, what stood before them now was the very worst combination of temptations.

A priceless treasure, and a beautiful woman.

Calum felt a tugging on his shirtsleeve. It was only then he managed to tear his eyes away from her to look at the slight figure standing at his side.

"Laird? Laird? Is it true? Is she really"—his voice dropped to a whisper—"is she truly a *mermaid?*"

Calum ruffled Hamish's mop of hair. "Now how could she be a mermaid, lad? Hae you e'er seen a fish walk down a flight of stairs?"

"But look at her dress, Laird. Mungo says that's her green tail skin, and if we can steal it, she'll not be able to swim away."

Calum chuckled. "Just you leave the lass—and her tail skin—to me, eh?"

But his levity fell off the moment the lass came to stand before him.

"Good e'entide to you, lass."

"And to you, Mr. Mackay."

"'Tis quite a pretty frock you've got on."

"I'm afraid other than my traveling habit 'tis all I have. Your men took my trunks when they ransacked the ship."

Beside her, Hamish was staring up at her as if she truly were some mythical creature come to life before his eyes.

It was easy to see why. She was so lovely that she even had Calum's own breath hitching in his throat.

He noticed the two men standing closest to him trying to suck in their stomachs before she might chance to notice their swelling girths. Most of the others in the room were just staring.

Staring, and wanting.

It was the very last thing Calum needed.

"The chair is called a tête-à-tête," she said. "It is a French courting chair. 'Tis the latest fashion in Paris. It allows young courting couples to converse facing one another—tête-à-tête—rather than turned one up close against the other, which can be a bit too intimate for some of the more protective papas."

The men continued to stare at her as if she'd just recited a magic incantation.

It was M'Cuick who finally got hold of his fleeting wits.

"Och, leave it to those Frenchy frogs to come up wit' something quite as kae-witted as tha'. Wha's a mon t'do wit' it after he's wed the lass, eh? Chop it up for kindling? Nae, I've a better use for it than tha'. I'm thinking it would make a fine chair for arm wrestling."

The lass stared at him. "Arm wrestling? But—"

Where moments before she had held them all in thrall, they all but ignored the lass now, immediately won over to M'Cuick's idea.

"C'mon, M'Cuick, you old sod. Let us show these lads wha' a real man's about, eh?"

It was Mungo, and he was rolling up his shirtsleeves in preparation for the first match.

M'Cuick, all too happy to oblige, started untying the strings of his apron.

Wagers were struck as a circle formed around the chair in anticipation of the match.

"But, wait!"

It was Hamish who spoke, his lad's voice struggling

to rise above the din of the others. "What'll the prize be for the winner?"

"Aye," agreed Hugh. "There's got t' be a prize."

The men glanced around. Since they all shared in the wealth from the raids, none of the booty seemed an attractive enough reward.

"What about the chair?" offered Hamish.

"Wha' the de'il would I be doing wit' a dae-na-gude piece o' fluff like tha'?" Mungo countered.

Opinions were given, and just as quickly they were rebuffed.

"Wait, lads . . . wait! Listen t'me now . . . I know just wha' should be the prize!"

It was M'Cuick once again, and he stood on the hearthstone as he had moments before, waiting for his audience's full attention.

"The winner," he said a moment later, giving a grin, "gets a kiss from the bonny lassie."

Tell a bunch of men they are vying for a pretty parlor piece and they would rather spend their time drowning in ale.

But tell those same men, men who hadn't been in the company of a woman in . . .

. . . in so long they couldn't even remember, that they were wrestling for a kiss from a pretty woman, and utter pandemonium breaks loose.

"Aye!" came the collective cheer.

They would have toasted the idea with a round of ale, but they were already tussling just to be the first to get into the chair, shoving, cursing, pulling hair even. It wasn't a matter of who they were going to get to wrestle first, but rather who they were going to convince *not* to.

The lass, Calum noticed, was standing by quietly

chewing her lower lip, those blue eyes as wide as if a
pack of wolves had gathered before her and were inch-
ing forward to take the first bite.

"Lads!"

Calum rarely yelled, and the uncustomary sound of
his voice raised above their own had them halting mid-
scuffle, some still holding fistfuls of another's shirtfront.

"Hae any of you considered tha' the lass might not be
so willing to bestow this prize?"

All eyes shifted at once from Calum . . . to the lass.

She glanced quickly at Calum, caught with indecision.
She would certainly refuse. There was no earthly way
this Sassenach lass was going to—

"I will."

Now it was Calum's jaw that went dropping.

He clamped it shut as his men let out a whooping bel-
low of approval.

And it was then Calum realized there was no earthly
way *he* was going to allow anyone to kiss the lass . . .

. . . other than him.

"I'll be sitting first," he said, shirking off his coat and
shooting a glare of unspoken warning to them all at one
time. "Who'll challenge me?"

Now, instead of rushing for the chance, they stood
mute and still as statues. No one dared oppose him.

Calum was just readying to disperse them all, send
them back to their ale for the night, when a voice suddenly called out from the back of the room, strong and
sure.

"I'll face you."

Chapter Ten

It was Fergus.

Calum should have known.

If anyone was going to come forward to challenge him, it would only have been him.

Fergus Bain came across the room at a saunter's pace, absorbing the stares of the others like a great oak collecting the rays of the sun, all the while keeping his own gaze fixed upon Calum. Calum knew that look, knew the defiance that sparked behind it. Though they were as close as if they had been born blood brothers, like brothers, there had been times throughout their upbringing when Fergus would suddenly and unexpectedly challenge Calum's place, a reminder to him that while he might be the clan chief's nephew, his place in the Bain family hierarchy was at best inadvertent.

When Calum had been a lad, five or six years old perhaps, he had fallen, as most five- or six-year-old lads do, only the fall had been severe enough to have left Calum with a fractured arm. Summoned by his cry, Uilliam had raced to help him, taking a hollering Calum into his arms and then walking him slowly, gingerly, all the way back to the house to tend to him. Unfortunately, it had happened on the very day that Uilliam had promised to take Fergus out deer stalking for the first time. Instead of packing up their muskets and heading for the moors as father and son, Uilliam had spent the afternoon splinting Calum's arm with a stout slat of wood and then sitting by his bedside through the night to watch for any signs of a fever.

It wasn't that he ever set out to favor Calum over Fergus or Lachlann, but Uilliam had taken a clan oath to serve as Calum's guardian. It was an honor that he had graciously accepted and that he earnestly carried out. Sometimes, unfortunately, it came at the expense of his own two lads.

Fergus had been just a lad of four, and Lachlann not yet born, when Calum had been delivered to the Bain household. There had been no warning, no hint of Calum's coming aforehand. Calum's uncle, the Mackay chief, had simply brought the just-toddling infant to the Bains' modest croft, and then had just as swiftly left him there to be raised. For a lad who had had his father all to himself those first formative years of his childhood, it must have been difficult, Calum realized, for Fergus to have had to share Uilliam's affections so suddenly and so unexpectedly. But he'd done his best to accept and get on, with only occasional lapses of jealousy.

He'd certainly made his feelings known the day Calum had broken his arm. It had been just as Uilliam had finished tending to Calum's splint that he'd realized Fergus was nowhere to be found. Fergus had orchestrated other schemes in an effort to draw his father's attention away from Calum before, but they had been nothing compared to the magnitude of what he would do that day. He stayed away for three days and nights, hiding out in a cave that was close enough to hear his father's worried voice calling out for him but far enough away not to be found. He timed his return well. By the third day, Uilliam had settled the blame for it all fully upon himself so that when Fergus finally did surface, tired and hungry and shivering with cold, he was quite assured of his father's favor for some time afterward.

"Calum," was all Fergus said as he came to stand before him. He shrugged off his coat, pushed back his sleeves over his solid forearms. His face, Calum noted, was etched with a steely determination, expressionless—until he happened to catch a glance at the lass. It was only a brief glance, but in that moment, the harsh lines, the glint in his eyes, suddenly softened.

It was then Calum knew it wasn't just the opportunity of proving his strength against Calum that had compelled Fergus to step forward.

Fergus had fallen under her spell as well.

It was dangerous, that look. And Calum knew it. He found himself wishing he could just walk away from the challenge, while at the same time knowing he could not.

"Are you ready then, lads?"

M'Cuick stepped between them, diffusing the knot of tension tied between them into nothing more than a healthy bout of male swaggering. He clapped them both on their backs and led them to the peculiar French chair across the room. The delicate carved wood on its spindly arms would not provide enough elbow room for the two men, so a makeshift tabletop was hastily improvised by way of one of M'Cuick's cast-iron griddles. It would call for an added degree of dexterity on the part of the competitors, for if either of them so much as shifted their weight from the platform, the entire thing would teeter, immediately forfeiting the match.

Calum rolled back his shirtsleeves, then took his place at the chair where Fergus was already seated and waiting. He leaned in. Calum positioned his arm in front of him. It was the very one he'd broken that long-ago day.

They locked gazes. The men clasped hands and waited for M'Cuick to call the start of the match. All the while, they watched each other like two wolves who were not about to share the same prey.

"A'right, lads. Now you both ken what to do. Soon as I pull my hand away, the match is on." M'Cuick glanced at them both. "Are you ready?"

"Aye," Calum said, giving a short nod.

"Aye," echoed Fergus.

M'Cuick's hand fell away. Calum and Fergus engaged. The match was on.

The room became charged with an almost palpable anticipation. The rest of the company pressed in around them.

At first there wasn't a sound, just a tense, expectant silence as the two forces met, collided, and held, each refusing to give way to the other. It seemed as if every man present was holding his breath.

But as the match stretched on—one minute into two— and neither showed signs of relenting, the men standing around them began to stir. Soon they started to fidget. Some muttered words of encouragement, directing them neither to Calum nor to Fergus, but to them both at the same time. Others tried to guess how long the match could go on. Fortunately, they knew better than to divide into rival sides.

Between Fergus and Calum, their clasped hands labored, trembling from the force of the one meeting another equally. His jaw was tight, his teeth clenched, and Calum refused to yield.

He could not lose.

The room grew warmer. Sweat began to sheen on Fergus's brow. He blinked twice, a split-second slip of concentration that allowed Calum's fist to inch slightly forward. The others noticed this and responded with a collective, indrawn breath. Fergus broke his gaze from Calum's and dropped his focus downward as he summoned every ounce of strength within him in an effort to try to regain his lost position. The muscles in his jaw worked and flexed as he strained his strength to its furthest ability. His face began to color a deep wrenching red.

The others started chanting—

Go . . .

Go . . .

Go . . .

Calum scarcely heard them. When Fergus had dropped his head, Calum had caught sight of the lass standing a space behind him. Their gazes met, held. He focused only on her. The prize of that one kiss from her became a reward Calum couldn't allow anyone but himself to claim.

He garnered every last bit of his strength, determination, and will, and concentrated them onto the object of their clasped hands.

He *would* win.

He knew the moment he began to gain the advantage. He felt Fergus's fingers slip just slightly. He saw the darkness of uncertainty cloud his eyes. With a final surge borne on an audible breath of release, Calum propelled his arm forward and seized the victory.

The mob erupted with a triumphant whoop, and immediately started giving them both congratulatory claps on the back.

Calum stood. His arm and every muscle within it throbbed and burned. Where moments before it had felt invincible, it now went as weak as bog mud. He shook it off, flexing and working his fingers, tightening his fist as the company surrounded them both. Finally, he offered his hand to Fergus in a gesture of recognition and respect.

Fergus stared at him through a long moment that seemed to stretch into several. Everybody fell silent. Calum hoped Fergus wouldn't bear the grudge of losing like a weight upon his shoulder. The two of them would need to be united if they were going to see their mission through to free Uilliam.

Fergus obviously realized this as well, for he finally took Calum's outstretched hand in a single, conciliatory shake.

The mob cheered.

"'Twas a fine match," Fergus said as they turned and started to walk together toward the center of the room.

"Aye, it was." Calum glanced at him. "My arm feels like a limp piece of seaweed though."

Fergus grinned. "Next time, you'll let me win, aye? I winna want the lads to think they can shove me about should they take the notion."

Calum chuckled and nodded. He was just glad it was over.

The men seemed to be, too. They had already started for the ale tub and kegs of wine in the corner to celebrate, until . . .

"Wait!"

M'Cuick called out, summoning them back. "What about the laird's prize?"

"Aye," said Hamish. "You're supposed to get a kiss from the merlass."

The merlass.

"She's not a . . ."

Calum turned, half expecting her to have vanished in all the uproar after the match. It would have been the perfect time for her to have made her escape.

But she hadn't.

She was standing by the hearth, alone, limned by the warmth of the firelight and looking more lovely than should have been possible.

That was what he had fought for . . . and won.

With all eyes upon her, the lass came across the room to meet him.

"You are the victor," she said softly.

"So it would appear." Calum felt suddenly hesitant, and decided it was the presence of that stone hanging around her neck that was making him uneasy. He'd dreamed about it all his life, dreamed of having it, holding it in his hand, and now, to have it so close, yet untouchable, was something he'd never planned for.

Nor had he planned to have it nestled against the breasts of a mysterious lass who called herself a mermaid.

"You dinna have to do this," he said, offering her the opportunity to change her mind.

Hamish and a couple of the others standing nearby overheard. They fell silent, waiting to see if she would.

She glanced fleetingly about the room, at the sea of faces watching them. Then she looked at Calum with those eyes of brilliant blue, lifted a brow, and said, "Perhaps are you intimidated by the notion of kissing a mermaid, Mr. Mackay?"

Calum heard someone chuckle. It sounded suspiciously like M'Cuick.

That chuckle, and the whisper of her soft startled gasp as he pulled her against him, were the last sounds he heard before his mouth covered hers.

Intimidated, she'd said.

He bent her back over his arm, kissing her hard. And then everything else—the room, the dozens of men standing around them—simply ceased to exist.

He'd meant to be done with it quickly, a swift and sudden sort of thing that would show her just how unintimidated he really was.

But once he'd drawn her against him, felt the warmth of her body pressed to his, felt the rapid staccato pulsebeat in her throat beneath the fingers that had lifted to caress her there, that sudden swift thing became something else entirely.

It became a long, hot, wet kiss that shot straight to his groin and somehow simply refused to end.

If he were to guess, Calum would have sworn it was her first kiss. When he first took her against him, her mouth was clamped tightly closed, and her body felt like a taut string stretched nearly to the point of breaking. Easing that tightness became a priority, and Calum stroked a hand along the column of her throat, skimming her jaw and letting his fingers get lost in the silky dark riot of her hair at the back of her neck. After a few moments, she eased just the tiniest bit, and he deepened the kiss, tasting her, teasing her . . .

. . . tutoring her.

She was an apt student. She slackened against him,

letting him bear her completely in his arms as she sur-
rendered her mouth to his, slowly, tentatively opening
her own. Their tongues met, caressed, and he seduced
her, nipping her bottom lip, refusing to pull back, kissing
her long and relentlessly.

He had expected he'd become aroused by it. It had
been some time since he'd kissed a woman, and quite
possibly a lifetime since he'd kissed one so incredibly
enchanting. What he hadn't expected was how deeply
the kiss would reach inside of him, seeping like honey
through every limb and taking hold of his most guarded,
most protected place.

His heart.

In that moment, Calum knew what all the poets had
meant by their pretty words hinting at the *zing* of
Cupid's arrow.

He knew, because in that moment, he'd been hit.

Calum lifted his head. He looked at her. His own
pulse was pounding in his ears, his breath hitched, and
he watched as her eyes slowly drifted open. She blinked
at him, her mouth still wet from his kiss. He wanted her.
Oh, how he wanted her. He wanted to take her almost as
much as he wanted to take that stone that hung around
her slender neck. He wanted to bury his hands in that
wild black hair and kiss her again, and again, and he
very likely would have, had there not been a room of
hairy leering Scotsmen surrounding them.

So instead he eased her up before him to stand, and
reluctantly slid his arms away.

The gaping bunch of idiots let out a resounding cheer.

Someone brought the lass a tankard, and then another
to Calum. Mungo prepared to let loose on his fiddle.

Until Hamish called out, pointing at the lass.

"Look! Look at the stone! 'Tis glowing!"

And indeed it was, a bright brilliant hot red more radiant than the light of the fire.

"Och, but she truly is a merlass," he heard someone whisper.

"Aye, just like the one who came to the Mackay in the legend . . ."

Calum spun around. "No, she's not a . . ."

But it was no use. The theory blew like the seawind, sweeping through the hall and stirring everyone in its path to expressions of awe and wonder. Mungo cocked his bow and started improvising a tune, his rich tale teller's voice singing out about "The Lass Who Came From Beneath the Sea." Ale was swilled. A celebration was begun.

"Laird?"

Calum looked to where Hamish was standing before him. The lad looked bright-eyed, nervous. "Aye?"

"I was after wonderin' . . ." His face colored as red as that stone. "Would it— Could I—" He stammered, glancing down at his bare toes.

"What is it, lad? Out wit' it."

"I was after wonderin' if I might ask the lass to dance."

It had taken every ounce of his sixteen-year-old courage just to ask him, Calum knew. He glanced at the lass, who stood watching Mungo at his fiddle. "You certainly dinna need my permission to do it, lad."

"Aye, but I do. She's your merlass, Laird. She has your magic stane and you've just kissed her. 'Twould be like courting anither man's wife, it would . . ."

Calum was just getting ready to educate the lad about the nonsense of myths and mermaids, but stopped himself from it. The match with Fergus had been confirmation aplenty that having the lass amongst all these men could be a dangerous thing. If Fergus had taken a notion of her, others no doubt would as well. But as Hamish had said, by winning her kiss before them all, Calum had all but claimed her for his own. It was the Scots way. And her best protection while she was there would be in having the others believe she—and that stone she wore—truly were *his*.

Calum knew his men, knew them to their bones. No one would harm her, and they would protect her with their lives just as they would him. So he simply answered, " 'Tis up to the lass, then."

"My thanks, sir." He started to turn, then stopped. "Uh, Laird?"

"Aye, lad?"

"I'm not knowing her name. What should I call her?"

It was a question Calum wanted the answer to as well. "She calls herself Maris, Hamish."

"Maris." The lad nodded. " 'Tis a bonny name, it is."

However false it may be.

Calum stood back, watching as Hamish straightened his backbone, squared his bony shoulders, and then started toward where the lass was standing, chatting with M'Cuick by the fire.

Hamish bowed his head. It took him some effort, but he finally made his nervous request. Calum found himself holding his breath for the lad, hoping she wouldn't rebuff him. It was undoubtedly his first experience in asking a lass to dance, and Calum couldn't help the feeling of relief that took him when he saw the wide nervous grin spread across the lad's face.

Hamish turned to Calum and nodded, indicating she had consented.

Together the two of them walked to the center of the

room. The others noticed them, took their cue and pushed back, clearing an area. Hamish put up a hand and the music slowed to a stop.

Hamish took up the lass's hand, showing her the basic steps of one of the Scottish country dances he'd no doubt learned on the dirt floor of the croft house he'd shared with his mother and sisters. She listened and watched, and then practiced the sequence slowly with him once. Then, when she appeared to have it, she nodded.

Mungo struck up a chord, opened into a lively tune, and they started dancing.

The mermaid's dance.

She was a quick study, because to watch her, Calum would have never known she had only just learned the dance's steps. She matched Hamish's feet step for step as they skipped and hopped around the center of the room in time to the music and the clapping hands and stomping feet of the others. The mood grew livelier the more the ale poured. After a short while, Hamish found himself being called off the floor, only to be replaced by another, this time M'Cuick, who despite his great size soon proved himself to be quite nimble of foot. 'Twas a good thing, too, for he would likely crush her toes if he happened to misstep.

The music played on, and the dancing kept up. They whirled and they turned, pranced and circled. One partner replaced another. All the while Calum stood and watched and wondered.

Just who the devil was this lass?

She called herself a mermaid, yet she spoke with the Sassenach's tongue. She dressed and conducted herself politely, nobly even, yet she deigned to pass her night dancing with a bunch of drunken Scotsmen. And she had the stone of his ancestors hanging around her neck, but she refused to reveal where she'd gotten it.

And then he remembered something she'd said when she had arrived in the hall earlier that evening and he had remarked upon the fineness of her dress:

'Tis all I have. Your men took my trunks when they ransacked the ship . . .

Her trunks.

The trunks that Fergus had told him were awaiting him even now in his study. Perhaps there would be something there that would reveal her identity, finally telling him whether she was related in some way to Lord Belcourt as he suspected, a mermaid like she claimed, or someone else entirely.

Setting down his ale tankard, Calum stole a final glance at the lass. Then quietly, he slipped away.

It was some time later that Isabella held up her hands in a gesture of outright surrender when yet another of the men stepped forward to claim a dance. Her sides were stitching beneath her stays and her hair, plainly arranged as it had been, had tumbled from its pins after the first few turns about the floor. It now fell down her back in a tangle of black. But she didn't care. It was a night for adventures and she had enjoyed herself immensely.

"Miss Maris, you look as if you might like a wee drink . . ."

"Oh, yes, thank you . . . Hamish, is it?"

The lad dimpled that she had remembered his name. "Aye. I hope this will do."

He handed her what appeared to be a tankard full of ale. Isabella had never had ale in her life. It wasn't something customarily served to the daughters of a duke. She was so parched, she drank it anyway.

In fact, she drained the entire tankard.

As she set the vessel down with a clank on the table, she wondered what her mother, the duchess, would say if she could see her now?

Dancing with rough Scottish men . . . swigging ale . . . sharing her first kiss with a notorious pirate? And what a kiss it had been . . .

It had been everything she had ever dreamed a kiss should be, unbelievably, undeniably breathtaking. For the rest of her life Isabella would remember that kiss, would remember, too, the way it had felt as if her legs and arms had turned to pudding, and how her senses had been sent soaring to the stars. Were all kisses that way? Or was it simply the adventure of the night, the fact that the one kissing her had been a handsome, exciting honorable pirate?

When she was older she would tell her daughters, and her daughters' daughters, about that kiss. They would sigh dreamily and giggle about it over tea and wonder if they, too, might one day be given such a first kiss.

She didn't know what had come over her to agree to kiss him as she had. The Bella she had always been would never have dared such a thing. But somehow, there was just something about him, something about the way she felt when she was with him. She felt like a new and different person. She was not the same *boring* Bella Drayton. She was someone else. She was Maris, a pretend mermaid, and for the first time in her life, she was *reckless*.

Elizabeth would be so very proud of her.

Dunakin Castle, the Isle of Skye

Lady Elizabeth MacKinnon was not known for her patience.

She was, however, rather *re*nowned for her impatience,

and it was that trait alone that had her muttering, "Bloody blooming hell . . ." as she stared out the rain-dotted windowpane looking out onto the misty Kyle of Akin.

Where could Bella be?

Had her husband been there, he would have looked at her with a reproving lift of his brow. Douglas didn't like it when Elizabeth swore. And truth be told, at that moment, she would have welcomed that scolding glance over having another day pass with no word from Douglas.

He had promised he would write when he found Bella.

Which only meant he hadn't yet found her.

Damnation!

Any number of horrors could be happening to her at that very moment as Elizabeth stood there, miles away, helpless to do anything to save her.

It was the very worst sort of feeling Elizabeth had ever known.

She closed her eyes, leaned her head against the cold windowpane, and tried to summon up a mental image of her dear sister.

Sweet, innocent Bella, who more so than any of her sisters had been sheltered the most by their upbringing. While Elizabeth had been off riding her father's stallions pell-mell across the Northumbrian hills, Bella had stayed behind at home, content just to write in her journal. When Katie and Mattie had staged mock dramas for the duchess in the garden and Caroline, bored with having been relegated to the lesser parts, had turned her attention to climbing the duke's prized fruit trees, Bella had simply sat off to the side, sketching them all in her sketchbook. Bella was meek. She was timid. And now she had been thrust into the very midst of a most dangerous situation, alone, no doubt frightened out of her wits, and with no one knowing where to find her.

Bella, we will find you. If it takes looking across every brae and burn in Scotland, I promise we will find you.

Elizabeth had never known a fear like the icy empty chill that had seized her when that ship, the *Hester Mary*, had arrived at Leith harbor without Isabella on it. Aunt Idonia had been beside herself, hysterical as a madwoman as she stumbled down the ship's gangplank, breaking into tears the moment she saw Elizabeth and Douglas and the others standing there.

She had scarcely been able to relate the events that had taken place, events that seemed somehow unbelievable despite the fact that the captain, crew, and the other passengers had all corroborated them.

Pirates had taken her sister.

Scottish pirates.

They had no clue as to who they'd been or why they had taken Isabella, no clue that is until Douglas had asked Lord Belcourt to repeat his version of the story a second time, this time concentrating on the things the pirates had said and, more specifically, the banner they had flown from the flagstaff of their ghostly ship.

Bratach Bhan Clann Aoidh.

It had been their war cry, and the clan standard for the clan Mackay.

And once they had deciphered that part of it, Douglas had known just where to begin searching for her.

"In Sutherland," he'd said, in an effort to reassure the duke, who had been on the very verge of calling out the king's army.

Sutherland, in the very northern part of Scotland.

Even from where Elizabeth was on Skye, it was some one hundred fifty miles distant.

Douglas had prepared to leave immediately from Edinburgh, chartering a sloop to sail after them. It was when Elizabeth had announced her intention to go with him that she learned just how inflexible her husband could be.

"No."

"But, Douglas, she is my sister!"

"She is my sister, too, Elizabeth."

"But she was my sister long before she ever was yours!"

That comment hadn't pleased him, although he had to know it was only the almost unbearable fear that had made her say it in the first place.

"Elizabeth, I love Isabella just as much as if she had been born a sister of my blood. Which means I will look for her just as diligently as you would, and with much greater means, I might add. I know the country. Being Scottish, I am much more likely to have success talking with them than you would."

Elizabeth tried, but failed to find any argument against that. "But you have to find her!"

"And *I* will. *You,* however, will travel with my brother to Skye where you will see to the safety and well-being of our unborn bairn. Aye? On board a ship that might very well come up against another in combat on the high seas is no' the place for an expectant mother."

He was right, and Elizabeth knew it. She'd only another two months before the babe was due. But that didn't mean she had to like it.

It was on that thought that Elizabeth repeated, "Bloody, blooming hell."

"Now is tha' any way for an expectant mother to be talking?"

Elizabeth spun around, half expecting to see Douglas standing there, somehow miraculously returned with Isabella beside him.

But it wasn't Douglas, not at all, although the man who stood there was as near as one could possibly get.

His younger brother, Iain MacKinnon, strode into the room to stand beside her at the window.

"Dinna worry, Bess. Douglas will find her. I know some of the Mackays from marching with the prince's army in the rebellion. They were all honorable, respectable men who would ne'er think to harm a woman."

Elizabeth looked at him. "Then why did these honorable and respectable men take her in the first place?"

"I wish I knew." Iain shook his head. "All I can think is that whoever took her must be some sort of rogue, an outcast of the clan. You dinna need t' worry though because he will only live long enough to regret ever doing it. Douglas will make certain of that."

And if he didn't, Elizabeth vowed, *she* most definitely would.

Chapter Eleven

Calum closed the door to his study behind him, shutting away the music and the revelry that were still well under way in the hall below.

He hadn't wanted to leave, but he'd had to. He'd had to because he had been afraid, truly afraid, that if he stayed, he just might kiss her again.

And if he kissed her again, he knew there was no way on earth, or in heaven or hell for that matter either, that he would stop.

So he turned the key, locking the door for good measure.

In the center of the room stood a half-dozen traveling trunks of varying sizes.

Among them, one would hold the secret to where Uilliam was imprisoned.

The other would solve the mystery of who the lass truly was.

The question was, which one did he want the answer to first?

After the kiss he'd just had, and the way it had hit him, hit him like a boulder hard in his belly, he wasn't entirely certain. The enigma of the mysterious Lady Maris was only growing more complicated. He wanted, nae, he *needed* to know who she was, where she had come from.

He also needed to find Uilliam.

Throwing chance to the wind, Calum crossed to the nearest trunk, pulled a chair up beside it as he set about opening its lid.

It was hers.

He knew it the moment he lifted its latch, jimmied easily enough with the point of his dirk. The very scent of her, subtle herbs and sweet spices, overwhelmed him as soon as he lifted its lid, as if she were standing just behind him in the room.

Fate had apparently decided for him.

Calum pulled away the layer of scented tissue paper that covered the trunk's contents and was greeted by swaths of fine silks and satins and laces arranged neatly before him. He took up a candle and set it atop the trunk beside it and started rummaging through, pulling out bodices and fichus and ribands embroidered with silver threads. These were not the trappings of any ordinary lass. They were costly fabrics and finely stitched furbelows. When he dug farther inside, beneath the clothing, he found a small box that contained her jewelry, fine pieces set with jewels and pearls that only served to feed his initial suspicion that she was in some way related to Lord Belcourt. If not his daughter, then a niece or cousin, perhaps. In any case, a genteel lady—and not any mysterious mermaid.

Calum noticed a single pair of white stockings, silk

and very finely woven, tucked away inside the trunk. He reached for them, picking one up and letting it fall to its full length. It was made to the shape of her leg, clocked with a trailing ivy design that had been embroidered along the lower calf. He imagined that bit of silk caressing the curve of her leg, tying at her knee with a wisp of silk garter. *Red* silk garter. He breathed deeply, slowly, as he ran the sleek fabric between his fingers, and pictured her wearing them, pictured her wearing *only* them, just the stockings and the Mackay stone dangling between her breasts.

Nothing else.

His body jolted at the very thought.

She would be lovely, he knew, her pale skin radiant as she stood before the fire, her breasts lush and full. He imagined her waist, small as it was, flaring to the hips she had hidden beneath those panniered skirts. He imagined her standing before him, a seductive smile on her lips as she snaked one hand around his neck, and pulled his mouth to hers. He imagined taking her up against him, against the hardness of him, and carrying her to the fire to lay her down on the great rug before it.

He would kiss her from temple to toe, taste her scented skin, and run his hands along the silken length of her thigh.

He would bury his face in her hair, nuzzling her neck as he made love to her throughout the night.

He imagined her looking at him with those soft eyes of blue and whispering his name . . .

Calum.

He imagined her taking that chain from around her neck and giving him the stone that would finally give him the answer for which he had waited a lifetime.

He imagined, because he knew . . . it was a dream.

Naught but a dream.

Calum set the stocking aside and continued searching through the trunk for his answers.

It was in the second, smaller trunk that he found something infinitely more intriguing.

A journal.

Her journal.

Calum sat back with the candle burning beside him and turned to the first page, reading the words written there in a fine and elegant script:

> *Today I received the news that Bess is with child. Whilst I was immediately elated for her, and thrilled at the prospect of becoming an aunt, I must confess to a certain envy. All her life, Bess swore against the trappings of love and marriage, yet she has found her greatest happiness in just that. And now, she is to become a mother, whilst I, whose only dream has ever been of having love and marriage and children, am left empty and alone. I feel terrible. And then I feel terrible for feeling terrible. Am I a horrible sister? I love Bess with all my heart, and am thrilled at her new happiness, but at the same time I cannot help but weep inside at the unfairness . . .*

For an hour or more, Calum sat and read through the pages. Her thoughts. Her feelings. Her innermost dreams. And while he didn't come any closer to discovering *who* she really was, he certainly had an understanding of *what* she was made of deep inside.

She was vulnerable.

She was romantic.

She was intelligent.

She was uncertain.

She loved art and poetry, and was deeply, *deeply* devoted to her family, of whom he counted at least four sisters, a father and a mother, and two others named Agamemnon and Homer, who were probably some sort of pets.

She dreamed of more. She dreamed of love and excitement and adventure, but when it came time to play a part, she seemed to linger offstage, allowing the brighter brilliance of her sisters, most particularly the one named Bess, to shine instead. She had been the second daughter and so she felt she had somehow disappointed her parents for not having been born a son. So she stayed quietly out of the way, never causing worry or trouble. She lived her life across the pages of her journal, all while watching the rest of the world tumble on around her.

And she was willing to sacrifice her own happiness for the contentment of her parents by agreeing to wed a man she didn't even know.

I received a letter today, read one of the passages near the end of the book. *It comes from Mother and Papa. It promises to reveal the name of my future husband. I have not opened it, nor will I, until I am certain all hope for someone else is truly, truly gone.*

She was a dreamer.

When he turned to the next page, something fell from inside, fluttering to the floor. He looked and found what appeared to be a folded letter, yet sealed. He picked it up, turned it over. Was this the letter she had written of? The one that was to contain her future husband's name?

He look at its front. It was addressed simply to "Bella."

Bella.

So that was her name. It described her perfectly—*beautiful*—suiting her far better than the invented Maris.

Calum set aside the journal and studied the letter closely, turning it front to back, front to back. The red wax seal held the impression of a crest. He looked at it closely and recognized the coronet of a duke.

He exhaled heavily, closing his eyes. She was not Lord Belcourt's daughter.

But that information did not make him feel any better. It only made matters worse.

He shouldn't open the letter, he knew. But at the same time, Calum couldn't keep himself from holding the blade of his dirk over the candle beside him, and sliding it under the waxen seal to loosen it—loosen it, but not break it.

He had to know who she was. If her father was a duke—an English duke—they would have more trouble than they could possibly imagine. Calum needed to know what he was facing.

But in the back of his mind, a small part of him also needed to know the name of the man she was going to wed.

The heat of the blade pulled the seal cleanly away from the parchment.

Calum slowly unfolded the letter.

Dearest Bella,
Your father and I have spent the past months whilst
you have been away considering quite a number
of suitable candidates for your future husband. It had

seemed so easy when your father was forever threatening Elizabeth with an arranged marriage, but in truth, it is the most difficult decision a parent can ever make. Your father especially had a terrible time of it. No one ever quite measured up for his Bella. However, just as we were preparing to concede defeat, the very perfect candidate appeared quite unexpectedly at our door. He had come, in fact, to call on you. Knowing the fondness you held in your heart as a young girl for him, I know you will be thrilled to learn that we have made arrangements for your marriage to Kentigern St. Clive. His father, the earl, has readily consented, particularly after your father offered rather many acres of the property adjoining his as part of your dowry. All that remains is your consent, dear Bella. Though we cannot think of a reason why you shouldn't wish to wed him, we did insist on the condition of your full and willing agreement to the match, else all stipulations already agreed upon are null and void. You may tell us your answer when you arrive in Edinburgh, although I suspect I already know what it will be. We shall be there to meet you at Leith, dearest.

It was signed simply *Your Loving Mother*, giving Calum no further hint of who the family might be.

Calum stared at the name one more time. *Kentigern St. Clive.* A thoroughly noble, thoroughly Sassenach sort of name.

The perfect sort of name to marry the daughter of a duke.

Calum folded the letter. He heated the blade, softening the wax to once again seal it.

When he was finished, he stared down at the letter that looked just as it had moments before he'd opened it. He was filled with discontent, both at what he'd read and the fact that he'd done it so surreptitiously. He'd had no right to invade her privacy as he had. He'd stolen into her most personal thoughts by reading the pages of her journal, thoughts that most people rarely examined about themselves, let alone committed to paper. And then to make matters worse, he had read something even she didn't yet know.

Needing to make some effort, however insignificant, to atone for what he'd done, Calum slipped the letter back into its place in the journal, closed the book, and placed it back inside her trunk.

He would read no further.

And he would try, try very hard to forget everything that he'd just read.

Even as he knew that would be impossible.

Just as impossible as it would be to forget her when she finally left.

It was nearly midnight when Isabella managed to slip away from the hall. Most of the men had dozed off, their ale tankards tipped precariously against their shirtfronts or dangling from motionless fingertips. Others had retired to the far corners of the room for cards and dicing.

After the dancing had finished and Mungo had played his last jig, she had sat with M'Cuick, discussing various ways of dressing a roast, until his eyes had grown heavy, and his lids had finally closed in defeat. She hadn't the heart to wake him, even to send him off to his bed, so she'd left him, with his head at rest atop his beefy forearms, snoring softly as she'd tiptoed away.

Now in her chamber, Isabella took her sketching pad and chalks from her traveling valise and retreated to the chair that sat beside the hearth. Someone, she knew not who, had stoked a fire for her and it was burning sluggishly in the grate, throwing shades of amber and gold across the page. She was not yet ready for sleep, her thoughts too abuzz from the excitement of the evening.

It was an extraordinary thing. In the space of one evening, she had watched as two men had battled for her favor, she'd been kissed for the very first time in her life, and she had danced with more men than she could possibly keep count of. Danced and enjoyed herself immensely.

But it wasn't just that one evening. It had been ever since the *Adventurer* had come sailing out of the mists. At a time when she should have been fearing for her life, she had instead felt truly, genuinely alive. It was a heady, addicting thing, this feeling, and she suddenly understood why her sister had always done so many outrageous things.

Elizabeth must have known what it was to feel this same way. It was as if the very world around her were suddenly splashed with vibrant, radiant color. There was an element of fear, yes, but it only heightened the even more palpable element of excitement. Things felt differently, smelled differently, even tasted differently. Every sense, it seemed, was sparked with a new and brilliant fire. Isabella could only imagine that once she'd experienced it, this magic, Elizabeth had been reluctant to let it go, so she had just done more and more outrageous things in an effort to recapture that thrill, that giddy sense of invincibility.

Isabella had just done the same thing, only it had

taken her twenty years longer to discover it. Now, however, she found herself just as reluctant to let it go.

She had been absently sketching while she'd been thinking and as she pulled the chalk away from the page, Isabella suddenly found herself looking down onto the image of Calum Mackay. Though roughly sketched, there was no mistaking those eyes, that clandestine stare, the mouth that had so completely overwhelmed hers. She rubbed a fingertip along the curve of his lip. She had never known what it was to have a man look at her the way he had, kiss her, want her. When he had taken her into his arms, Isabella had felt her heartbeat skip, had sucked in a breath, and had steeled herself for what she had hoped would not be too frightening an experience.

She had never been kissed by a man before. She hadn't known what to expect. She could never have been more mistaken.

The only frightening part of it had been when he'd pulled away. Deep down she hadn't wanted him to. And if he hadn't ended it when he had, she would have kept on kissing him all night.

She didn't know when Calum had gone from the hall. She'd been so busy dancing with her swift succession of partners, it had been some time before she'd looked, only to see him gone. She'd been disappointed. She'd wondered why he'd left. Had he not felt what she had when they'd kissed?

And then she scoffed at herself for even thinking such a thing. Calum Mackay had doubtless kissed many girls before her, probably kissed them all in the same way. She was foolish and naïve to think that it should have meant to him anything close to what it had meant to her.

As she sat there with the flickering light of the fire

dancing across the image of his face, Isabella enhanced the image, scuffing in his shadow of beard, straightening the slope of his nose. She refined the image until it looked as close to Calum as possible. And then she went over it with pen and ink, making it permanent so that when she told her granddaughters about this night—and that kiss—she could show them the image of the man who had given it to her.

Their kiss may not have meant anything to Calum Mackay. But Calum Mackay had meant quite a lot to Isabella.

Because Calum Mackay had shown her what it was to live.

And Isabella would never forget him for that.

Chapter Twelve

It was early the following morning, just after the break of day, when Calum found Bella sitting in the hall. She was alone, perched upon the window seat. She had a cup of tea balanced on her lap as she stared out at the sea glittering under the sun through the arched window.

She was the picture of loveliness. Her hair was drawn up loosely on her head with curls framing her face. The sun shone in behind her, framing her in brilliant soft light of gold. Yet even with the radiance of the day, her face was somehow dim. Just the set of her shoulders and the shadow in her eyes told of her mood: distant, withdrawn. She looked rather like a forlorn princess imprisoned in a tower, awaiting her knight errant to come and rescue her from the wicked villain.

To rescue her from *him*.

Calum leaned against the doorway, crossed his arms loosely over his chest. " 'Tis too fine a morn to be sitting in here all alone, lass. Why d'you no' take a turn outside? We rarely get a day such as this and M'Cuick promises me the skies will hold fair all the day. He is never, ever wrong about these things."

She turned, looked at him. "But I thought I wasn't to leave the castle."

Her voice was soft, timorous, as one would expect from any imprisoned unhappy young princess.

"Och, lass. I may be a pirate, but I'm no' as heartless as all tha'. We're surrounded by ten miles of empty moor. The nearest settlement is some fifteen miles distant, and tha's wit' knowing how to get there. E'en if you were of a mind to take flight, you'd no' make it very far. There's the wolves, the bogs, and aye, e'en the midges to contend wit', too. The perils far outweigh any chances of success." He readied to leave, pulling on his coat. "You're free to wander at will. Just be sure to wear a cloak. The sunlight is deceptive, it is. 'Tis still a bite to the wind. And be certain to keep the castle in sight at all times. It is easy to get lost out on the moors."

The dullness that had shadowed her eyes seemed to lighten as she considered the idea. She even smiled. "Thank you, Mr. Mackay."

"Calum, lass. My name is Calum."

She looked at him. "Calum."

He liked the way his name sounded on her lips, liked it too much, perhaps.

He turned quickly to leave.

"Perhaps it is better that I stay here," she said on an audible sigh, and more to herself, he suspected, than to him. "I wouldn't know where to go, what to do. I'm really not the daring sort."

Like Bess, Calum thought, remembering the many passages he'd read in her journal the night before.

He turned back to the room. Her discontent with herself, and the fact that she wasn't the "daring sort" was a matter she'd written about more than once. She'd all but canonized her sister for her misadventures, admiring her, envying her, while never once herself trying to break out of her self-imposed shell.

But perhaps, in the face of her flamboyant sister, she'd just never had the chance to.

"Would you . . ." He hesitated, wondering if he should ask what he was about to ask—or just turn and walk away. "Would you like me to show you about the castle and grounds? Perhaps it would help you to feel a little less disconcerted if you were to acquaint yourself with the place more first."

She looked at him, considering his offer, as uncertain as he no doubt. He half expected her to decline until finally, she smiled. "I think I would like that very much, yes. Thank you."

She stood, taking a moment to put her skirts in order, smoothing down the folds of brocaded fabric over the bulk of her dress panniers. Nonsensical things, panniers, he thought. 'Twas like having as pair of fishing creels, bottom side up, one strapped to each hip. Intended to give an impression of elegance and grace, they really just made for rather a lot of maneuvering when a lass needed to get through a narrow doorway—when a lass needed to do much of anything really other than sit at a spinet or needlework frame, poised like an elegant figurine. They certainly weren't suitable for traipsing about the Highlands.

And her shoes, he thought, taking in the cocked heel and narrow pointed toe. They looked torturous. No wonder most lasses took such tiny, mincing steps. If they didn't, they'd end up tumbling headfirst, and their fishing creel panniers would end up slung around their necks instead of jutting out from their waists.

There wasn't much elegance in that, now was there?

"You might want to consider a change into something simpler," he suggested. "Have you anything a wee bit less . . . eh, structural, perhaps?"

She laughed, a sweet and mirthful sound, and then lifted her hand as if to cover her mouth.

It was then he noticed her fingertips. They were colored nearly black.

What the devil had she been doing? Crawling about in the soot of the hearth?

"I'm afraid I've only a few gowns from which to choose," she said, pulling his thoughts back.

"You've your trunks," he finished. And then before she could say the opposite to it, "I had them taken to your room this morn."

"You have?" Her face lit up. In fact the entire room seemed to have brightened.

"Aye. And it's sorry I am that your things were taken from you as they were. 'Twas a grievous mistake."

"Thank you, Calum." She crossed the room, stopped, kissed him quickly on the cheek. "Thank you very much."

Did she realize she had just kissed the man who had been responsible for having the trunks confiscated in the first place?

And did she realize that in doing so, she had just warmed the room by several noticeable degrees?

Calum stood and simply stared. It was all he could do.

She stopped, and turned at the door before leaving. "You'll wait here while I go to change then?"

He nodded wordlessly, and she vanished through the

door, leaving him blinking and mystified, as if he'd just been taken by a sudden burst of sunlight.

After she'd gone, Calum crossed the room to the window to look outside. M'Cuick had been right. It was a fine day, much too fine to be locked away inside these stone walls poring through books. Tonight he would start the search for Uilliam's name. It wasn't as if they could go after him immediately anyway. The *Adventurer* had just returned, and she would need to be checked thoroughly before they set out again. The hull needed careening, sails mending, decks needed to be swabbed, and bilges needed to be dried. Tonight would be soon enough for checking Lord Belcourt's records. Calum thought of the other things he could be doing that morning, plans he could be preparing, decisions he could make, but somehow none of them seemed as appealing at that moment as walking about with her.

Out of custom, Calum checked the horizon for sign of any unfamiliar craft. It was a thing that had become a habit over the past year since he'd been at Castle Wrath. There was a part of him that wondered if the day would come when he would see a fleet of the whole Hanoverian navy approaching to arrest him and his crew. It was a possibility he had had to plan for; only a complacent fool didn't prepare for every inevitability and it was only a matter of time before someone somehow recognized one of the men. And if that day ever came, Calum had decided long ago that he wouldn't be one to flee, no matter if they sent in five hundred troops to take him. He would stand and he would face them, he would defend this place, and he would likely die—but he would die a Scotsman, not a prisoner of the counterfeit king, and certainly not an exile displaced in a foreign land.

When he looked down from the window, Calum noticed something sitting on the ledge, a sheet of parchment that had been turned facedown. Beside it lay a slender stick that looked like kindling wood charred on one end, obviously from the candle that sat yet burning beside it. Calum picked up the sheet, turned it over. There was a scene drawn upon it, the same scene he had just looked upon outside, the castle ruins, the rocky cliff, and the stretch of sea beyond.

It was no casual depiction, but an accomplished piece embellished with mood and texture and shading. Calum ran a finger lightly along the drawing's edge, inadvertently smudging one corner. He lifted his hand and rubbed the blotch of dark ash away with his finger and his thumb. He remembered Bella's fingers, how black they'd been.

So the lass was an artist.

It didn't surprise him.

Bella returned a short time later, dressed in a simple sort of gown with full skirts that were unhooped, and a fitted bodice made of soft gray. The plainness of the gown suited her, and the color turned her eyes a stormier shade of blue, a lovely complement to her dark hair. Where most lasses preferred brightness and vibrant color, she favored the colors of nature, the shades of the sea . . .

. . . *of the merfolk.*

Calum shook his head at the thought.

"Will this do?" she asked.

Calum turned. "Aye, lass. Very well." In truth, she could wear a scrap of ragged woolen and still look lovely. "Are you ready then?"

They stopped in the kitchen to tell M'Cuick they'd be

going about. Calum ignored the cook's speculative glances and asked for a small basket with some bannocks, cheese, and fruit that they might take along with them. He didn't know how long they'd be gone, or how far they would go, so he thought to prepare for any eventuality. He certainly wasn't in any hurry to return.

They started out taking a turn about the castle courtyard. Calum explained what each of the ruined buildings had once been, trying to give her a picture with words of the great fortress of Castle Wrath. Rather than a simple polite nod, she listened to his every word, and asked questions—thoughtful, intelligent questions that showed her genuine interest in what he had to say.

Though he regretted having done it, in having read her journal, he found it easier to talk to her. He already knew the things that interested her and it was that trait he appealed to, her love of imagery, her sense of artistic beauty.

They came to the stables where Hamish stood just inside, seeing to his duties in feeding and watering the ponies and mucking the stalls. He beamed when he saw the lass.

"Good morning t'you, Miss Maris," he said, doffing his straw hat.

It was quite obvious the lad had fallen for her.

"How do you do, Hamish?"

"Oh, fine. How can a man no' be fine on a day as today?"

Calum grinned to himself at the lad calling himself a "man."

"It is a fine day, is it not?" Bella said.

"Aye. The skies are clear and the wind is soft. Are you and the laird of a mind for a ride then?"

"A ride?" Her face immediately dimmed. "No. I do not ride."

"Och," Hamish hit himself on the forehead. "I should've thought of it myself. To be sure, you winna ken how to sit a horse, being of the merfolk as you are."

Calum glanced at her.

The lass merely smiled and said to them both, "Yes. You are right."

Minx.

"Perhaps it is time you learned to ride then, lass," Calum said.

"Oh, no. Really, I—"

But he ignored her. "Fetch the Trakehner, aye, Hamish?"

"And one of the ponies for Miss Maris?"

"Nae. Just the stallion. This first time, she'll ride with me."

Her eyes went wide as blue china saucers when Hamish led the glistening black beast outside the stables moments later. "You want me . . . to ride him?"

"There's naught to worry over, lass. He's a well-mannered mount."

"But he's so . . . big."

Calum led her over to the horse while Hamish saddled him. "You just need to get a wee bit acquainted, is all." He took her hand. Their eyes caught and held for a moment before Calum lifted her fingers slowly to the horse's muzzle.

"Just give him a bit of a stroke and he'll do anything you ask of him."

Just like the rest of us . . .

Calum watched as she tentatively ran her fingers over the horse's cheek. The stallion lowered his head and nudged against her for more, nearly knocking her backward.

She laughed. In minutes, she had eased and was scratching him behind his pricked ears.

"We'll be off then."

Calum swung up and settled into the saddle.

"But I don't even know how to get up on his—"

Calum tightened his knees and swept her up from the ground with one arm. In a moment she was sitting before him, her feet dangling over one side.

"Oh," she said, looking at him, startled. "Goodness."

Their faces were so close he had felt the soft rush of her breath against his cheek.

The horse danced a bit beneath them and she dug her fingers into Calum's sleeve. Her face had paled. Her eyes were wild. She looked frightened half to death.

She really was afraid.

Certainly the daughter of a duke would have ridden a horse before?

"Easy, lass. I'm no' going to let you fall. We'll take it slowly. Now just hold to my arm and we'll start it at a walk, aye?"

She looked as if she'd rather be anywhere, anywhere else on earth other than seated on that horse before him. Yet, after a second or two of consideration, she nodded.

Calum urged the horse away from the stables, keeping a tight rein on him. He could feel the tensing of the beast's muscles beneath him, the barely contained prance in his step, and knew the horse was anxious to take off across the moors at a gallop. It was a thing Calum often did with him, to stretch the beast's legs and soothe his own restless spirit as well, racing at breakneck speed along the soft sands of the shore with the wind ripping against his face and stinging his eyes to tears.

But not today.

They walked about the castle courtyard, letting the lass get used to the feel of the horse beneath her. After a while, Calum felt her begin to relax, and she finally eased back against him.

The soft scent of her hair, the gentle sway of her body against his, were a heady, potent combination, filling his thoughts with the memory of the kiss they had shared the night before, the way his body had responded to that kiss, like a starving man would hunger for the tiniest crumb.

It was craziness, he knew, to even allow himself to be in her company. She was the daughter of a duke. And she was already promised to another man, another man who, if her mother's letter was any indication, she already had tender feelings for. If she had read that letter, knew she was betrothed to the esteemed Kentigern St. Clive, would she e'en deign to ride upon the horse with him now?

He should forget her while she was there, go on as he always had. But at the same time Calum just couldn't seem to resist her. Perhaps it was because he knew in time she would go. She would leave and she would wed her Kentigern St. Clive, so why shouldn't he enjoy what time he had with her?

He took her down the hillside, away from the castle. They trotted through the moor and cantered along the sea path, and she laughed, a full, throaty sound that warmed him despite the chill in the air.

Her hair brushed against his cheek soft as a silk ribbon when the wind blew. Her body melded to his and they moved as one with the movement of the horse. Slowly she let down her defenses, she lost that assumed mermaid persona and Calum began to see the Bella whose words he'd read in that journal emerging . . . blossoming . . . living.

She asked him about his childhood and he told her, not everything, but he told her about his father falling in battle, and how he'd been sent in fosterage to Fergus's father. The hours passed quickly. He lost track of the time. He lost track of where they went. Somehow it didn't surprise him when he looked up suddenly to find they had arrived at the small bay where he had come as a lad.

The lad who had been looking for his mermaid.

He pulled the horse to a stop and slid from the saddle, then reached for her waist to help her down.

She slid against him. He didn't immediately let her go, but stood with his hands spanning her waist, his eyes drinking her in.

Even the wind seemed to have stilled.

"Calum . . ." she said, and her voice held a nervous edge, as if she knew he wanted to kiss her.

But he didn't give in to the temptation.

"Come, lass," he said, taking her hand. "I want to show you something."

He let the stallion graze on the *machair* while he led her down the path, straight to the stone where he used to sit and watch the placid bay.

"'Tis lovely," she said, and he watched as she closed her eyes and turned her face to the sun. With her dark hair blowing in the breeze, she looked just like the mermaid he'd always imagined.

He wanted to tell her. He wanted to tell her how he

had come there as a lad and had watched the water for her, his mermaid. He wanted to tell her he knew the truth about her, that she did not need to hide from him, that he would never hurt her. Instead he simply stood with her, hand in hand, and looked out to the sea.

He showed her the isles of Lewis and Harris, mist-ringed in the distance. He pointed out the distinctive call of the curlew as it soared overhead. He picked her a fragrant sprig of broom and slipped it behind her ear.

"That tall column of rock there," she said, pointing to the bay. "It is so narrow. It looks as if it might topple over with the strike of the next wave."

"Oh, I dinna think tha' will happen, lass. He's been standing that way for nigh on five hundred years at least. 'Tis Am Buachaille."

"Aum Bo'ach-elly'a," she repeated carefully. "What does it mean?"

"He is the herdsman."

She cocked her head, looking at the stack. "He looks . . . lonely, somehow."

Calum smiled inwardly. If only she knew how lonely he'd been.

"Come," he said. "Let's walk to the water's edge."

It took little coaxing to convince her to shed her shoes and stockings and dip her toes into the surf. She gasped at the chill of the water, and danced back to keep the waves from wetting the hem of her gown as she gathered the many layers up in her hands. She never even realized she had exposed her lovely ankles and calves to his view, putting him in mind of the stocking he'd taken from her trunk the night before. In the end, when he'd put back all the ribbons and furbelows, he hadn't been able to make himself return the stocking with them. She had countless other stockings, and he reasoned that she would never miss the one. So he'd tucked it back far into his desk drawer. Pitiable, perhaps, but he'd always have that scrap of silk to remember her by, even after she had gone.

"Calum!"

Her animated call had him turning, jogging to join her where she was bent at the waist, fishing in the surf with both hands. Whatever she'd spied had apparently taken her mind off keeping her skirts dry, for the hem now dragged heedlessly in the water, swirling about her legs.

"Look!"

She fished a hand beneath the water's surface and then pulled it back, holding up a single gold coin.

She was grinning as Calum took it. He looked at it closely. " 'Tis Spanish."

"A Spanish coin? Here?"

"Aye, lass. 'Tis from a shipwreck. There's countless many of them in this bay. The sailing up on the cape can be difficult, especially to those who aren't familiar with the waters. Many a vessel has been lost. After time, they drift down here where they bury themselves in the sea-bed." He pointed outward. "If you look, you can see some of the masts yet sticking up from the surface."

She shaded her eyes against the sun, eyes that were the very blue of the water before them. "Oh, yes. I do see." She turned back to face him, her eyes alight and her face as lovely as a thing should ever be. "Thank you for bringing me, Calum. This is a special place."

Calum's voice had grown heavy in his throat. "Aye, lass, it is."

And she was a special lass.

There was something about her when she'd turned,

her hair pulled loose by the wind, her face kissed with color from the wind. Whether it was the place, or the lass, or the mixture of the two he did not know. All Calum knew was he couldn't resist himself as he pulled her against him, tipped back her head, and lowered his mouth to hers for a kiss.

She didn't deny him. She sighed softly and melted into him.

It was the only persuading he needed.

Calum lifted his hands to her face, fanned his fingers against her neck and jaw, and deepened the kiss, kissed her as if it were the last time he ever would.

Because he knew it very well could be.

His belly clenched and he molded his mouth to hers, losing himself, kissing her with long and passionate strokes, relentlessly tangling his tongue with hers. *Dia*, but it was incredible. She gave every bit as much as she took, sliding her hands up against his chest and splaying them against the linen of his shirt. He wondered if she could feel how fast and how hard his heart was beating.

He pulled his mouth away, but only long enough to drag it along the curve of her jaw to the hollow of her slender neck. He heard her suck in her breath as his fingers slid back to cradle her as she dropped back her head, moaning softly in her throat. He sought out her warmth, wanted to steal her breath, he wanted to take her, make her his, and he knew she would let him until—

Calum was taken by a sharp and sudden shove. It instantly broke them apart, had him staggering, staggering headfirst into the surf.

He landed, sprawled flat, with a resounding splash.

When got to his feet, and the red flash of his anger

and dripping of his hair had cleared from his vision, he saw Bella looking at him. She had a giggle in her eyes and a grin on her lips. The same lips he had moments before been kissing.

She was grinning because beside her stood the lagging tongue and grizzled dim-witted face of Fergus's deerhound, Fingal.

He'd been named for the famed Scottish giant, an appropriate name given that when the beast stood on hind legs, the dog was taller than M'Cuick.

And then Calum peered beyond the dog and the lass, and spotted Fergus standing on the bluff overlooking the bay. Standing and looking none-too-pleased at what he'd undoubtedly seen.

"Bluidy *cù* . . ." Calum muttered to the dog as he dragged himself out of the water, his shirt soaked and clinging to his skin, and his trews dripping a trail behind him.

The drenching had served to do one thing. It had certainly doused the fervor that had seized him.

And somehow, as he looked at him standing up on that bluff, Calum suspected it had been Fergus's intention all along.

Chapter Thirteen

A quiet wind drifted in off the isolated shore, causing the thick tufts of marram grass to whisper and sigh. The sun was veiled, lost behind a murky haze of slumbering clouds, and the sea seemed not to move, not even to ripple. The air was damp with morning's mist, the hour early. And it was silent, so silent in fact, even the birds weren't calling.

A perfect day for sitting amongst the dead.

Isabella had spotted the tiny burial ground when she'd been out riding with Calum the day before. He had called it Balnakeil, which meant, he'd told her, Bay of the Church. Indeed, the scattering of headstones and their picturesque sanctuary lay on the curve of a quiet little bay, inland from the sea above a wide stretch of sand that was so white it glittered. There had been a church at the site for over a millennium, he'd said, since 722 when St. Maelrubha had first founded it. The church building itself was in ruins, its roof partially missing, its stone walls crumbling in some places, seemingly held together in others by only the drape of rich green ivy that covered it like a shroud.

Graveyards had always held a fascination for Isabella. Some people saw them as dark and depressing, but Isabella looked on them as she looked on a museum, with the stones as the works of art. She could spend hours gazing at them, trying to interpret the meaning of the symbols and the words carved upon them. She would wonder at the lives that had been led and then had ended—who they had been, how they had lived. She would pull away the weeds that threatened to eclipse them and smooth away the debris, as if to somehow assure them they hadn't been forgotten.

When she'd seen the place the day before, and had learned of its ancient history, she had taken note of where they'd been and had woken that morning with the sole aim of returning there. Calum had gone off at dawn, Hamish had told her, though the lad didn't know where or when his laird would return. So she'd gathered her sketching tools and papers, and had set out just as the sun was climbing over the moor.

The outing also gave her the opportunity to practice her riding skills. It was a daunting step for her. Calum could never know what he'd done when he'd swept her up onto the back of that stallion, ignoring her protests against it. When she'd been a child, eight perhaps nine years old, Isabella had not been reluctant to ride at all. She had ridden most every day and she had loved it, surrounded by the scents and sounds of the seasons.

But much as she loved it, she hadn't been the rider Elizabeth was.

Reckless, wild Elizabeth was a born horsewoman. Where Isabella rode for leisure, to soak in the countryside and reflect on the day, Elizabeth had ridden at one speed—a breakneck gallop over the rolling Northumbrian hills around Drayton Hall each day. As was her nature, Elizabeth had one day challenged her younger sister to a race; and for once, not wanting to be left behind, Isabella had accepted.

They'd crossed the first field neck-to-neck, hooves flying as they laughed into the wind, their pert riding hats swept from their heads to flutter behind them. They were heading for the second field when Elizabeth veered her horse, a spirited young stallion, toward a low drystone wall. It was as if danger called her name. She'd cleared it easily.

Isabella was hesitant, but unwilling to concede without even trying—after all, she was still a Drayton and had her pride. She pushed Clover to follow, but the mare had neither the strength nor the experience of the other horse. Her back hooves clipped the wall and the two of them went tumbling into the ditch that awaited on the opposite side.

Isabella was thrown clear, but Clover was left with a broken foreleg.

The duke had had no choice but to put Clover down. Isabella would never forget watching the poor animal's suffering as it lay, helpless and twisted in that ditch, its eyes rolled back in its head in shock. Nor would she forget the echo of the musketfire that had ended her life. It had been the last time Isabella had ever ridden.

Until yesterday.

The sheer power of the stallion had been a frightening thing, but somehow, with Calum at the reins, her fears had quickly melted and she'd begun to remember how much she had loved the feel of the wind against her face, the thunder of galloping hooves pounding in time to her racing heartbeat. It was as close as a person could get to flying and she'd reveled in it. So when she'd woken that morning, Isabella had summoned up the courage to ask Hamish to saddle her a biddable mount. She would take it a step at a time.

The small sweet garron pony Hamish had selected plodded her way happily over hill and moor; she almost seemed to sense Isabella's nervousness and kept to an easy pace. She was a dun-colored mare with a body much more compact than that of the stallion, lower to the ground and sure of foot across the rugged Highland terrain. Hamish had told Isabella the horse's name, but it had been in Gaelic and sounded in English rather like he had just insulted her, so Bella simply called her "girl."

It was a little odd at first, taking to the saddle, for Isabella rode astride; the sidesaddle wasn't a thing commonly found in the Highlands. But she'd managed to hitch her skirts through her legs breeches-style in a manner Elizabeth had often done (away from the eyes of the duke and duchess, of course) whenever she'd wanted to ride particularly recklessly.

Along with her sketching tools, Isabella had taken a basket from M'Cuick. He was planning a new dish for supper that evening with a roast of beef and mutton collops and had asked if she would gather him some primrose and purslane to spice it with. She had agreed, though she would see to the task later. Right now, however, she was far more interested in the study of the headstones that surrounded her.

There were tall Celtic crosses, standing stones weathered by the sea, and huge granite slabs carved in Latin.

Some displayed winged angels with cherubic faces, others had chilling images of stark skeletons holding the hourglass of time. Many showed the occupations of the deceased through symbols of their trade, blacksmiths, farmers, and mariners especially. They were ancient and beautiful, the carvings upon them telling the life story of the departed soul through intricate symbols with decorative intertwining plaits and knots.

Even now her drawing pencils and chalks were scattered on a cloth beside her as she bent her head close to the pages of her sketching book, slowly, painstakingly copying the ornate designs.

She was so engrossed in her task, she didn't even notice when she was no longer alone in the graveyard.

She simply looked up, seeking the next design.

And she saw him.

It was Calum.

He was weaving his way through the headstones and crosses with a destination obviously in mind. He hadn't seen her. He had passed where she was hunched behind one of the larger crosses and had kept on walking, no doubt never expecting there would be anyone else there that early in the morn.

Isabella remained as she was, motionless, watching as he stopped at a stone that stood on the very edge of the graveyard, closest to the sea. He crossed himself, bowed his head, and closed his eyes reverently. Everything seemed suddenly to still. Isabella herself scarcely dared to breathe. Until the wind softly ruffled his hair, and he reached out slowly, gently placing a hand against the weathered stone. The obvious emotion that came with that one small gesture nearly brought her to tears.

He turned and she saw his face in profile. His expression was stark, hollow, and filled with a terrible grief.

Isabella felt she should leave, felt an intruder on this obviously private moment. But leaving would only alert him to her presence. He'd obviously wanted to be alone; why else would he not have told Hamish where he was going? It would be better, she decided, to simply wait until he'd gone. So she remained where she was, although she glanced away as if to allow him his privacy.

She waited. When she chanced a look back, he had lifted his hand and she saw that he held a single flower, a wild rose, white and lovely, in his fingers. He hunkered down, gently placed the flower at the base of the stone, stared at the stone a moment more, then stood to leave.

Isabella remained hidden among the stones until he turned, walked away, and had been gone for several minutes.

She hadn't seen him much since they'd returned from their ride the day before. All along the ride back to the castle, he had been quiet, his mood remote. Somehow she had sensed it was more than just having been plunged into the sea by Fergus's dog, even though that had been the definite turning point of what had been a most wonderful day.

She'd asked Calum, but he'd just shaken his head, telling her it was time for them to get back to the castle. She'd heard later from M'Cuick that Calum and Fergus had exchanged words, heated words behind the door of Calum's study. Had it been because Fergus had found them together? It only seemed to support the feeling she sometimes got that Fergus wasn't pleased at having her there, even though it was he who had brought her.

Stepping quietly through the graveyard, Isabella went to the stone over which Calum had prayed. The flower he'd left had blown from where he had laid it into the weeds below and Isabella bent to retrieve it. It was a simple stone, gray and weathered from the sea, with the carvings of a double heart and a flower that looked very much like the wild rose Calum had brought.

As she placed the bud back upon the base of the stone, she read the words that were carved in Latin upon it:

Here lieth the mortal body of Moira,
wife of Artair Ros Mackay of Wrath,
the great Jacobite lately fallen at Sheriffmuir.
She joineth him in eternal slumber
the 2nd of June 1716.

There was more carved underneath it, obscured by the overgrowth. Isabella knelt closer, pushed away the tall grass and read:

Taken this day a wife ever true,
And a mother for naught more than a moment.

The words left Isabella with a chill that had nothing at all to do with the weather.

This was Calum's mother's grave. And she had died giving birth to him.

As she sat back, wrapping her arms around herself, Isabella stared at the stone, this stark monument to a life cut tragically too short. She realized she had been so very blessed. She had had parents all her life who loved

her and had raised her in a blithe and secure environ-
ment. War, rebellion, human loss, those things had never
really touched her. She had read about them, heard them
discussed, but they had never threatened the safety of
her most cherished circle.

Her family.

Yet Calum had lived with those things almost from
the very moment of his birth. He had never known the
comforting touch of a mother's loving hand smoothing
against his brow. He'd never had a father to turn to for
guidance and strength. He had been orphaned twice
over, left alone in the world. 'Twas no wonder he had
turned to rebellion. It was all he'd ever known.

Yet, somehow, despite the misery, it hadn't tarnished
him completely. He still brought a flower to his mother's
grave site. And he still said a prayer for her soul.

Isabella spent the next quarter hour pulling away the
tall grasses from the stone, cleaning the slate. She didn't
know why; she had never known the woman, but she
had somehow inexplicably been touched by this memor-
ial to her. She tried to envision what Moira Mackay must
have looked like, what her life must have been. She
wondered if Calum's dark hair and warm eyes had been
a feature he'd inherited from her. She wondered how she
must have felt, carrying her dead husband's child, only
to be herself taken from her son at the very moment of
his birth.

Calum had told her he had been given in fosterage to
Fergus's father shortly after he'd been born. Had he been
loved? And even if he had, had he always been plagued
by a sense of displacement, of not truly belonging?

It was a thing Isabella had never had to experience.
She had always known her place in the order of things at

Drayton Hall, had always been comforted by it, yet somehow she sensed how he must have felt.

At sea, without a port to call home.

When she finished with the weeds, Isabella stood, wiping her fingers on the cloth she used while she was drawing. She looked out onto the sea. The day had moved on. The sun had come out and was struggling to shine its light down through the clouds. A single heavenly beam of light reached out to the little bay and its ancient church like the hand of an angel. It was a most blessed place, and Isabella couldn't understand how it had been left to ruin.

With a last glance to the headstone, Isabella gathered her pencils and chalks and wrapped them carefully in the folds of the cloth. She tucked them into her basket and headed over the hill to where she'd left the pony to graze.

She was so lost in her thoughts, she never realized that someone stood watching her departure from afar, watching and waiting till she'd gone. That same someone went to that same graveyard, and stood before that same headstone. Another hand set a second pale wild rose beside the first one.

Another prayer for the soul of the departed was offered.

Isabella was perched upon a boulder, her sketching hand scribbling at a furious pace as she sped to capture the odd-looking bird pecking at the pebbles along the burn's edge.

It was a large bird, and all black except for a brownishness to its wings and the brilliant red that surrounded its eyes. Its tail feathers were glossy and sleek, and they stood in a wide fan like that of a peacock while it strutted around, emitting odd little *click-clock* noises from its hooked beak.

Isabella had never seen such a bird, so she was racing to sketch it so that she could ask M'Cuick what it had been. But when it suddenly squawked and took flight, its wings beating it a hasty retreat over the grassy stretch of moor, she couldn't help but groan aloud.

"No!"

She tried to quickly finish the sketch while the bird's features were fresh in her mind, until a movement caught her attention from the corner of her eye. She turned just as a small boy was snatching her picnic basket.

Their eyes met.

And the boy ran.

"Wait!"

Isabella was a good runner. She always had been, had always beaten her sisters in the foot races they would have along the ancient bowling green at Drayton Hall. She took hold of her skirts and sprinted after him, calling out for him to stop, that she wasn't going to hurt him, that she just wanted to speak with him.

But he just ran on.

He fell once, sprawling headfirst into the heather, and the contents of the basket went tumbling down the braeside. He looked at her in terror as she ran to meet him, his eyes white on a dirty face. He grabbed up whatever he could of the food, the apples, oatcakes, and a round of cheese, and started running again.

Isabella charged after him, trying to ignore the stitch in her side.

He headed for a rocky outcropping that jutted above

the burn, slowing when he had to pick his way over the boulders and brush.

Isabella called after him. "Please, stop! I won't hurt you! I just want to talk to you!"

But he didn't listen. He just babbled something at her in Gaelic, and she realized he couldn't understand that she meant him no harm.

He must have been terrified.

When he ducked into the low opening of a cave, Isabella thought she finally had him. She heard him call out something in Gaelic, and lowered her head to follow. But it was black as night inside the cave and she stopped a short distance inside, fearing she might not find her way out without a light. She could hear him hurrying deeper into the cave, and then very soon there was no sound at all.

She had lost him.

Isabella returned to the castle late that afternoon, her basket filled with the purslane and primrose she had promised M'Cuick, along with fragrant rosemary, heather, broom, and gorse that she'd clipped to freshen the castle. After the incident with the boy, she had waited outside the cave for a while to see if he'd emerge. She'd wanted to see if she might somehow communicate with him, deduce where he was living and how. He was obviously hungry, and the way his tattered clothes had hung on his bony frame, she could tell his meals were few and far between. What if he was alone, surviving only on the benevolence of nature? What would he do for shelter and warmth once the winter months approached?

But he hadn't come out and with the sun beginning to

wane in the sky, Isabella had had little choice but to go back, collect her sketching tools where she'd left them, and head for the castle.

When she arrived, Calum was waiting at the stable. His arms were crossed and his expression was quite fierce.

His words, when they came, were equally as fierce.

"Where the devil have you been?"

He practically growled at her.

"Good day to you, too, Calum," she said lightly, handing Hamish the reins and patting the mare on her nose. "She was lovely, Hamish. A perfect mount. Thank you for choosing her for me. I'll ask M'Cuick for an apple treat for her after supper."

Hamish tugged on his hair for want of a cap to tip. "She's a sweet lass, she is, Miss Maris." He called when she started away. "Miss Maris, can I carry your basket for you?"

"I'll get the basket," Calum glowered. "You see to the pony."

Hamish nodded and turned, reluctant to goad his laird, even for Isabella.

"You needn't have been so harsh with him," Isabella said when he'd gone. "He was only trying to be helpful."

"I'll ask you again, lass. Where have you been?"

"I beg your pardon, Mr. Mackay, but I seem to remember you telling me I was free to wander about at will."

"Aye. But you were gone all the day, lass." He frowned. "We cudna find you anywhere. You took a mount and I knew you were—" He stopped himself. "You only just rode with me yesterday . . ."

"You were worried," she said.

"I simply thought— I mean to say, you've the stone and—"

"You were worried," she repeated, and he looked at her, reluctant to reveal any emotion.

So he said nothing.

Isabella decided not to tell Calum of the boy's thievery. He might forbid her to go out again, might send out Fergus's dog after the lad, and she wanted to return to the cave again to bring more food.

"Thank you," she said and smiled. "I am sorry to have caused you any alarm. I was simply enjoying myself so much I forgot the time. In fact, I forgot even to eat. I'm starved and I'm sure Malcolm is anxious for his purslane. Care to join me for some tea?"

She didn't wait for him to answer. She shoved her basket into his arms, sending stalks of broom and heather smacking into his nose. Then she turned and headed for the kitchen.

Calum did the only thing he could.

He followed her inside.

Supper was late that evening, and the men's mouths were grumbling nearly as loudly as their stomachs. By the time M'Cuick brought out his roast of beef and mutton collops, they had been on the very verge of civil unrest.

The tastiness of the food, however, soothed their hungry palates and soon they were so busy shoveling forkfuls of rosemary potatoes and tender roast into their mouths, they never even noticed that the chair at the end of the table reserved for the lass stayed empty.

But Calum did.

He was sitting there frowning at that empty chair,

ignoring his supper plate as he wondered if she'd been slighted by his harsh words earlier and had stayed away because of it. He hadn't intended to sound like such a tyrant. It was just that he'd been waiting for her, for hours it had seemed, and when he'd seen her riding into the courtyard on that pony, her face pinked from the wind and her hair windblown about her shoulders, he'd forgotten himself, forgotten himself completely.

She'd been right. He had been worried. And it was a thing he'd not been prepared to feel.

It had been foolish of him to tell her she could wander at will. While he liked to think of this part of the Highlands as his own private island, in truth it was not. What if she'd been set upon by some renegade rebel soldier? Or by a wolf? Or even worse, a Hanoverian detachment of soldiers who would rescue her and take her away?

What if she just hadn't come back?

It would be better if he had someone accompany her in the future. Hamish perhaps. Yes, she liked Hamish and if he made it seem as if Hamish was only accompanying her to be useful, to carry things or show her about, then perhaps she wouldn't be made to feel as if she were being watched over.

"Oy, Calum." The voice pulled him from his thoughts. "Have you made any sense of Belcourt's books yet?"

Calum glanced at Mungo, who sat down the length of the table. "Nae, not as yet. 'Twill take some time to get through, I'm thinkin'."

Mungo nodded, took a swig of ale.

"Why d'you no' ask Calum if he's e'en taken a look at the books as yet, Mungo?"

It was Fergus who had spoken. Calum looked at him.

He didn't say a word, but his expression offered a warning.

Fergus, however, wasn't daunted.

"And while you're about it, Mungo, why d'you no' ask Calum why he's frolicking his time away with his wee merlass whilst my da rots away in a Sassenach prison, eh?"

The room silenced. A tension descended, thick and sudden as a hot summer thunderstorm. Calum took a deep breath, let it out slowly. He set down his fork and knife and was about to respond, when the door across the room pushed open, and the very object of their conversation stood framed within its opening.

She walked into the room, oblivious to the scene she had just come upon, carrying what appeared to be a covered dish. She had changed from her riding clothes into a gown that was a dark wine color, silk and fitted low over her breasts. She looked especially lovely in the candlelight, and her full skirts brushed the chairs of the men as she walked the length of the table to Calum's chair. The rustle of her petticoats was the only sound in the room.

She set the platter before him.

"What's this, lass?"

She grinned, cocked her head softly to the side. "Remove the cover and you'll see."

Calum looked down the length of the table, catching the eyes turned his way. Everyone else seemed as ignorant of what she was about as he. Everyone, that is, except M'Cuick, who was grinning as if he'd just paid a visit to Jenny Sinclair in Durness.

Calum lifted the cover to reveal a cake, garnished with wild berries—brambleberry, strawberry, and cloudberry—and topped with a custardy cream. In the center of the cake stood a single small candle.

He looked at her, bewildered beyond belief.

"Happy Birthday, Calum."

Calum blinked. "What did you say?"

"It is your birthday, isn't it?"

In that moment, he might very well have been knocked to the floor by just the flutter of a feather. How? How could she have possibly known? Nobody, not even Fergus, knew the significance of the day.

If he didn't know better, from having read that journal, she might just have convinced him to her mermaid story right then.

"Thank you," was all he managed, and even that was an effort. He was staring at the cake, as if he'd conjured it up in a dream.

"Did you know," she said, breaking the awkward silence that had descended, "that in ancient times it was feared evil spirits searched out people on their birthdays? To protect the birthday person from harm, friends and family would gather around them and bring good thoughts and wishes. And giving gifts brought even more good cheer to ward off the evil spirits."

Calum looked at her.

"I regret I have no gift to offer you, other than this." She took the blossom of a rose that she had tucked in her hair. " 'Tis significant. The rose is the good luck flower for your birth month of June."

Calum took the rose. He didn't know what to do with it. He felt rather stupid just staring at it, so he set it on the table beside his claret glass.

"You made this cake?" he asked, anything to break the silence.

"I wish I could say that I had, but that was Malcolm's doing."

The big Scotsman sat at the opposite end of the table, grinning ear-to-ear.

"Why is there a candle?"

"Have you never had a birthday cake before, Calum?"

Realizing from his silence that he had not, she explained. "Baked inside the cake are three pieces of paper, each folded into a tiny square. On each note is written a wish. One is for wealth, another for health, and another for your heart's desire. We must light the candle, and the smoke from it will take your wish up to the heavens. Then, whichever of the notes you find first will be the wish that is granted." She smiled. "Or so the tradition goes."

She took up one of the candlesticks that lined the length of the table and used it to light the one on the cake. She waited until a brilliant flame danced before him, then she said, "Now you must blow out the candle."

Calum looked at her. "Isn't this a bit . . . foolish, lass? I'm a grown man of one-and-thirty years."

"*Two* and thirty," she corrected. "Your friends are already gathered here. Can a pirate not celebrate his own birthday?"

This brought a round of encouragement from the others.

"Oy, come now, Calum! Make yer wish!"

"Aye, we're waitin' for a bite o' that cake . . ."

Calum finally bowed to the weight of popular opinion and quickly, and without ceremony, extinguished the light. Everyone around the table broke out in a cheer.

"Cut the cake no'," called a voice that he recognized as M'Cuick's. "See what will be your wish!"

More encouragement followed this suggestion until
Calum had picked up his knife and sliced through the
spongy pastry. He cut a wedge, pushed the cake open
with his fork, and spotted what appeared to be a folded-
up piece of paper nearly hidden amongst the crumbling
layers. He looked at the lass.

"Take it. Open it, and read what it says," she said, her
eyes alight.

Calum took up the note.

He read it.

And then, without saying a word, he folded it back.

"What's it say?" Hamish asked, thoroughly caught up
in the reverie. "What's your wish to be, Laird?"

"Oh, he cannot say," Bella interrupted. "For if he
does, then his wish will not come true."

"Well, we wouldn't want that," Calum said, half smiling as he tucked the folded note inside his coat pocket.

He pushed his chair away from the table and stood.

"You're leaving?" she asked.

"Aye, I'm afraid I am. I've work to do in my study,
lass. But you stay, have some o' the cake with the lads."
And then he lowered his voice to a near-whisper. "Thank
you for this, lass."

Calum turned before he could see the shadow of disappointment cross her face.

He'd had to. Because if he hadn't, she, and every one
of his men, would have seen how deeply her gesture had
touched him.

It was sometime later, after the supper had all been
eaten and most of the men had retired to their beds, that
Isabella sat at the table in the hall with M'Cuick.

She had taken out her sketching book with a thought

to show him the drawing she'd made earlier that day of
the peculiar bird. The fire was burning sluggishly in the
grate, throwing long, glowing shadows on the walls and
in the rafters. The clock on the wall was ticking its way
quickly past midnight, and at the opposite end of the
table, Fergus, Mungo, and Hugh sat nursing their late-
night whiskys before heading off for bed.

"'Tis a capercaillie, lass," M'Cuick said. "A rare bird
it is to find, too. They've been hunted so much they're
believed extinct in many parts o' the Highlands."

He looked up from the sketch as the others got up
from their chairs to leave. "Oy! Fergus, Mungo . . . look
at wha' the lass drew. She's quite a good hand, eh?"

Fergus glanced at the drawing with a scarce amount of
interest as he headed for the door. "Aye, she does."

"She's made drawings of some of us, too," M'Cuick
went on, pulling out the other sketches in her book.
"Look, 'ere's Calum, Hamish, and e'en meself!"

The image of M'Cuick standing at his stewing pot by
the kitchen hearth was placed on the table alongside the
others.

Fergus stopped, picked up the drawing, then took a
moment to glance through the various other sketches. He
took up the drawing of Calum and was studying it
closely. When he finally set it back, he glanced at Isabella without saying a word. Hugh was looking through
the images she'd drawn while in Paris.

"Shinna you be gettin' off to bed yoursel', M'Cuick?"
Mungo said.

"Aye. Just as soon as the lass and I finish our tea.
Dinna worry yourself about it. Your breakfast will be
ready when you get up."

Isabella watched as the men turned and left, muttering

farewells. She felt a shiver along the back of her neck and wondered if it had been the dying fire, or Fergus's frigid stare, that had given it to her.

"Och, lass, 'tis a lovely thing, your drawing as you do. Nae matter where you go or wha' you do, you'll always have your sketches to look at, to remember things, auld times . . ."

Memories.

M'Cuick's expression had grown misty, and Isabella suspected he was thinking about his family.

It gave her an idea.

She took up a blank page, removed a chalk from her bundle. "Tell me about Mary, Malcolm."

He looked at her, startled that she'd read his thoughts so easily. "Wha' do you mean?" He looked down at the blank page, her pencil poised above it. "Ye're goin' to try to draw her? But you've ne'er seen her."

"Yes, but you have. So I want you to tell me. Draw me a picture of your own with your words. You can start by telling me what she looked like on the day you married her."

M'Cuick blinked, and in that blink, his expression slowly changed. Though he was looking at Isabella, in his mind he was somewhere else, standing in a small village church, nervously awaiting his bride. "She had the blondest hair I'd ever afore seen . . ."

For the next hour or more, M'Cuick told Isabella everything about his Mary, how he'd met her, standing at the market in Inverness. She'd been wearing a blue ribbon in her hair, and the moment he'd seen her, Malcolm had fallen completely and utterly in love with her. He told of their wedding, of the simple home they had made. He reminisced about dancing beneath the stars on

Beltane, crying like a child when she told him she was expecting their first child.

He described the way she would shoo him out of her kitchen whenever he tried to steal one of her bannocks. He told Isabella everything, the births of their children, the disagreements they had had over the silliest things, and the fun they'd had later making up. He knew her down to the smattering of freckles that dusted her nose and the dimple she would get when she smiled. Isabella asked questions, details about her, and Malcolm answered. And all while he talked, Isabella sketched, sweeping the red chalk pencil across the page.

When he'd finished talking, M'Cuick looked up to see that Isabella was sitting with her chin resting on her hand, just watching him. The red chalk pencil lay on the table before her.

"You're no' drawing anymore?"

She smiled. "I finished a little while ago."

He shook his head. "I dinna e'en notice."

Isabella took up the drawing, holding it so that it faced away from his view. "Do you want to see it?"

He looked at her, took a breath. He nodded.

Isabella handed him the page.

She watched his face register an expression of pure and utter wonder. "'Tis her . . . 'Tis my Mary."

"I wasn't sure if I had her nose just right, but that is why I drew it in the chalk. I can rub some of it out if need be, redraw it before I ink it over to make it permanent."

"Nae, lass. Nae." He shook his head. "'Tis perfect as it is. You've drawn her just as she was." He looked at her. "You drew in the bairns, too, Tomas and wee Mary."

He sniffed. "You e'en drew in Mary's pigtails. How d'you do it, lass? How'd you make them look so real?"

"I just listened to you, Malcolm," she said. "I just listened to your heart."

His eyes glistened with emotion in the low light. "'Tis a wondrous gift you have, lass. Wondrous." He set the drawing aside and reached for her, crushing her to him. "Thank you for it," he said against her cheek. "'Tis the most precious gift I could e'er have received."

Chapter Fourteen

It was late, more than just a couple of hours past midnight. The candlestick he read by had burned to a guttering stump, and Calum was still poring through Lord Belcourt's "bibles."

He'd been at it since leaving the hall earlier that night.

His hair was mussed from the countless number of times he had raked his hands through it in frustration. His eyes were heavy and stinging with fatigue as the names had begun blurring before him on the page.

MacLeans.

MacLachlans.

Clanranalds.

Camerons.

His countrymen. His brethren.

Now inmates in a foreign land.

So many had been taken away, countless many. Calum's only consolation was that he had recognized a good many of the names on those pages as men whom he had freed.

Not all.

Not most.

But some.

And for Calum, even having saved one was a victory.

Mungo, M'Cuick, Hugh, Fergus—they, along with all of the others, had been entered into the ledger book like just another boll of meal or hogget of sugar on a market list, their intended fates checked off with sterile assiduousness:

Hanged.

Beheaded.

Transported.

Each one signed with the same four words:

At His Majesty's Pleasure.

There were hundreds of names scribbled in each of the four books. Not only men, but women, even children who had been labeled rebels for merely wearing the white cockade. All Calum could think as he continued to read those words—*At His Majesty's Pleasure*—time and time again was that "His Majesty," the usurper George, must be quite pleased.

But there was one name he'd yet to find in the ledgers, the one name Calum sought more than any other.

Uilliam Bain.

He wouldn't give up till he found him.

"You look tired."

Calum's eyes shot up with an alacrity that belied his fatigue. He'd been so concentrated upon his task, he hadn't even heard her come in the room.

"Lass," was all he said, and glanced wearily at the clock.

It was past three of the morn. Dawn would soon be breaking.

Was she a dream?

"I saw the firelight shining underneath the door. I didn't want to disturb you, but I thought you might like a cup of tea and perhaps a taste of your birthday cake. It was a difficult thing, rescuing you a bit of it before the others devoured it all."

While she spoke, she had emerged from the shadows of the doorway on bare feet, carrying a tray with a small teapot and two cups. A plate with a wedge of the cake stood beside it.

She wore a simple night chemise and had draped a length of tartan woolen around her shoulders to ward away the chill. Her hair was down, tumbling about her shoulders and neck. She looked like an angel sent to earth.

"Thank you," he said as she set the tray on his desk, poured them each a cup of tea. He felt badly for having left the gathering earlier that evening, and so quickly on the heels of her bringing him his birthday wishes. He took the cup of tea she offered, and then took her hand. She looked at him.

"Thank you for the gift of the cake, lass."

She stared at him and simply nodded. "'Twas no trouble. Everyone should make a wish on their birthday," she said, and slowly pulled away to sit.

Calum sipped his tea, closed his eyes to savor it. It was just what he needed. It was warm and strong and it eased the weight of the fatigue that had settled over his shoulders during the past hours.

"The tea is good."

He opened his eyes to see she had lowered into one of

the chairs in front of his desk. She had her knees drawn up with her toes peeking out from beneath the hem of her chemise. She was cradling a cup of tea in her hand, sipping gingerly at the steaming brew.

"What keeps you awake at this hour?" he asked.

"I couldn't sleep," she said. "Would you mind if I were to just sit for a spell? I won't bother you. It's just that it's rather . . . cold in my room."

"Cold? Why did you no' say something sooner? I could have Hamish come in to stoke the—"

"Not cold in that way, Calum. Just lonely."

He looked at her. "You're welcome to sit for a while if you'd like, though I doubt I'll be much in the way of company. I'm half asleep myself and I've these books to get through."

He turned his attention back to the page in front of him and started scanning the next column. He tried very hard to concentrate, but he was consciously aware of the fact that she was sitting not five feet away from him, watching him.

"You're welcome to look through the shelves for something to read," he suggested.

He watched as she glanced behind him to where the wall was lined with books.

"Perhaps that would help you to sleep," he added.

She nodded, set her cup on his desk, and got up. The ticking of the clock and the sound of her pulling books from the shelf was the only sound in the room for several minutes.

Calum turned a page in the ledger.

"Anything I can help you with?"

He turned his head to see her suddenly leaning very

closely over his shoulder, looking down at the ledger that was opened before him.

They were so close his face nearly brushed hers. He could feel the warmth of her breath on his nose, could smell the scent of her. All he had to do was close his eyes and . . .

"Nae," he said, more to himself than to her. "Thank you, lass, but 'tis a task I must see to myself."

"What is it?" She narrowed her eyes, peering at the page. "It looks like some sort of account book."

Calum blinked at her, but didn't immediately answer.

"Calum, I just want to help." She frowned when he continued mute. "Why will you not trust me?"

"The question should be why *should* I trust you, lass?"

He tried to ignore her wounded look as he pressed on. "You arrived here knowing my name, knowing even my birth date. You want me to tell you everything, yet you won't even reveal your true name."

"I already told you. My name is—"

He held up a hand. "I'm not a suggestible lad like Hamish, lass. I know bluidy well you're not any mermaid."

She looked at him. A moment stretched into two.

Finally she said, "My name . . . is Isabella. *Lady* Isabella Drayton."

It was nothing more than he had already suspected. "So you are a Sassenach."

Her face darkened. "And so that makes me the enemy?"

"Everyone is the enemy, lass."

He looked at her, stretched the truth just a little. "I've heard of the name Drayton. Your father is a duke."

He only really knew this because of the crest imprinted on the seal of her letter.

Isabella straightened. "Yes, he is a duke. An *English* duke, or as you prefer to call it a Sassenach duke. My sister, however, is married to a Scot. Douglas Dúbh MacKinnon of Dunakin on Skye."

Calum was unable to hide his surprise. This was the "Bess" she had written of?

"Your sister is the Lady MacKinnon who helped the prince make his escape?"

Now she was the one surprised. "How do you know about that?"

"Everyone knows of it, lass. It is legend about the Highlands. Lady MacKinnon is said to have entertained a Hanoverian general and his captain in her parlor while at the same time her husband helped to spirit the prince away right under their very noses."

"So you see not everything is either black or white."

She referred to the two cockades of the rebellion. White for the Jacobites, and black for the Hanoverians.

"Your sister put her life at great risk to help the prince," Calum said.

"What else was she to do? Elizabeth knew if they caught him, he would be killed. She would do anything to protect her family."

"Family?"

Isabella nodded, moved to sit on the edge of his desk. "Yes. Although *officially* my father's lineage is known to history to have descended from Sinclair Drayton of Parbroath, in truth, his great-great-grandfather was the only surviving male child of Henry VIII."

Calum considered her words. "He was a bastard?"

"He was one of the lesser known illegitimate children

of the king. For that he was granted a dukedom upon his reaching his twenty-first year. Society, it seems, is kinder to the by-blows of a sovereign. So although it isn't a legitimate connection, it is widely known that my father descends from the house of Tudor, thus we are connected by blood to the Stuarts, who also descend from the Tudors through Henry's sister, Margaret."

"As do the Hanoverians."

She merely said, "This is true."

Calum tried to take this all in. She, and her family, were in a unique position, for at any time they could claim allegiance to each of the warring sides. And then he realized, "So had the union of Henry and his paramour been legitimatized, your father could now be king, and you could very well be a crown princess."

She took a breath. "Yes, I suppose you are right."

A princess. Calum took a moment to adjust to the idea. She had told him more, far more than even he had expected. She wanted his trust very badly. He wondered how much more she would be willing to reveal.

Calum stood, facing her, facing her so closely her knees brushed his thighs beneath the fabric of the kilt he wore. He reached toward her, saw her swallow nervously as he lifted the stone from where it lay against her breast, nearly hidden behind the folds of her nightdress.

She didn't even flinch.

"Who gave you the stone, lass?"

His voice was nearly a whisper. He looked into her eyes, watching as she blinked.

She didn't respond. She didn't want to tell him, perhaps had been told not to, yet she was seeking a way to convince him he should trust her. Finally she said, "It was a man called le Comte de St. Germain."

He shook his head. "I have never heard of this man."

"Nor had I. I was traveling back to England from Paris and stopped for a night at Versailles, to convey my father's regards to the king."

"You met Louis?"

"Yes," she said as if she had just told him she had met a flower seller on the corner of the village high street. "My father had sent the king a gift, which I was to present to him. After my introduction to the king, Madame de Pompadour invited me to supper. It was there I met Monsieur le Comte de St. Germain. He is, apparently, quite close within the king's circle."

A man, quite close to the French king, had had the stone of his ancestors, the stone his father had died carrying into battle. The tale was only growing more mysterious.

"What did he look like, this comte?"

"He was a most intriguing man. They claim he does not age, that he has lived for centuries, and that he can manufacture potions to sustain youth, can even make precious jewels out of stone. He is an accomplished artist. It was he who gave me the stone. He told me it needed to be returned to the rightful MacAoidh, that it had been taken from the clan. He charged me with the task of bringing it back. That is how I knew who you were."

"But why did he choose you for this task?"

"He said the stone had chosen me."

Somehow, Calum believed her.

He leaned in closer to her, his fingers still holding the

stone. "So then why do you no' give the stone to me? I
am Mackay, and the stone has led you to me."

Their faces were close, so close that their breaths min-
gled. Calum wondered if he should kiss her, crush his
mouth to hers and kiss her until she was breathless and
swaying against him.

Kiss her until she gave him that stone.

But he didn't.

She blinked. "I cannot give you the stone, Calum. The
comte said I would know when it was time, when it was
right. He said that I would have to make a choice, between two. He said it would become clear to me in time,
but that until it did, I daren't take the stone from around
my neck. Else . . ."

"Else what?"

"Else the circumstances would be dire for all concerned."

"And you believe him?"

He could already see that she did, but he asked it
anyway.

"At first, I admit, I thought it all an elaborate ruse. But
too many things have come to fit what the comte told me
that night. You. How the stone disappeared. And there is
no accounting for the glowing of the stone when I touch
it. The only thing that doesn't fit is the reference the
comte made to the need to make a choice. *Between the
two,* he said." She shook her head. "Try as I might, I just
cannot decipher what that means." She looked at him.
"Can you?"

Yes, he could.

Calum gazed at her deeply. He wanted to tell her,
wanted to tell her everything. She had been so honest
with him and perhaps, in the end, what he might tell her

wouldn't matter. Perhaps the stone would come to him and then he would know. Even so, in the end, he held back.

He lied.

"No, lass, I cannot."

It was the only answer he could offer her.

The face that answered the door upon their knocking was far from a welcoming one.

It was old and it was weathered, lined from decades of glowering at the world into which it had been born.

"Who're you?" the man said, his fierce gaze traveling up and then down the intruders standing before him.

He wore a servant's clothes, plain shirt and plain breeches with stockings that were dingy above scuffed and worn shoes. His hair, what there was of it, was thin and white, sticking out from his head like the bristles of a brush. He was apparently unimpressed by what he saw, because the grimace on his mouth only twisted all the more.

"MacKinnon of Dunakin," Douglas said, unaffected by the man's rudeness, although he was surprised by it. Highland hospitality was a thing of honor, a matter of great pride and tradition. This dour reception was markedly out of place. "We request to see the chief."

The man didn't move, didn't so much as blink. "The Mackay is not receiving any visitors."

Douglas opened his mouth to respond, but found himself suddenly getting shoved aside by the thickheaded Kentigern St. Clive, who came charging forward, dangerously in the face of the sentry.

"Now see here, old man. My affianced wife has been stolen and we've information that your *Mackay*"—he accented the word in a taunting mimicry of the Scots brogue—"has knowledge of her whereabouts. I demand to see him. And I demand to see him *now*."

The man looked at St. Clive briefly, then turned his glance amusedly to Douglas. "Who's the whelp?"

"Whelp!?" St. Clive nearly screeched. "Do you know who my father is, you Scottish piece of—?"

Douglas took him by the arm and pulled him back before he ended up with a claymore running through his fine brocaded waistcoat. "Silence, *amadan*."

St. Clive's face turned red. He didn't know what Douglas had just called him, but he was perceptive enough to know it wasn't anything at all flattering. "Who do you think you—"

Douglas rounded on him, grabbed him by the lace of his cravat, and pulled him forward until his face was just inches away from his own. "I said silence. Whether you like it or no' you're in Scotland now, you ignorant *gheeho*. Your father's title and name have no significance here."

Douglas had spoken no louder than a whisper but it had the effect of a menacing war cry. St. Clive narrowed his eyes hotly, but didn't say another word.

"Douglas."

Douglas looked over St. Clive's trembling shoulder to where his father-in-law stood, watching the exchange. The look on the duke's face questioned whether he should step in.

"I'll manage this, your grace."

The duke simply nodded.

Douglas released St. Clive and then turned back to the door. The sentry was looking at him with a newfound appreciation in his eyes.

This time when Douglas spoke, he did so in Gaelic.

"What the *amadan* says is true, man. A lass has been taken and we've reason to believe the Mackay can assist us in finding her. This lass is the sister to my wife, Lady MacKinnon. I'm very concerned about her."

"The prince's Lady MacKinnon?"

And in that moment, Douglas knew they'd be admitted, for while the House of Mackay was famously Hanoverian, courage and cunning held a special place in the heart of every Scotsman, Jacobite or no.

"Aye, she is the one. Now I give you my word we only wish to speak with the Mackay to see if he might be able to help us identify who the perpetrators might be."

The man gave it an extra moment's consideration for good measure, then he said, "Wait here."

He'd only been gone a moment before St. Clive was piping up again.

"That was wholly unnecessary, MacKinnon. You could have—"

"Shut up."

Douglas decided right then that if Isabella so much as considered marrying this *dowf,* he would kidnap her himself . . . and lock her in a tower. A very high tower. On a deserted island . . .

Douglas had never seen his wife more beside herself with indignation and outrage as she had been when her parents had announced to the whole of the family who had gathered in Edinburgh to meet Isabella of their choice of St. Clive for her husband.

Elizabeth had been so very angry, she had nearly thrown her slipper across the room.

"You cannot have her marry *him!* Anyone, heaven's

sake, even Caroline's pig Homer would be a better husband than *him!*"

She had practically shouted it at the duke and duchess, without the slightest concern that the very object of her aversion had been standing right beside her, in the same room, having traveled with the Draytons in their coach to propose to Isabella formally.

In the duke and duchess's defense, they had had no notion of the events that had taken place that long-ago summer. Even Douglas wasn't entirely clear about what had happened, although he knew it had something to do with Isabella having had her young heart crushed after finding St. Clive frolicking amidst the fields with someone named Maggie the Deflowered.

The duke and duchess had simply remembered that Isabella had once held tender feelings for the blond future earl, thought, too, that she would be overjoyed that they had arranged for her to become the wife of the young man she had always pined for. They were sincerely astonished when Elizabeth revealed all in candid detail (down to the man's grass-stained breeches) of what had taken place that day at the fair.

The duke and duchess, however, were suddenly left with a most awkward dilemma.

Because they had thought him the best candidate, the Duke and Duchess of Sudeleigh had already entered into a tentative and somewhat legal agreement of marriage with St. Clive and his father, the Earl of Chilton. Faced with the Draytons' sudden and obvious disapproval of his past behavior toward their daughter, St. Clive, blackguard that he was, had tried to wave the entire episode off as a boyhood sowing of oats, nothing more, all while

Elizabeth stood there with unquestionable murder in her eyes.

But there was a way out.

Blessedly, Douglas's in-laws had included as part of the marriage agreement the requirement of Isabella's consent to the match. If Bella was to refuse St. Clive's proposal—which she certainly would, or Elizabeth would likely kill her before she could ever marry the cad—the contract would be off.

St. Clive, however, was not so certain of Isabella's refusal.

He actually believed he could gain her consent, if only he could talk to her. And it was his confidence in himself that had made him insist upon accompanying Douglas and the duke to the north to search for her. St. Clive was merely posturing, Douglas knew. It wasn't Isabella, or her love, that he sought to secure. The dowry he'd been promised consisted of some thousands of acres of the land that lay between the Chilton and Drayton estates, fine arable land that would assure him a healthy yearly allowance. It wouldn't have mattered to him if Isabella had been abducted by Hades himself. St. Clive only wanted the land, and would, Douglas suspected, beg, plead, and threaten Isabella so he could get it.

Douglas, however, was determined not to give him the chance.

He'd promised Elizabeth that when he found Isabella—which he fully intended to do—he would bring her straight to Dunakin, and would not allow her to make any decisions about the marriage until she had spoken to Elizabeth first.

"You can follow me now."

Douglas looked up to see that the Mackay guard had

returned. He led, followed after by the duke, with St. Clive bringing up the rear.

Where he belonged.

They were led into a room at the back of the house that appeared to be of use as a study. The walls were paneled in dark oak, and a fire burned in the hearth despite the warmth of the day. Across from the door, the windows were opened onto a sun-dappled garden. There was a chaise set there where a man sat, his legs propped up upon the footrest and covered by a woolen blanket.

"The chief will see you now," the sentry said and turned to leave them.

Douglas approached the chair slowly.

"Come, come," beckoned an age-gnarled hand. "Come around here where I can better see you."

The Mackay chief was a man who looked a full decade older than his seventy years. His hair was white and thin and hung about his leathery-skinned face in fragile wisps. His eyes were rheumy and red, and his breathing came in labored rasps. He was not, it would appear, much longer for this life.

"Sir?"

"You're MacKinnon, I am told?"

"Aye, sir."

" 'Twas your clever wife who outfoxed Campbell of Mamore and Fergusson, aye? She must be quite the minx, that lass."

Douglas smiled. "That she is, sir. I've her father with us, the Duke of Sudeleigh."

The duke took his cue and came forward, leaving a fuming St. Clive to lurk in the long shadows cast through the windows like a ghillie.

"Mr. Mackay," the duke greeted him. "It is a pleasure to make your acquaintanceship."

"Your grace. I hear good things of you. You are known for your political neutrality. A difficult thing to maintain in this day and age I suppose."

"Yes, sir, it can be."

The chief nodded slowly. "So tell me about this lass, the one who is missing . . . she is your daughter?"

Affined by both their age and experiences, Douglas backed away and allowed the two men to converse.

"She is my second daughter, with Elizabeth, Lady MacKinnon, being the eldest. Isabella was making a channel crossing from France when her ship was waylaid by pirates."

"Pirates?" The chief was suddenly seized by a coughing spell. The besieged man's body was wracked with such force that Douglas feared his bones might break. He crossed to the sideboard to pour the man a glass of water.

"Thank you, MacKinnon." The chief took a sip. His coughing quieted. He settled back against the chaise once again. "You've reason to believe one of these pirates was a Mackay? My clan is known for many things, your grace, but piracy isn't one of them."

"If I may," Douglas interjected. "From the accounts told us by the witnesses, these pirates were flying the *Bratach Bhan.*"

The chief was understandably surprised by this bit of news. "The Mackay banner?"

"Aye, and I'm told they used the clan war cry."

His weathered face grew troubled. "The Mackays have many enemies, MacKinnon, particularly with the part we played in this last rebellion. How can you be certain this wasn't one of our rival clans trussed up to make it appear as if it was the Mackays?"

"It is a possibility, sir."

The chief shook his head. "But this matter of the banner disturbs me. It vanished, you know, after the death of my brother, Artair Ros Mackay at Sheriffmuir. But it did appear again. Just once. At Culloden."

"Do you know who carried it into battle, sir?"

"Aye. But it canna be him. He's dead. He was killed on the battlefield."

"That is true, Uncle. But his body was never found."

Everyone turned to the door where a stranger suddenly stood. He was tall, dark-haired, perhaps thirty years of age. He came into the room and knelt beside the chief, paying his respects.

"Ah, gentlemen, allow me to introduce Alec Mackay, my nephew."

The newcomer greeted the others.

"Are you suggesting you might know who took my daughter?" asked the duke when the introductions were finished.

Alec nodded. "I've a notion, your grace."

"Who?"

Douglas had asked it, but it was a question they all wanted the answer to.

And Alec provided it. "I believe it was my brother, Calum Mackay of Wrath."

The chief started coughing again, this time worse than before. Alec returned to the chaise, and patted the man gently on the back in an effort to try to loosen the rattling that was making it so difficult for him to breathe.

The chief held up a hand, and eased back in the chair. "He is alive? Calum is alive?"

Alec nodded. "Aye, Uncle."

"H-how long have you known?"

"Some months now." He looked at his uncle. "I promised him I would not tell anyone of his existence. He needed it to be believed that he was well and truly dead."

"But where has he been living all these months?"

"Up at Castle Wrath."

"Wrath? How on earth is he surviving? It's a ruin . . . there's no food, no stock."

"The man's a bloody pirate! He's living off his spoils!"

Douglas shot St. Clive a look that would have quelled a raging bull.

"Who was that?" the chief asked, puzzled at the introduction of a new voice behind him. "Is someone else in this room?"

"Kentigern St. Clive, Mr. Mackay," he said, coming forward to shake the man's frail hand. "My father is the Earl of Chilton."

The chief shook his head. "Never heard of him."

Douglas, standing off to the side, suppressed a grin.

"Well, from what I have just heard, it seems your nephew is very likely responsible for abducting my affianced wife against her will."

"Oh, I dinna know about that," Alec said. "She didn't look all too upset about it."

Everyone turned toward him.

"You've seen her?" Douglas asked. "You have seen Isabella?"

"Dark hair, lovely face, likes to sit in graveyards and draw the stones."

"Good God, that's my Bella!" The duke came forward. "Where did you see her?"

"At the churchyard between my house and Castle Wrath."

"He's locked her in a church?"

Alec shook his head. "Nae. She was quite free to wander. In fact, she had a pony with her."

"A pony?" The duke waved him off. "That's not Bella. It cannot be. She's been terrified of horses since she was a girl."

"Begging your grace's pardon, but not any longer she's not."

"It has to be her," Douglas said to the duke. "Who else could she be?" He turned to Alec. "Perhaps she had taken the pony to escape from your brother?"

"I suppose 'tis possible, but when she left, she was headed back in the direction of Castle Wrath. And she didn't seem to be in any hurry. She looked like she was just out enjoying a summer's day."

"It doesn't make sense," St. Clive cut in. "Perhaps he's brutalized her. Perhaps she is too traumatized to know to escape on her own."

"If I may, gentlemen . . ."

Everyone turned to look at the chief yet seated in his chaise.

"The only way you're going to get any answers to your questions is to go to Castle Wrath and find out for yourself. But let me tell you this. When you do go, you'd best go prepared with a strategy. A good strategy. Calum Mackay is one wily and tenacious lad. He'll fight to the death, if need be."

"That's perfectly fine with me," St. Clive said, cracking his knuckles with all the bravado of a peacock.

"Think of Bella, St. Clive," Douglas warned. "We don't want to put her in any unnecessary danger. We've no idea what this man will do if we go charging in there declaring war. He had crew enough to sail a ship. For all we know he has a small army living up there with him."

"So what will we do?" St. Clive sneered, his lip curling derisively. "Shall we just sit back and wait until he and all his men are through with her?"

Alec stepped before him, his voice dropping with a note of ill-concealed warning. "My brother may be many things, sir, but he's no defiler of women. He's a Mackay, and thus he has honor."

St. Clive scoffed. "Forgive me if I disagree. This is my wife we're talking about."

"*Potential* wife," Douglas stated. "She hasna agreed to any match."

Nor will she, he thought to himself.

Douglas turned to Alec. "You know this Castle Wrath very well?"

"Aye. Played there as a lad. 'Twas to be our father's legacy, had he not perished."

"Do you think you can help us come up with a way to breach it?"

Alec thought about it a moment, then nodded. "I've an idea. Come, gentlemen, let us allow my uncle to rest while we discuss things further in the garden."

Chapter Fifteen

"That is the one."

Isabella pointed up the rise to the almost indistinguishable opening of the cave where the boy had vanished the day before.

"You're certain of it, Miss Maris?" Hamish asked.

They had ridden ponies, with baskets filled with bannocks and cheeses, milk and fruit and fresh water. If they couldn't find the boy, Isabella had decided she would leave the baskets for him at the opening of the cave. At least he'd have food to eat.

"Yes, that is the one. You see, I marked it with a ribbon from my hair."

And indeed the red bit of silk yet fluttered from the gorse that clumped near the opening.

They dismounted and climbed the path to the cave where Hamish bent to light the lantern they had brought with them.

"You stay here, Miss Maris," he said. "I'll go in first

and have a look around. There's no telling what might be inside."

Isabella nodded, realizing his need to play the role of the male protector, and not just the stable boy. She had known from the moment she had decided to tell Hamish about the boy and the cave and her intention to return there that she would need to appeal to him as an equal, a cohort. So she waited while he vanished inside the yawning mouth of the cave, and turned to watch for the boy herself out on the moors, lest he was already out and wandering.

She listened to Hamish's retreating footsteps, heard him calling out in Gaelic, his voice echoing against the cragged rock walls. His voice grew distant the farther he delved into the cave. Still he called. Still there was no responding voice. Until . . .

Gabh uam!

Isabella spun around, listening.

She heard the exchange of two voices in Gaelic, a rapid, heated clash of words that gurgled from the opening of the cave.

Her heartbeat quickened. She stood. And waited.

A short time later she spotted the swaying light of the lantern approaching. In moments Hamish had emerged, his hand clutching the boy's shoulder.

"Hamish, you found him!"

"Aye, miss, but he's like to run. He thinks you want to send him to the gaol for stealing your basket."

"No, no, no." She shook her head in an effort to assure him. "We just want to help you."

The boy, who appeared to be about seven or eight years old, looked at her in timid and utterly oblivious silence.

"Please tell him for me, Hamish."

Hamish said something to the boy in Gaelic. The boy glanced at her, suspicion written across his dirty face.

"What is his name?"

" 'Tis Druhan, miss."

"Ask him where he lives."

A moment later, Hamish had his answer. "In the cave, miss."

"He lives in the cave? This cave? Alone?"

"Nae. His mammie lives with him."

"His mother?"

"Aye. Seems his da fought in the rebellion and was killed. The soldiers came from England and burned their house and all their things. They've been moving along from place to place ever since, wherever they could find shelter. They've been at the cave here for about a fortnight."

"But if his mother is with him . . . where is she?"

Hamish spoke with the lad, and the boy immediately started to weep as he gave his answer.

"She's in the cave. She's ill, he says. He only stole the food to try to help her to get well."

"Oh, Hamish, we must get her from that cave. It is too damp and cold. If she's unwell, she will die in there." Isabella quickly thought. "Tell the boy we want to bring them back to the castle with us, to shelter them and tend to his mother. Tell him he does not need to be afraid."

Hamish blinked. "But . . . , Miss Maris, the laird, he has a rule. No wives and no children allowed at Castle Wrath."

"Nonsense. She will die if we do not help her. Calum would never turn away someone in such dire straits. I know he wouldn't. Now give me the lantern and tell the boy to show me where his mother is. Then you ride to the castle quick as you can and fetch a litter that we can hitch to one of the ponies to transport her. Tell no one what you are about. It is much more difficult to turn someone away when they are standing right in front of you. I will speak with Calum when we return. If he is angry, I will tell him I insisted that you help me."

Hamish spoke to the boy who nodded, staring at Isabella with uncertainty. Then Hamish turned for the ponies.

"And, Hamish, bring blankets. And tea. And some *uisge-beatha*. 'Twill help to warm her till we can get her to a bed and a hearth. And hurry!"

While Hamish galloped one of the ponies back to the castle, Isabella and the boy entered the cave guided by the glimmering light of the lantern. The boy said nothing as they went, just kept glancing at Isabella as if to assure himself she really meant him no harm. She smiled at him, touched him softly on the top of his matted hair, and he seemed to ease.

Isabella couldn't imagine how the boy and his mother had sheltered there for one night let alone fourteen. The walls inside the cave were damp and covered with moss. The air was thick with an unhealthy moisture that clung to everything it touched, chilling Isabella despite the layers of her clothing. It was no wonder the woman had taken ill.

They followed a series of tight twists and low turns until finally they came into a cavern chamber. The ceiling here was higher than the passage they had traveled, the air icy without any fire to warm it. The only light came from a small fissure in the rock overhead through which the daylight filtered—along with the rain, it would seem, for a puddle had formed directly beneath it. Bunches of heather and other brush had been stacked into the shape of pallets, numbering two. One of the pallets was vacant. The other was covered by a thin blanket, beneath that lay the slumbering figure of Druhan's mother.

She couldn't be many years older than Isabella, but her condition had aged her markedly. Her eyes were hollow sockets on a gaunt face, the skin paper-thin. Her hair, probably once a lovely blond, was now a gritty shade of brown and very thin. She opened her eyes wearily as Isabella approached, sucking in a sudden and labored breath when she realized it wasn't her son, but a stranger standing beside her.

"Leig leam . . . leig leam . . ." she gasped.

She started to lift herself, as if to attempt to flee, but Isabella put out a hand and whispered, "Nae . . . *shh*."

The woman seemed to sense that Isabella meant her no harm and eased back onto the pallet, but not without wincing from the effort.

She was indeed very ill, though it appeared to be more from malnourishment than for any other reason. She likely gave whatever they managed to find to eat to her son, and he was too young to realize by doing so she was slowly starving herself. She wore what amounted to little more than a tattered chemise and Isabella suspected she had given up some of her own clothing to fashion coverings for her son. The pallet she lay upon smelled of urine and stagnation. Isabella wondered if she had grown too weak to relieve herself properly.

Isabella reached inside the basket she'd brought and removed a skin of water, touching it to the woman's cracked and dried lips. She sipped, closing her eyes as she labored to complete even that one simple task. Isabella wiped the bit that had dribbled down her chin with her handkerchief, then she smiled as she took the woman's hands and covered them with her own to warm them.

The woman responded with a weak and fragile smile, closing her eyes out of sheer, interminable fatigue.

Isabella decided against giving the woman any food, not until they had gotten her to the castle where M'Cuick could prepare her a healing posset. If she hadn't eaten in some time, as Isabella suspected, her stomach might rebel at the sudden introduction of ordinary food. The effort of vomiting it back up would only cause the woman far more pain and exhaustion than it was worth. So instead Isabella continued to offer her sips of water while waiting for Hamish to return.

He did not keep her waiting very long.

Hamish arrived with a litter and the supplies Isabella had asked for, along with something else utterly unexpected.

M'Cuick had apparently come upon Hamish brewing the tea and had questioned him until he'd revealed what they were about.

Isabella met them outside the cave.

"Miss . . ." M'Cuick began.

"If you're going to tell me Calum won't be pleased about this, Malcolm, I have no wish to hear it." Her concern over the woman's condition had steeled her resolve.

"Nae, miss. That isna what I was going to say at all. I was going to tell you if there was to be any retribution for bringing them to the castle, I would take it upon myself."

"Oh." Isabella smiled at him. "You needn't worry,

though. I don't think there will be any question about it
once Calum sees how in need these two truly are."

She led them back inside the cave and waited while
Hamish spoke to the woman, explaining who they were
and why they had come. Her name, he translated, was
Kettie Munro, and she had traveled there from Tain,
from which she had been aimlessly wandering the moors
for over six months.

Hamish and Isabella gathered up what little was worth
keeping from the cave while M'Cuick gently picked up
Kettie and carried her to the litter.

In the daylight, Kettie's condition showed even more
starkly.

It took them some time to return to the castle. Every
bump and rut seemed to jar Kettie's fragile bones, and
though she fought to keep from crying out, the strain
of it showed on her face. She was a brave woman. Isabella would very soon learn just how far that bravery
extended.

The first thing Isabella did when they arrived back at
the castle was hasten to her chamber to fetch Kettie
some clean clothing. M'Cuick set to arranging a chamber for the two newcomers off the kitchen, where they
would have the warmth of the cooking hearth to keep
them, and would be close enough to see to throughout
the day. Two small beds were set up with mattresses
stuffed with heather and herbs, and laid with fresh
linens. Then while M'Cuick went off to prepare one of
his healing possets, Isabella helped Kettie into a much
needed bath.

The Scotswoman was embarrassed at first, and fought
with what little strength she had against having herself
undressed, but Isabella did everything she could to pre-

serve her modesty while reassuring her with words of comfort in Gaelic that Hamish had quickly taught her. She helped her to pull the soiled chemise over her head, promptly tossing it into the hearth, and then blinked back tears of dismay at the many sores that marred her skin, the absence of flesh that caused the skin to stretch dreadfully over her ribs and shrunken breasts.

But none of this caused her as much concern as the one that had her leaving Kettie to soak a moment while she went into the kitchen.

"She is with child."

M'Cuick looked up from the pan of milk and whisky he was stirring over the fire. "Nae, lass . . ." He shook his head. "She canna be." And then, "You're certain?"

Isabella nodded. "She's far enough along that there is little doubt of it. And if her husband fell at Culloden as they have told us, it cannot possibly be his child. The only explanation I can come up with is . . ."

She didn't want to say what she thought had happened to the woman.

"She was raped?"

Isabella nodded solemnly. "How else could she have gotten with child? No doubt it was when the soldiers came and attacked her house. I'm not so sheltered to think such things are not happening all across the Highlands. There's no telling the horrors she went through. Oh, God, Malcolm, do you think Druhan was there? Do you think he saw what happened to his mother?"

Tears were spilling from her eyes and her voice broke with emotion. M'Cuick left the fire to put a comforting arm about her shoulder.

"There's no point looking back," he said. "We canna

do a thing about it. What we can do is see that she and her bairn are given the best of care now."

Isabella looked up at him. He was right. They needed to see Kettie through to a healthy and safe future. She nodded slowly.

Isabella washed Kettie's hair and scrubbed her skin with an herbal soap that M'Cuick had given her made with thyme and lousewort. It would kill any vermin and would also serve to help heal the sores that covered her body from having lain as she had, unmoving for so many days on that unhealthy pallet. M'Cuick kept a steady supply of the stuff for the prisoners they freed from the English hulks, who were often left for months in the most inhumane conditions.

By the time she'd finished, Kettie's skin had begun to pink up and her hair glistened once again. She squeezed Isabella's hand weakly, whispering a soft *"buidheachas"* that Bella needed no translation to understand.

Druhan, however, was less enthusiastic about his turn in the bath. He shook his head furiously when told, and then when Isabella tried to approach him, he darted underneath the huge trestle table in the kitchen and refused, absolutely refused to come out. It finally took M'Cuick snagging him by the ankles and hoisting him up, dunking him in the tub headfirst, to get him there.

The resulting yowl echoed throughout the castle, and even had Fergus's dog, Fingal, bolting for the door.

After she'd helped Kettie from the bath, Isabella slipped one of her own chemises over her head and then took her to sit by the hearth fire, to sip on M'Cuick's restorative posset while Isabella slowly and carefully combed the knots and tangles from her hair.

It was thus Calum found them when he walked into

the kitchen a handful of moments later. He'd been summoned by the echo of Druhan's cry. He stopped in the doorway. He didn't say a word. He didn't have to.

His expression said it all.

"Calum."

Isabella stood, crossed the room to meet him. "Before you say anything, I would like to tell you that if there's to be any recourse for having brought them to the castle, it should be directed at me. No one else. I am the one who insisted upon bringing them here."

He looked at her. "The only *recourse* you're to receive, lass, is my gratitude. Hamish told me everything. Had you not done what you have, I shudder to think what would have become of them."

Isabella smiled, and blinked. "Thank you."

She poured Calum a cup of tea and told him everything, including her suspicions about the origin of Kettie's unborn child. When she'd finished, he sat for several moments, silent, thoughtful. Then he walked over to where Kettie yet sat by the fire, took her hand as he hunkered down before her, and spoke with her in private, hushed Gaelic.

"You were justified in your suspicions about the child," he said to Isabella later, after they'd gotten Kettie and Druhan off to bed. Kettie had eaten very little, her stomach too weak to accept much more than a few spoonfuls of a thickened pap of meal and milk. Druhan, however, had eaten and then had asked for more, cleaning his trencher of M'Cuick's kidney stew, three bannocks, and finishing off two servings of lemon pudding afterward. It was his reward, he'd been told, for submitting so "generously" to his bath.

The hour was late. They were sitting in Calum's study,

poring through the prisoner ledgers together. Calum had decided to tell Isabella the truth of his quest to uncover Uilliam's whereabouts and free him before he was transported across the sea. Though Fergus would likely tell him he'd been a fool to trust her, after her undertaking on behalf of Kettie and her son, Calum couldn't help but believe that he could trust Isabella with anything.

Including the one thing she deserved to know, but that he had purposely kept from telling her.

He would tell her about his brother.

"What will Kettie do?" Isabella asked, as Calum tried to think of the words to say to her.

Even though he had decided he would tell her the truth about Alec, he was reluctant, because he feared once he did, she would very likely leave. She would have to go to Alec to see if it was he who was the rightful holder of the stone. And once she did, she might never come back.

So he waited, allowing himself one last night with her.

"What else can she do?" he said. "Kettie will bear the child, and if it is a son, she will give it her husband's name. She will tell Druhan that it was his father's last gift to them. She will teach it to speak the Gaelic tongue and she will raise it as a Scot. It is the only thing she can do to prove to the English bastard who sired it and to the rest of the world that their brutality did not conquer her."

"You hate the English so very much," Isabella said, her voice nearly a whisper. It was not a question, rather a statement of fact.

"They killed my father, lass. They have imprisoned my foster father. They have violated my country in every manner possible. They have murdered our children, and they have raped the mothers of Scotland. They thieved the crown of my forefathers. I fear they will not rest until they have driven out, killed, or enslaved every last Scot."

"I am English, Calum."

"Aye?"

She looked at him, utterly hopeless. "Does this mean you hate me as well?"

Calum looked at her, just looked at her, and he felt something tighten inside of him, deep inside of him, deeper than he'd ever felt anything before. He gave her the only answer he could. He gave her the truth.

"I could never hate you, lass."

Because the truth of it was, he was falling in love with her, every day a little more. From the moment she had arrived, she had captivated him just as she had captivated every man with him. The selflessness she'd shown in risking his anger to bring the rebel widow and her son into the castle was only one of the many reasons.

He loved her for the way she had so effortlessly conformed to their simple way of life at the castle, how she treated the men, every one of them with respect, breaching the barrier of English versus Scottish with just the soft curve of her smile.

He loved her belief, her utter belief in the legend of the Mackay stone, how she defended it, refusing to give it up even to him, how she hadn't scoffed or ridiculed what could only seem to others as ridiculous.

He loved her for the way her hair curled softly around the back of her ear, how she tucked it there when she was reading.

He loved her for the way her eyes sparkled when she laughed.

He loved her.

It was the first time Calum had ever loved a woman. And it was that more than any other reason that brought him to turning his head, and brushing her lips with his.

He'd only meant to kiss her, softly and quickly, as a way of thanking her for the compassion she'd shown to Kettie and her son. But somehow that kiss got lost as he drew her into his arms and felt the warmth of her body calling for him.

She had dressed for the night in a delicate lawn night-dress covered only by a woolen wrap. And he looked at her before him as he slowly pulled away the tartan folds.

She didn't move, just stayed there, staring at him with those blue eyes wide and wondering. He could see the rapid rise and fall of her chest beneath the stone that yet hung there, sparkling against her skin.

He took her hand, led her to the hearth, and urged her down to sit with him before the dancing light of the flames. She was nervous he could tell, perhaps a little frightened, but she lifted one hand and reached for him, touching the side of his face with her fingers, and coaxed him to kiss her again.

She opened her mouth to him, tasting him with her tongue in the way he had taught her as she lowered her-self back to lie against the rug, taking him with her. Calum lingered above her, framing her face with his hands and staring down at her in the firelight.

She only seemed to grow more beautiful with each day that passed. Would that still be the same ten years on? Twenty? He would give anything to know.

He kissed her nose, her forehead, and her chin, then he trailed his mouth down along her jaw to nuzzle at her neck. Slowly, gently, he loosened the ties of her night-dress, listening to the soft expectant hush of her breath as he finished the last one and slowly, and with care, parted the fabric.

Lying beneath him, Isabella closed her eyes and willed her thunderous heartbeat to calm. She could feel Calum's eyes drinking in her naked breasts and fought against the instinct of embarrassment at being thus bared before a man for the first time. She bit her lip, and prayed that he would touch her, prayed that he would run his hands against the very flesh that was aching, aching for his warmth.

He obliged her, smoothing his fingers against the curve of generous flesh, and Isabella sucked in her breath, arching her back and lifting her breasts upward so that he filled his hands with her.

She thought she had never felt something so wonderful, so torturously sweet as when he glanced his thumbs softly over her nipples, giving her vibrant, tingling shocks of sensation. Until Calum lowered his head, his breath hot against her skin, and covered her there with his mouth.

Isabella gasped, arched her back again, and dragged her fingernails through the threads of the rug. "Calum . . ."

He suckled her, drawing on her nipples with his tongue and his teeth and his lips, filling her with such jolts of pleasure that she wondered if she could stand him to continue.

Then she wondered if she could stand it if he stopped.

She knew a need to feel him, to feel his bare hot skin rubbing against hers, and so when he finally lifted his head, releasing her from his tender torment, she reached for him, grasping his shirt in her hands and pulling on it until she had slipped it over his head. He knelt before her, his skin aglow in the light of the fire, and Isabella devoured him with her eyes, the hard, muscled planes of his solid chest, the steely strength of his sinewy arms. She ran her hands over him, feeling the heat of him, the tightening of his flattened stomach. She had never seen a creature more beautiful, more perfectly formed and molded, more utterly and completely male.

Isabella rose up, standing on her knees, tilted her head to look up at him, saying nothing. Needing to say nothing to convey the depth of love she was feeling.

Calum cupped her chin with his hand, kissed her, and drew her against him until her breasts were pressed against his bare chest and their heartbeats pulsed in perfect rhythm.

She felt his hand slide down along the line of her back, cupping her bottom and pulling her tightly against him. She felt the hardness of him, the delightful pressure and friction of him. Her body responded with a heat that surged through her every limb, surged and met and pulsed deep within her womb, all while he continued to kiss her with long and deep strokes of his tongue.

His hand glanced her thigh, slipping beneath the hem of her nightdress that pooled at her knees. He slid up and underneath, scorching the soft and untouched flesh of her leg until he splayed his fingers at the angle of her hip and caressed her there softly, gently. When he released her mouth, and dragged his tongue down along the side of her jaw, suckling her neck, Isabella dug her fingers into the hard flexing muscle of his arm and clung to him as she dropped her head back on a soft outrush of breath, and a moan of complete and utter pleasure.

That moan turned quickly to a gasp when she felt his fingers delve downward, parting her, stroking the heated wetness that beckoned for his touch. She rocked backward and he held her with his arm, supporting her fully as her legs threatened to give beneath the unrelenting caress of his fingers. He explored and he stroked and she raked her nails across his shoulder, dropping her head forward and burying her face in his neck, breathing in the essence of him and fearing she would melt into a pool of liquid heat while unwilling to stop the movement of his hand against her even for a moment. She clung to him as if she were drowning, drowning on a turbulent sea of need. She felt his finger slide inside of her, felt the muscles of her body contract around him as a surge of wetness slickened her, swelling her around him. He used his fingers and his thumb, working her in exacting, intensifying strokes, tormenting her, fulfilling her, taking her higher and then higher still to the heavens until she felt the unexpected shock of her climax and cried out, muffling her cry in the hollow of his neck as sensations she had never imagined rocked her entirely, body and soul.

Wave after exquisite wave of pure sexual pleasure fused itself within her. She wanted him to stop. She wanted him to go on. She spasmed against him and then at the moment she nearly begged him to stop, he stilled and merely held her, held her tightly to him.

She hadn't even noticed that as the heat of her passion drifted slowly back to earth, so had she as Calum gently laid her back onto the rug beneath them, covering her mouth and kissing her with a hunger that matched her own.

She blinked up at him when he lifted his head to gaze down at her in the hearth light.

"Calum."

His eyes softened and he kissed her on her forehead. "Aye, lass?"

"I never knew . . . never could have imagined . . ."

He smiled. "I know, lass."

"But you did not—"

"Shh . . ." He leaned on his elbows above her, framing her face with his hands and smoothing the tiny tendrils of hair that curled about her ear. "It would be the furthermost desire in my heart to make love to you right now, right here, Isabella. I don't think I have ever wanted anything else more in my life. But I cannot."

She blinked. "Why?"

He looked at her, looked at her deeply, and said, "Because there is no honor in taking that which has been pledged to another."

Isabella felt her body go awash with an icy chill, banishing the delicious warmth that had settled over her but moments before. "What do you mean, Calum?"

"You are betrothed to someone else, Isabella."

She felt her throat tighten, constricting her next words. "How do you know that?"

He closed his eyes a long moment. When he looked at her again, his expression had gone from the tenderness of their loving to a guarded, shadowed mask. "I am ashamed to say that I read of it in your journal."

He had read her journal?

Isabella instinctively stiffened, felt the beginnings of tears in her eyes, and squeezed them shut in refusal. She took a deep breath, letting it out slowly. "How? Why?"

"The night of the feast, after I won your kiss from Fergus. I slipped away from the hall . . ."

"I wondered where you had gone."

"I came here, to the study. I was going to start looking

through Lord Belcourt's ledgers. Fergus and the others had brought the trunks they had taken off your ship here. They were waiting when I arrived."

"My trunks," she stated.

He nodded slowly. "Though it can never justify my invading your privacy as I did, I only sought to find out who you really were. I dinna know if you were Lord Belcourt's daughter. I dinna believe you were a mermaid. So when I found your journal, I decided to read it. To see if it would reveal who you really were."

Isabella closed her eyes, unable to look at him, unable to endure the knowing that her personal thoughts, her innermost private dreams, had been exposed without her knowing it.

"I canna tell you how very sorry I am, lass."

She swallowed, trying desperately not to cry. She knew if she did it would break him. She looked at him. She could see how very much this had troubled him. She could understand his reasons, and it was that which she focused on in an effort to dispel her own embarrassment.

And then she remembered what he had said to her, why he had not taken her, made her his. Why he had not made love to her.

You are betrothed to someone else, Isabella.

"You . . ." She didn't want to ask the question even as she knew that she must. "You read the letter? The letter from my parents? The one I had tucked inside the journal?"

He stared down at her blankly. Finally he nodded.

She bit her lip. "So you know? You know who I am to marry?"

"Yes, lass."

She swallowed hard, locked her gaze to his, and asked

on a whisper that was filled with impending dread, "Who?"

"His name is St. Clive."

Isabella's vision blurred. "Kentigern St. Clive?"

Surely she had heard him wrongly.

But when he solemnly nodded his head, she knew she had not.

"It cannot be." She shook her head. "You must be mistaken."

But how could he have been mistaken in *that* name?

Calum lifted himself off of her, moved to sit on the rug beside her. "Nae, lass, he is the one. He is the one who your parents have made arrangements for you to marry. I'm certain of it."

Isabella stared up at the ceiling for several moments, silent, still, as she tried to understand what she'd just been told. Then she turned, looked at the door, and got to her feet, rushing from the room, heedless of the fact that her nightdress was loose and open and free.

She hastened up the stairs to her chamber, crossed the room to the bed where the candle she had left burning earlier yet glowed. She took up her journal from where she had set it earlier that evening on the side table, opened it to the page where the letter yet lay, tucked away. She took up the letter, broke the seal with trembling hands, and read the words her mother had written.

When she got to the final line, she lowered to sit on the edge of the bed, and stared for several moments at the uncompromising stone wall before her.

Calum had been right.

It wasn't until she read the letter a second time that she realized exactly why he had stopped making love to her completely, why he had not made her his.

Knowing the fondness you held in your heart as a young girl for him, I know you will be thrilled to learn that we have made arrangements for your marriage to Kentigern St. Clive.

Calum believed she would want to marry Kentigern.

Dear God, he couldn't be more mistaken.

Taking up the letter, Isabella dashed from the room, racing down the stairs once again. She was nearly breathless when she reached the study door.

"Calum, it does not matter. I would never—"

But the room was empty.

He was suddenly gone.

Chapter Sixteen

Calum was in the stables later that morning, brushing down the Trakehner after having ridden him hard across the moors.

He looked up when Fergus came walking in. Their eyes locked.

"I want to talk to you," Fergus said.

"I already ken what you want to say." Calum turned, hanging up the tack to dry. "And I can tell you it's no' what you're thinking."

"Isn't it now? I saw you. With her. Last night." He lowered his voice. "In your study."

Calum whirled around. "You've taken to peepin' in on a man's private moments now, have you, Fergus? Like some sort of pathetic keeker?" He closed his eyes, took a breath, and reined in his emotions. Fergus was his brother and he was coming dangerously close to saying something he would later come to regret.

He looked at him. "I love her, Fergus."

"Love her? But you dinna e'en know who she is!"

"I know everything I need to. She's compassionate. She's intelligent. She's—"

"A Sassenach."

Calum scowled at him. "Aye, so she is. What of it?"

" 'Tis a foolish man, Calum Mackay, who beds down with his enemies."

"Is it tha' which really bothers you, Fergus? That she's a Sassenach? Or is it tha' she chose me instead of you that first night in the hall, eh?"

"Is tha' what you . . . ?" Fergus shook his head, obviously fighting to control his own troubled emotions. "What I think, Calum, is that she could be a spy."

"A spy?" Calum scoffed. *"Dia!* Where the de'il did you come up with that one? 'Ave you and Mungo been at the *uisge-beatha* early this morn?"

Calum turned, started out for the courtyard. He was finished with the conversation.

"Listen t' me!"

Fergus went after him, grabbed his arm. "She makes drawings, Calum . . . of people. Of us. She has drawings of you, M'Cuick, some of the other lads. She's drawn the castle, some of the places around here."

"Aye. She's an artist. Tha's what artists do."

"Aye, she's an artist who only need hand those pictures over to the government and we'll all end up gibbet bait."

Calum shook his head. "Isabella would never do that."

"Isabella?" Fergus stared at him. "So is tha' her name then? At least the name she told you?"

"Aye. And she told me aught else as well. You've no need to worry where her loyalties lie. I do and I trust her, Fergus."

"And you know this after wha'? Less than a fortnight of acquaintance with the lass?" Fergus frowned. "For your sake and the sake of every man who's with us, I certainly hope you're right."

He turned with a disgusted sweep of his arm.

"Wait."

Fergus stopped, looked at Calum.

Calum came to meet him, his voice growing quiet. "Hae you no thought for what you'll do once this is all over, once we've finished with this life on the seas?"

"Aye, I have. I'm for America."

"America?"

It was the first time Calum had ever heard Fergus speak of it.

"Aye. There is nae Scotland anymore, Calum. Not the Scotland we fought for. We lost on that bloody moor and we canna get it back."

"We lost a battle, Fergus. Not the rebellion."

"Look around you, Calum Mackay! There is no rebellion. The prince has nae made any attempt to return in o'er a year now. He's left us at the mercy of the government and now 'tis said the French are talking of peace with the Hanoverian. Already the clan estates of our brethren have been given over to the Sassenach nobles. It is only a matter of time afore they come to remove the rest of us, too."

"So you'll make that task all the easier by abandoning your homeland and going to the very place we have worked to keep your father and the others from? 'Tis a good thing Wallace and Bruce dinna surrender so easily as you, Fergus Bain, else we'd all be wearing breeks and eating kippers for breakfast."

Fergus frowned at him. "Aye, but I'll go on my own terms, Calum. Not as a prisoner, not as a servant indentured to another, but as a man free to choose."

Calum shook his head. "I'll ne'er turn my back on my heritage."

"And what do you think you're doing by bedding the Sassenach lass?"

"I intend to wed her."

"Wed her?" Fergus drew up, taking a deep breath and letting it go slowly. He stared at Calum for several moments. Finally, he shook his head.

"Answer me this, Calum. Do you wed her because you truly love her? Or do you wed her because you want that bluidy relic of a stone she's got hanging 'round her neck?"

Calum never got the chance to respond.

A moment later, he heard Isabella. She was calling his name, calling it loudly, over and over again.

Fergus and Calum both dashed for the castle door.

They found her in the study, sitting at the desk with Belcourt's books strewn in a sloppy half circle around her. Her hair was piled up loosely atop her head, as if she'd pinned it there simply to get it out of the way. When she looked up and saw them, her face lit up like the sun just breaking through the window behind her.

"I found him!"

"Who, lass?"

"I found your father, Fergus. Right here. 'Twas in the third book. Nearly the last page. 'Uilliam Bain of the Mackay regiment in Sutherland.' " She read further. "It says here he was taken at Culloden, and was held at an infirmary while his injuries healed. That is why you couldn't find him listed with the others taken on the battlefield, Calum. He was tried and found guilty of being a rebel. He was to be contained aboard the HMS *Signal* until such time as he is to be transported to the American Colonies."

"Does it say when he is to be transported, lass?" Calum asked.

"I'm looking . . ." She read through the columns. "It doesn't. But they are to anchor off Carlisle until such time as they do. When they do set off, it will be with stops in both the ports of Belfast and Londonderry, which means they will be traveling by way of the Irish Sea."

"Only a few days' sail from here." Calum turned to Fergus. "If we set a course along the Hebrides, we can intercept them."

"But what if he's sailed for America already?"

"I don't believe he has," Isabella answered. "The notes indicate that the ship that departed before this one was anchored for over four months waiting for their transport clearance and all the documentation to be completed. Your father's entry is dated just two months ago. And without this ledger, Lord Belcourt and the Privy Council will have to re-create most of the documentation. Even if by some chance he has sailed, his destination port is listed as Boston in the Massachusetts colony. You could look for him there. There certainly would be some record of his whereabouts."

"We'll just hope he hasn't gotten that far yet," Calum said. He looked at Fergus. Their differences of that morning were forgotten in the face of this long-awaited news. "We've a ship to prepare."

"Aye."

Calum slipped easily into his role as captain. "Send for Mungo, Hugh, Lachlann, our best lads. We'll meet at the bay and start kitting out the ship straightaway. If we hurry, we can be ready to sail in three days' time."

Fergus turned to see to his task. He stopped at the door, turned back. "Miss?"

Isabella looked up from the ledger.

"I wanted . . ." He faltered, glanced at Calum, then he said simply, "Thank you. Thank you for finding my father."

She smiled. "I'm happy I was able to help, Fergus."

He was gone a second later.

Isabella and Calum were suddenly alone.

And they both had something they wanted to say.

"Calum, about last night . . ."

He held up a hand to silence her, shaking his head. "Come here to me, lass."

Isabella circled the desk to join him. He took her hand, clasped his fingers with hers between them, and looked deeply into her eyes. She felt her heartbeat skip just looking at him.

"When you left me in the study earlier, I dinna know what to do. I dinna know what to think."

"But I just—"

"Shh." He touched two fingers to her lips. "I needed to sort things out, lass. For myself. So I saddled up the stallion and I rode, rode like the very devil was chasing after me. I rode until the thoughts in my head were clear and when I finally stopped, I was at the bay where you found the Spanish coin."

She smiled at the memory while he went on.

"I sat on that rock looking out o'er the water and I remembered how you'd looked that day." He brushed a loose tendril of hair from her eyes. "You were dancing about the water with the sun in your hair. You were my mermaid somehow magically come to life."

Calum reached inside his coat, removing something. It was a small scrap of paper. Isabella looked and saw that it was the same small scrap of paper she had baked into his birthday cake.

He held it out to her and she took it, reading the words upon it.

"Your wish," she whispered. "It was for your heart's desire."

"Aye. Did you know when I was a lad I would go to that same bay and sit on that rock for hours watching the water, wishing and praying my mermaid would come to me?"

She shook her head.

"Aye, I did. I would go because somehow, from the very moment I could, I knew that if I wished it hard enough, she would eventually come to me. So I wished . . . and I waited." He looked deeply into her eyes. "I am not waiting anymore, Isabella. Because my wish has come true. You are here."

Isabella felt her eyes begin to sting with tears. She bit her lower lip as he took up her hand, still clasped in his, and kissed it softly. "I know that the letter your mother wrote says you've a life elsewhere, waiting for you to return to it. I know that it says you had feelings for this man, this St. Clive."

"But that is—"

He placed his fingers to her lips once again. "I also know that if I never ask you what I'm about to ask you, I'll spend the rest of my life wondering. Wondering if perhaps, somehow, you might have said yes. So I'm asking you now . . ." He dropped to one knee. "I'm asking if you'll stay. Not only here, at this castle, lass." He opened the hand he held, splayed her fingers wide, and flattened it against the warmth of his chest. "I'm asking if you'll stay here, too. In my heart."

My heart's desire.

Tears fell freely down Isabella's face as she stared at

him, kneeling there before her, offering her more than she could have ever hoped for.

She didn't even need a moment to consider it.

With her hand still pressed against his pulse, she lifted her other hand, placed it on the side of his face, and whispered, "I'll stay."

They were the only two words she could manage to say.

They were the only two words she *needed* to say.

Calum rose to his feet. Isabella blinked, struggled simply to breathe. He cupped her face in his hands, tipped her mouth to his, and kissed her until her tears fell no more.

Then he drew her into his arms and held her.

"We've things to talk about, lass," he whispered against her ear. "There are things I must tell you."

She nodded into his chest.

"But not now," he said. "Tonight, when we can have the night to spend together. Will you come to me tonight?"

"Yes," she answered back.

And she knew when she did, he would make her his.

The hours of the day had never passed more slowly. Every hour, it seemed, Isabella was peering at the clock, glancing at the sky, wishing for the approach of night. In the morning, she took Druhan down to the shore and searched for winkles and partans in the tidal pools. She helped M'Cuick to roll out bannocks and took up the hem on two of her gowns for Kettie to wear. She took a nap, wrote a little in her journal. Still the minutes dragged. By afternoon, she was in the kitchen once again with M'Cuick and Kettie, "treading" the blankets in a washtub.

And she had never had so much fun in her life.

She had her skirts hitched up above her knees, and her legs and feet were bare, just like whenever Caroline went fishing for frogs in the duke's ornamental lily pond.

M'Cuick had filled the tub with warm soapy water and Isabella's task was to step about with the blankets underfoot, to "tread" the dirt from them. The trailing hem of her skirt was soaked and her petticoat clung to the back of her knees. Her hair was damp and sticking to the back of her neck. While she worked, Kettie softly sang a song in Gaelic. Although Isabella didn't understand a word of what she said, it had a gentle rhythm that harmonized perfectly in time with the work.

The improvement in Kettie's appearance in just the space of four-and-twenty hours was as near a miracle as one could hope for. Gone was the pallid cast of her skin. This morning her cheeks were even faintly sun-kissed from the short walk she had taken along the sea cliffs with M'Cuick, her hair pale blond, fluttering on the wind like a silken feather. Though still too weak to be on her feet for very long, she had refused to stay abed, and had insisted on sitting with them in the kitchen while they saw to the day's tasks.

And it wasn't just Kettie who had been transformed overnight either.

M'Cuick had been hovering about her like a mother hen from the moment they had brought her and Druhan to the castle. He had never looked so happy. It was as if, by Isabella giving him the gift of that sketch, M'Cuick had allowed himself to accept the fact that he'd survived the terrible ordeal that had taken the lives of his family. He'd no reason to feel guilty for having been spared. And the sketch had somehow provided him with a sense of acceptance, freeing him to move on with his life, to look to the future, even, Isabella hoped, dare to wonder that he might once again fall in love.

Love.

It was a word that immediately brought to mind an image of Calum. As she stood knee-deep in that wash-tub, Isabella wondered what her mother would be more upset about. The fact that her daughter was doing the laundry, or that she had fallen in love with a pirate. A noble pirate, yes, but a pirate all the same.

Her father would likely suffer an apoplexy. Another of his daughters, lost to a handsome Scotsman.

Elizabeth, however, would think it right grand.

Isabella looked up when she realized that Kettie had stopped singing and was looking at the doorway where someone had just come in. Isabella turned, and her heart jumped at just the sight of him.

"Calum?"

He looked so very different, she almost hadn't recognized him. He had shaved the scruffy beard from his chin, and had pulled his hair back neatly from his face, exposing the clean, stark lines of his jaw. The effect was stunning, making him look like a completely new man, unbelievably even more handsome than before.

Isabella stepped out of the tub and went to him on wet bare feet. She stopped right in front of him, hooked her arms around his neck, and planted him with a kiss that sent them both reeling back against the wall.

It wasn't until she pulled away a moment later that she noticed something not quite right in the way he was looking at her.

As if he had no idea who she was.

"Calum?"

"Lass, I—"

His words were cut off by the cocking of a pistol.

Bella jerked around.

"Calum!"

But how could he be standing there . . .

. . . when he was standing right in front of her as well?

She backed away, backed away from them both while her gaze shifted from one to the other—one, the Calum she had always known, the other, a near-perfect imitation.

"I . . . I do not understand."

And then suddenly, she did understand. She understood very clearly.

"You are twins."

"Aye, lass," said Calum, coming into the room. He wore his typical loose shirt and plaid with his sword and his flintlocks belted across his chest. His hair was tied, but loose, his face rough. He uncocked his pistol, tossed it on the table, pulled out a chair, and sat.

His brother did the same, taking the seat across from him.

"Take a seat, lass. And I'll explain it all."

And he did. He told of how his father's heir was to have been the next Mackay chief. But the night of their birth, in the confusion of their mother's fleeting life, the midwife had never taken note of who had been born first. Thus the two, and the need for the stone to decide the "real" Mackay.

Sitting between them at the end of the table, Isabella couldn't seem to stop staring. The differences between them were almost as astonishing as the similarities. They had the same nose, the same chin, the same dark and heavy brow. But where Calum let his hair fall unkempt about his forehead, his brother dressed it neatly, pulling it back from his face with an almost severe orderliness.

And their eyes. Calum's were a touch greener, and his face was darker, tanned from the sun.

Isabella didn't wait for any explanations.

"What is your name?" she said to Calum's brother.

"Alec," he answered. "Alec Mackay." He looked at her then and his face registered a genuine surprise. "That stone . . . is it?"

Isabella reached for the stone, covering it with her hand. As soon as she did, it started to glow once again with the pale red light it had the first time she'd seen Calum. In that moment, St. Germain's words echoed through her thoughts.

There are two of the Sons of Fire, very much alike, yet very different, too. It is your task to choose between them.

"Sons of Fire," she repeated.

She looked at Calum. "You knew?" She didn't even wait for him to answer. "You knew all along that there were two of you, even when I asked you, yet you didn't say a word. Why?"

Calum simply looked at her.

Isabella blinked. Was that why he had kept her there, kissed her, held her? Was it only for the stone?

"Calum!"

Fergus's urgent call summoned from above.

Calum ran for the stairs. Isabella, Alec, and the others followed.

When they reached the hall, Isabella found yet another surprise.

"Douglas?" she said upon seeing her sister's husband standing there with Fergus's pistol pointed ominously at his side. And then immediately she added, "F-father?"

"Isabella!" The duke started for her, until Fergus trained his pistol on him.

"Do not move, Sassenach."

The duke froze. "She's my daughter."

Isabella didn't wait for Fergus to respond. Instead she angrily pushed his pistol away. "How dare you point that at my father!" She turned into his arms. "Father, what are you doing here? Where is Mother and the girls? How in the world did you ever find me?"

"'Twas Douglas's doing." He looked at her, scanning her from head to toe. He touched her hair, mussed from the laundry work. "You are unharmed? Have they . . . ?"

"No, Father, I have been treated very well."

"That remains to be seen."

Isabella turned just as Kentigern St. Clive came forward. "If anyone has so much as touched a hair upon your head, Isabella, I will have them arrested and hanged for the brigands they are."

"Oh, really?" Fergus said, immediately rising to the challenge. "You and what army, Sassenach?"

"King George's army, Highlander. In case you haven't yet heard, he and his son the Duke of Cumberland know exactly how to deal with rebels like you."

The mention of "The Butcher's" name was all the prompting Calum's men needed. A dozen or more pistols cocked in unison.

"Temper your tongue, St. Clive," the duke warned.

"Pah!" he scoffed. "I am a peer of the realm. If they dared to kill me they would—"

A shot fired, burying itself in the gravel not six inches from the toe of his silver-buckled shoe.

Kentigern danced back on a shriek.

M'Cuick came forward. "Who's the pouf?"

"Pouf?" Kentigern drew himself up. "I'll have you

know you are addressing Kentigern St. Clive, the future Earl of Chilton."

M'Cuick shrugged. "Never heard of him."

Isabella saw Douglas suppress a smile.

"You filthy . . ."

With one swift sweep of his arm, Calum had his dirk out of his stocking and was pressing it dangerously close to Kentigern's nervously bobbing Adam's apple.

He lifted a brow in challenge. "Care to finish that thought, Sassenach?"

There was a look in Calum's eye, a dark, frightening look, that had Isabella taking a step forward. "Calum, please . . ."

Kentigern's wide-eyed stare swung suddenly her way. "Calum? You speak rather too familiarly with the man who had you forcefully abducted and carried off to this barbaric backwo—"

His last word was squelched when Calum lifted the flat of his blade an inch higher, pressing it into the soft flesh of St. Clive's lily-white throat. "Now unless you want me to cut out your tongue and choke you with it, I would suggest you heed his grace's warning and learn to temper it. Aye, Sassenach?"

Kentigern didn't say a word, just stared at Calum in stony silence.

"Good. Now I'll suggest we move this discussion to the hall." Calum looked at Isabella's father. "Your grace? Might I burden you with the task of keeping this one from any further unnecessary insults?"

The duke gave a nod. "Come with me, St. Clive. And endeavor, if you can, to keep your mouth shut."

Chapter Seventeen

It was a stony silent gathering that convened in the great hall at Castle Wrath.

On one side of the long trestle table sat Alec Mackay, the duke, and Douglas with a seething St. Clive sulking at the end. On the other, Calum, Fergus, Mungo, and M'Cuick.

Hugh and Lachlann stood ready at the door, just in case they were needed.

And Hamish had come in bringing the bottles of claret and brandy Calum had asked him to fetch.

The rest of Calum's small army of men had taken up posts along each wall, leaving Isabella with only one place to go.

She lowered into the chair at the head of the table.

Calum was on her right, Alec her left.

Neither seemed to know where to begin.

"Father," Isabella said when she was unable to stand the silence any longer. "How is Aunt Idonia?"

"Hm? Oh, she's well enough, I imagine. Went to

Drayton Hall with your mother and sisters after Edinburgh, just in case you should have turned up there."

"Your grace," Calum said then, looking at her father. "I wish to offer my apologies for the worry and concern your daughter's coming here must have caused you and your family. Though I wasna party to what took place on board the *Hester Mary*, my men were. I take full responsibility."

The duke frowned at him in precisely the same way he used to frown at Elizabeth whenever she'd done something particularly unruly. "It would help settle things in my mind, Mr. Mackay, if I had any idea *why* my daughter was taken."

"I can answer that," Isabella said. "It was because of this, Father."

She reached for the stone.

The duke lifted a brow. "That's rather a large bauble you bought for yourself in Paris, Bella."

"I did not buy it, Father. It was given to me, when I went to Versailles. It belongs to the Mackay clan."

"And when my men saw her wearing it on the deck of the *Hester Mary*, they recognized it."

Calum went on to explain about the legend of the stone, and how it had gone missing when his father had died thirty years before.

"That is all well and good, Mackay, but it still doesna explain why your men waylaid the *Hester Mary* in the first place," Douglas finally pointed out.

"MacKinnon," Calum said, looking at him, "you were at Culloden?"

Douglas frowned. "Nae, I was not."

"But your wife . . ."

"I was in London when the battle took place, Mackay,

fighting to win back the title and land my father had forfeited in the first rebellion. My brother, Iain, however, did march with the prince, along with other of my kinsmen."

Calum looked at him. "Did they all come home?"

"Of course they dinna. Some died. Others were—"

"Transported?"

"Aye."

Fergus nodded. "Aye, so was I."

"And I," added Mungo.

"Me, as well," echoed M'Cuick.

The echo continued, rippling around the room like a storm wind as each and every man of Calum's crew sounded off.

Douglas looked at Calum and nodded in understanding. "Lord Belcourt's missing 'bibles.'" And then he said, "You've got to know you can't save them all."

"I dinna intend to. Just one more."

Kentigern, whose patience had been stretched about as thin as it would, finally stood. "Enough of your attempts at justifying your unlawful actions. You abducted an innocent woman and I demand satisfaction as her affianced groom."

Isabella lifted her chin and looked at him down the length of the table. "I haven't yet accepted any proposal of marriage from you, Kentigern."

"Are you saying you would be foolish enough to refuse it, Isabella?"

As he stood there, staring at her down the length of that table, Isabella suddenly was taken by an image of him, of how he'd looked that day at the fair, standing on the hillside with his grass-stained breeches and bits of clover sticking out of his hair.

Poor Bella Drayton . . .
You're just a child . . .
A silly, foolish child . . .

Isabella stared at him, and wondered how she could have ever thought him a gentleman. "I do not accept you, Kentigern. There will be no marriage."

St. Clive's eyes went wide. "*You* do not accept *me*? You would throw away a marriage to the son of an earl? What are you saying, Bella? That you'd rather be some lawless pirate's—" He stopped, sucked in a breath slowly, then nodded. "That is it, isn't it? You've already slept with the filthy Scottish pirate. You gave your innocence to a fiend and a murderer and a traitor."

Calum stood, made to pull out his sword. "You bluidy bastard. She doesna—"

"You are right, Calum," Isabella said. She set her hand gently on his sword arm in an effort to calm him. "I do not have to tell Kentigern anything. I could simply marry him and never mention these past weeks again, leaving him to wonder for the rest of his life whether or not his accusation is true." She looked at St. Clive. "Are you willing to live that sort of life, Kentigern? Wondering, always wondering, whenever you might visit my bedchamber whether I preferred you, or whether I spent my nights longing for the arms of the *filthy Scottish pirate*? Is the dowry my father promised you worth more to you than your own pride?"

Every man in the room was staring at her, staring with a look in their eye she had only ever seen trained upon her sister.

It was the look of unquestioned respect.

Except for Kentigern, who was looking quite ill.

"You whore!"

Isabella didn't flinch, not even the slightest, at his insult.

Calum, however, was another matter.

He broke from Isabella's grasp, stalking the three steps it took to circle the table. He pulled out his sword with a *whish* and trained the point straight at the man's waistcoat. Isabella wondered if Kentigern's heart was racing wildly beneath the polished steel.

"Apologize to her." And when Kentigern didn't immediately respond, Calum repeated loudly, "Apologize!"

Kentigern then showed more guts, or more patent stupidity, than anyone had ever given him credit for.

"No," he said, turning a face that was twisted in a sneer. "Go ahead and kill me. Kill me right in front of her. Show her the sort of bloodthirsty savage she has given herself to."

Calum stared at him hard, his face set as rigid as a stone, visibly warring with himself.

"Calum, please," Isabella said. "He isn't worth it."

No one moved. Finally Calum glanced to the side of the room, summoning two of his men with a short toss of his head. "Take him. Lock him in the stables." He stared at St. Clive. "Better yet, put him in with the swine so he'll no' feel out of place."

"You'll regret this, Highlander," Kentigern said. He turned to look at Bella. "As will you, Bella Drayton. No one of any respectability will ever wed you now."

Isabella walked around the table until she was standing but a foot in front of him. "If you are to be considered an example of respectability, then I'm glad for it."

The two men who Calum had charged with taking him shoved him toward the door. "Get movin', Sassenach . . ."

Isabella stood and watched as they went.

When he'd gone, the room fell silent. No one seemed quite certain what to say or do next.

It was the duke, however, who broke the silence, sighing audibly from his end of the table. "I don't know what your mother could have been thinking when she talked me into the notion that he would be a fitting husband for you." He shook his head. "Addles my brain, that woman does. Thank God I had sense enough left to require your agreement to it." He looked at his daughter. "I am sorry, Bella."

She smiled. "You never could have known, Father. And I don't regret it. Had you not arranged the marriage, I never would have had the satisfaction of turning him down."

The duke grinned, his eyes shining proudly. "That's my girl." Then he turned to Calum. "As for you, sir . . ."

"Father—"

"Bella, the man was responsible, albeit indirectly, for abducting you. Once St. Clive gets back to London and starts the telling of his side of the affair, there will be a scandal. Scandal I can endure. Lord knows we've endured enough of them with your sister. Dishonor, however, I cannot. I mean to ask Mr. Mackay what he intends to do about that."

"That is simple, your grace," Calum said easily. "I intend to marry your daughter."

"I expected no less." He turned to his son-in-law. "Douglas, is it not the law in Scotland that a marriage merely requires the mutual consent of both parties before witnesses?"

"Aye, your grace."

The duke grinned. "Oh, yes, that's how Elizabeth got

herself wed to you, isn't it?" And then he laughed out loud at his own jest.

Douglas merely shook his head.

"Bella, dear," the duke said, looking at his daughter. "Is it your wish to marry this man?"

Bella smiled. "Yes, Father, it is."

"And you, Calum Mackay, are you willing to be my daughter's husband?"

Calum looked at Isabella. "I'm quite certain there isna a man present who wouldna be willing to wed her."

Calum's men responded with a resounding "Aye!"

The very loudest cheer came from Hamish.

"Aye, but I'm not asking them, Mackay, am I? I'm asking you."

Calum turned, looked at Isabella, who was waiting, along with her father, for his answer. He said, "Your grace, it would be my great honor to take Isabella as my wife."

"Well, then," said the duke, "I guess all that remains is for you to kiss her and be done with it."

Isabella looked at her father. "Now, Father?"

"Yes, Bella, now. Before the man changes his mind."

"Impossible," Calum said, grinning as Bella turned to him.

He lowered his head, and covered her lips with his in a kiss.

The resulting cheer had the windows rattling in their panes.

"Your mother will expect the thing done again, you know," the duke said when the kiss had ended. "She'll never countenance having not been present when *two* of her daughters were wed. Poor Catherine, I fear, will be locked away in her room until the nuptial morning."

Isabella grinned. "Unless Caroline devises a way to get her out."

The duke nodded. "Oh, and that she would. You know the little imp actually did race that pig of hers at the fair?"

"She didn't!"

"Aye, she did. Hitched him to a pony wagon, ribbons and all. Said I'd only forbidden her from entering the sidesaddle races. I apparently had neglected to include the buggy races in my instruction as well."

Isabella smothered a giggle.

"Daughters . . ." the duke muttered, shaking his head. Then he turned to look at Douglas. "Bear that in mind, MacKinnon, when my Elizabeth brings that child of yours she's carrying into the world. If she's a daughter you'd do best to prepare for a head full of graying hairs"—he turned to Isabella and smiled—"and a lifetime of the greatest joy you've ever known."

Isabella blinked, walked up to him, and kissed him on the cheek. "Thank you, Father."

He tipped a finger under her chin. "Just be happy, my girl," he said softly. "You deserve nothing less."

She glanced at Calum. "I am happy, Father."

"I know." The duke turned back to the table. "Well then, what's all this about Lord Belcourt's missing ledgers?"

Calum and the others spent the next hour telling the duke, Douglas, and Alec about the plans to rescue Uilliam Bain.

"This Uilliam Bain must be a special man," said the duke when they'd finished.

"He's as fine a father as a lad could ever ask for,"

answered Fergus, lifting his whisky glass in a gesture of salute to his father.

Douglas looked at Calum. "When do you leave?"

"On the morrow's evening tide. I expect it will take us two, perhaps three days' sailing to Carlisle. Depending on whether we are pursued, another three to return."

"Well, Douglas," said the duke. "I'm thinking there's only one thing to be done."

"Aye, sir," Douglas agreed.

"What is that, your grace?" Calum asked.

"Well, I certainly cannot let my daughter become a widow so quickly after getting wed. So Douglas and I are going with you."

"Father, no!"

The duke turned to her. "Hush, Bella."

"Your grace, Isabella's right. You canna—"

"Do not even think to refuse us, Mackay. As of about five minutes ago, we are now family. And *my* family looks after its own."

Calum looked at Douglas.

"Don't even try to fight him," Douglas said. "'Tis a losing a battle."

Calum blinked, at a loss for a response. He simply said, "Thank you."

"It is done." The duke nodded. "Now, I've a mind to partake of a bottle of your excellent Scottish whisky. And you—I would suggest you not waste any more of your wedding night, son. A man only has one wedding night. 'Tis a good idea to make the most of it."

"Father!" Isabella was mortified.

The duke grinned. "I know what I speak of, Bella girl. A man doesn't get himself five daughters by sleeping alone, you know."

"Yes, but . . ." She colored red to the tip of her nose, but only for a moment before Calum was sweeping her up and into his arms, and carrying her from the room with the calls and cheers of his men resounding behind them.

He carried her up every flight of stairs, stopping once, twice along the way to kiss her long and slow. Isabella couldn't believe that she was suddenly a wife, and to the man who had stolen her heart.

It was a true dream come true.

Calum kicked the door to his bedchamber open, carried her inside, and then locked the door behind them.

Nothing was going to disturb them this night.

He turned to face her. "Hello, my wife."

Bella looked at him. "Are we really wed? Everything happened so quickly. I feel like I should need to catch my breath."

He took her in his arms. "Are you regretting it?"

"No. Never."

He looked at her deeply, his expression suddenly turning serious. "I swear to you, on my honor, I will do everything within my power to assure that you never will regret becoming my wife."

Calum lowered his head and kissed her until Isabella was giddy and breathless.

He breathed into her hair. "I find myself anxious to see you. All of you."

Isabella felt herself begin to blush, but smiled shyly and closed her eyes as Calum nuzzled her neck. "That may take you some time," she whispered. "There are, after all, quite a lot of layers to contend with."

Calum lifted his head, his eyes sparking with a devilish light. "Is that a challenge, my lady?"

Isabella knew a delightful shiver when he looked at her. She smiled coyly. "Nay, my lord. It is an invitation."

The heat in his eyes took flame. He stared at her, unspeaking.

"Does my new husband not know where to begin? You could start with my stockings, I suppose . . ." She lifted a foot.

"Och, nae, my lady," he said, shaking his head slowly. "The stockings will be the verra last thing to go. You see I've this secret fancy to see you wearing your stockings . . . and naething else."

"Oh . . ." Isabella felt a tingle. "Oh."

"Now then," he said, stepping back, circling her slowly, his eyes taking in every inch of her. He stopped behind her. "I think that I will begin with this bit of muslin you have tucked around your lovely neck."

Isabella gasped when she suddenly felt the heat of his mouth descend upon the curve of her neck. She felt gooseflesh rise along her nape and closed her eyes, giving herself over to the most delicious of sensations. Calum's hand slipped slowly over her shoulder, tugging gently on the wispy kerchief, pulling it from where it was tucked inside the bodice of her gown. The soft muslin caressed her skin as it slid tantalizingly slowly over her breasts and neck, all while Calum continued to nuzzle her at her neck, shoulders, and behind her ear.

Isabella took a deep breath when he pulled away, and with it, took the kerchief.

"Now about that gown . . ."

He came around to the front of her, crossed one arm over the front of him to support his elbow while the other hand supported his chin. "I've ne'er seen a gown with that . . . what is it called?"

"A stomacher," she whispered, wondering if she could possibly melt from the heat in his eyes.

"Ah, yes. It appears somehow to be held in place by this row of pretty bows . . ."

He reached out and pulled on the first bow. It loosened, fell open. "Yes, that did seem to do the trick." He proceeded to untie the other four, plucking them one at a time, very slowly.

When he was finished, the robe of her gown fell open. Calum came to her, standing before her very closely, and slid his hands underneath the silk robe, pushing it back, off and over her shoulders, until it dropped on the floor behind her.

Isabella looked up at him, and waited.

She wore a quilted underskirt over a hooped petticoat that tied in the back at her waist. Still standing before her, Calum lowered his head to kiss her, kissing her neck and shoulder, while sliding his hands down over her back to the ties at her waist. He gave each tie a tug, and together the skirts collapsed to the floor.

Calum took her hand, helped her to step out of the pool of silk and tapes and whalebone. Isabella stood now wearing her stays and her chemise, which fell to midcalf. Calum came before her, his lips curved in a knowing and seductive smile, until he took a glance at the stays, and the intricate knot Isabella had employed to tie them.

His grin vanished. "What sort of Gordian puzzle is this?"

Isabella giggled. "We ladies cannot make it too easy on you." She arched a brow. "I should like to see how you manage this. The maid who taught me to tie it claims it cannot be breached."

"Oh, really?" Calum grinned again, took his *sgian*

dhub from his stocking, and very quickly and efficiently cut through the tie.

"Oh!" Isabella sucked in a breath. "I shall have to inform her that she was quite mistaken."

Calum unwrapped the stays.

All that remained was the chemise, the stone around her neck . . . and those stockings.

Calum took Isabella's hand, first one and then the other, and lifted them above her head. Then he knelt down before her, his gaze capturing hers, and slipped his hands beneath the hem of the chemise. Isabella held her breath, waiting as he ran his hands slowly, gently upward, caressing the backs of her knees, splaying his fingers over her thighs, her bottom, up along her back until he whisked the chemise over her head.

His eyes continued to hold hers as he reached up and slowly pulled the pins from her hair.

Her hair fell in a tumble down her back.

Calum stood back and feasted on her—wearing her stockings, the stone of his clan, and nothing else—with his eyes.

"You are the most beautiful vision I have ever seen."

Isabella felt herself blush, and had to fight against the urge to cover herself. She had never been naked before anyone in her life, except her maid. But the glow of pure appreciation she saw in Calum's eyes quickly allayed her embarrassment, made her feel as if she were indeed as beautiful as he claimed.

It was a heady, powerful feeling.

"There is, however, one thing wrong."

"What is that, my lord?"

"The garters on those stockings." He shook his head.

"They really need to be red. We shall have to remedy that."

Calum came to her, his expression no longer playful. He stared down into her eyes as if he was memorizing every detail of her face, tipped her chin, and lowered his mouth to hers, kissing her long and slow as he urged her body closely against his. Isabella felt the heat and hardness of his chest against her breasts beneath the thin fabric of his shirt, felt the undeniable rigidity of his erection pressing against her belly. She felt a heat between her thighs and sought to ease it, running her hands up over his back and pulling him all the way closer.

When Calum broke the kiss, trailing his mouth along her neck and over her shoulders, she dropped back her head and lost herself to the sensations of his lips and his tongue. He kissed her on her breasts, suckling her, and she moaned softly, raking her fingers into his hair as his mouth worked her sensitive flesh, drawing on her nipple, teasing it, making her blood surge through every vein.

He continued lower, kissing over her belly, her hip, until he was kneeling before her. Isabella closed her eyes, braced herself with her hands against his shoulders as he very slowly lifted one foot off the floor and into his hands.

"Hold tight to me, my lady . . ." he whispered, and Isabella gasped, jerking when she felt his mouth kiss her at the very top of her thigh, and keep on kissing, moving slowly closer to the very center of her.

And when his tongue touched her there, she thought surely she would die. The sensations were so new and unfamiliar, so intense, she felt her knee begin to buckle.

"Calum . . ."

"Hold tight to me . . ."

And Isabella gripped her fingers into his shoulders as his tongue entered her, tasting her, flicking delightfully across the swollen bud of her, again and again and again.

He consumed her while at the same time he pulled the garter tie that held her stocking, sliding the silk down and off of her leg.

When he pulled his mouth away, moving to her other leg, Isabella heard herself moan in protest.

He didn't deny her for long.

Calum lifted her other foot and placed it on his thigh, then he continued his sweet assault on her as he removed her other stocking. And when it was gone, that silk stocking, he opened her fully with his finger and did not stop until he had overwhelmed her, and her body was rocking with her climax.

Isabella swayed against him, strengthless, spent, clutching his shoulders as if they were a boulder on a stormy, turbulent sea. Her eyes fluttered open as he stood.

Sweeping her into his arms, Calum carried Isabella across the room and lay her gently upon the bed.

She watched, basking in the afterglow of her climax, as he hauled his shirt over his head, unbuckled the belt that held his plaid, never taking his eyes from her.

In moments he was naked. And he was glorious.

His body glowed in the light of the fire, defined and sinewy. His dark hair hung about his neck, free from its tie as it fell over his eyes. She lifted one arm, beckoning, and he slid onto the bed, moving over her. He pulled her into his arms as he covered her mouth and kissed her. Their tongues met and tangled and danced as his hand slid slowly down along her side, cupping her hip, lifting her leg. Gently he settled himself between her knees.

She felt the hardness of him pressing against the slickness of her, and knew there would be pain, but it was a pain she longed for, for the need to feel him inside of her was consuming her.

He looked at her. "I love you, my Bella." And she smiled and closed her eyes, kissing him, taking in a breath, waiting . . .

She felt the sudden sharpness of his thrust as it breached her maidenhead and squeezed her eyes against the shock of pain.

Calum lay for several moments, sheathed within her, allowing her body to accept him. She was so warm, so tight around him, he wondered if he'd expend himself that moment. Slowly he withdrew, the slick heat of her sending a rush of sensation through his body like fire. Gently he pressed back, filling her completely, moving in long and smooth strokes as the sensations within him began to build.

He gathered her into his arms and started to rock against her, thrusting now, again and again, moving faster, harder. His breathing grew labored as he concentrated his every muscle upon the joining of their bodies and the pleasure that awaited them. He would take them there. With each thrust he felt Isabella sway against him, taking the fullness of him, the power of him, the strength of him, deep, deep within herself.

She cried out when the raw potency of this, her second climax rocked through her, and he felt her body contracting around him. He felt the rush of his own impending release, felt his body stiffen above her. He called out her name as he took his final thrust, burying himself within her. As he emptied his seed on a ragged, strenuous gasp, Isabella wrapped her legs and her arms around him, holding him tightly to her as he fought to catch his breath against the softness of her neck.

It was the most glorious feeling either of them had ever known.

Later that night, much later, the fire had burned down to a listless glow and the castle was filled with a peaceful and wondrous quiet. Calum was sleeping against her, with his head nestled gently against her breast and his hand splayed possessively against her hip. As she lay there, marveling at the night, Isabella thought to herself that Elizabeth had been so very right.

Making love with Calum, lying with him in his bed, feeling his breath softly brush against her neck, was the most beautiful feeling she had ever known.

She was his wife.

She was his lover.

And someday, perhaps nine months from that night, she would be the mother of his child.

Heaven did exist on earth after all.

Chapter Eighteen

The morning dawned to a soft rain that trickled down the windowpanes and puddled on the flagstones that lined the castle courtyard. All throughout the castle Calum's men were scrambling hither and yon, loading the supplies and preparing the arms they would need to sail the *Adventurer* on that evening's tide.

In the hall, Isabella watched the flurried activity from the vantage of the window seat. She'd been sitting for hours, trying to dispel the dreadful sense of foreboding that had greeted her upon awakening that morning to find Calum gone from their marriage bed, already preparing to leave. She'd lain for some time, holding his pillow, breathing in the scent of him, remembering the touch of his hands against her skin the night before. It would be all she would have to sustain her after he left.

Though she knew she could never expect him not to go after his foster father, the fear of what could happen to him, to them all, hung on her shoulders like a leaden cape. And now her father and Douglas were involved.

Isabella thought of Elizabeth carrying Douglas's child.
Her sister would never forgive her if something happened to Douglas. Isabella would never forgive herself.
But she knew she could no more stop the three grown
men from doing what they intended to do than she could
stop herself from loving Calum. So she simply closed
her eyes, leaned her head gently against the castle's cold
stone wall, and said a silent prayer that they would all be
delivered safely back to her.

A sudden cheerful whistling had her turning toward
the open doorway where a moment later, the figure of
her father appeared.

"Well, my girl, what do you think?"

Isabella felt her mouth fall open. She didn't even
bother to shut it.

It would, after all, only fall open again.

"Father?"

The duke came into the room, only he looked about as
far removed from dukedom as he possibly could. Instead
of his usual tailored and brocaded waistcoat, he wore the
Mackay plaid and a loose saffron shirt with ties that
opened at the neck, and full sleeves that billowed about
his burly arms. A brace of pistols were belted at criss-
crosses over his barrellike chest, and his snowy white
hair, always impeccably dressed, was loose and hanging
wildly about his neck and shoulders. The most startling
feature, however, wasn't his dress, or the sight of his
lanky ashen legs sticking out from beneath the hem of
the kilt. It was the fact that to help disguise himself, he
had painted his face a rather fearsome shade of blue,
complete with the white saltire cross X'd across its
middle.

"For St. Andrew," he said, grinning beneath the paint.

"Scotland's patron saint. 'Twas Douglas's idea. I rather like the significance."

"Well, you needn't worry anyone will recognize you. No one in their right mind would ever believe you're the Duke of Sudeleigh now."

He glanced at himself in a looking glass, grinning. "I know. It's brilliant, isn't it?"

Isabella shook her head. "No, Father, it isn't brilliant. Not at all. It's dangerous and it's reckless and you should not be doing this."

"Nonsense, Bella. I'm a man grown and this is a worthy cause." He turned to look at her. "Do you think you should be the only one allowed to have an adventure?"

"But what if you get shot?"

"Tosh, dear . . . Calum says these things rarely result in any exchange of fire."

She let go a heavy sigh. "Well, that is certainly a comfort."

"Really, Bella, there's naught to worry over. We'll just cruise down the coast, sweep in unexpected, and be off. It'll be a snap."

He snapped his blue-tinged fingers for effect.

Isabella frowned at him, crossing her arms before her. Perhaps if she tried a different tactic, the one that always terrified the duke the most. "Is that what Mother will say when she learns of this?"

The duke's blue face froze, but only for a moment before he quickly recovered himself. "I'll contend with your mother after we've returned. There's a man's life at stake here, Bella, dear."

Bella couldn't disagree, just as she couldn't dispute the yearning for adventure that seemed to run in her family's blood.

It wasn't as if she couldn't understand it. Her father had devoted his life to his duty as the Duke of Sudeleigh. He had married the woman he'd been told to wed, had raised five healthy daughters, and had spent the better part of his life ensuring a quiet, staid, *safe* existence for them all. He'd not fallen into the turbulent trap of politics so many of his contemporaries had, and truth be told, Isabella didn't honestly know where his loyalties lay— Hanoverian or Jacobite. It just wasn't a thing talked about in the Drayton breakfast parlor. One thing that was certain, however, was that beneath that cerulean disguise, his eyes were alight with a fire she'd never seen before.

It was the fire of adventure.

At least they finally knew where Elizabeth got it from.

"Have you decided yet what you're going to do about that stone?" the duke asked, changing the topic quite effortlessly.

In truth, Isabella had been thinking about it throughout most of that morning. Now that she knew of Alec's existence, it became a matter of which of the two brothers the stone should go to. "I wish I knew. When the Comte de St. Germain—"

"Who?"

"St. Germain. He is an associate of Louis XV's. 'Twas he who gave me the stone to bring back to Scotland in the first place."

The duke took a seat beside her. "Bella, there is no Comte de St. Germain."

"Yes, there is, Father. I met him. At Versailles. In fact, 'twas the king and Madame de Pompadour who introduced us."

The duke considered this. "Interesting . . ."

"What is it, Father?"

"What else do you know of this St. Germain?"

"I know that he is rumored to have lived for many ages, centuries even, without ever growing older. They claim he possesses some sort of strange elixir that will maintain a youthful appearance, and that he can turn ordinary rocks into precious stones. He is an artist—"

"—and he can speak many languages, has traveled the world . . ." the duke went on.

"Yes . . . yes, that's him. So you do know him?"

"No, Bella, I don't know him. Nobody does. Because the man is a phantom. He's an aberration, a fictional identity created by the king to protect certain individuals who perform, eh, *delicate* services in his interests . . ."

"You mean a spy?"

"I didn't say that." The duke looked at her. "But you'll notice I didn't deny it, either."

Isabella took a moment to consider what she'd just learned. Suddenly it made perfect sense. "So that is why they claim he never ages? Why he speaks so many languages and has traveled the world over? Because he is not one man, but a succession of many?"

The duke merely looked at her. He didn't need to answer.

"That does explain a lot," Isabella said, more to herself than to him. "But it also just adds to the mystery of who he really is and why he gave me the stone. And it doesn't make the decision about what to do with the stone any easier. This man, whoever this St. Germain really was, told me that when the time was right, I would *know* what to do, that the stone would tell me. But the stone doesn't seem to be doing much of anything anymore. It hasn't glowed or so much as showed a spark."

The duke patted her hand. "Then you must just keep it

until somehow, in some way, you do know what to do with it. There is something mystical about the stone, there is no doubt. I spoke with Alec quite a bit during our journey here, he told me much about the history of this clan you've just married into. 'Tis a clan that has been divided since the Jacobite rebellions began. Their uncle, the Mackay chief, has no living heir, and since their father has died, the next in line for the chiefship is—

"Either Calum or Alec." Isabella took a deep breath. "It's a horrible position in which to be. I love Calum. And now I am his wife. Naturally I should choose him . . ."

"Yet something cannot allow you to disregard Alec's right to the stone as well?"

Isabella nodded slowly.

"Give it time, girl. You might even pay a visit to the Mackay chief. Perhaps he can help you find the answers you seek."

Isabella sighed. "Perhaps."

"Perhaps, what?"

Isabella turned just as Calum strode into the room. Her heartbeat quickened just to see him.

Like her father, he wore the Mackay plaid with a pistol brace. His hair was untied, loose but slicked back from his bearded face, and he wore a coat of deep, unfathomable black. His sword was strapped to his waist, and he wore a bonnet the exact same shade of blue as her father's face. On it was the distinctive white cockade of the Jacobites.

"Your grace," he said, and handed her father a sword. "You've experience with a blade?"

"What? Oh, yes, certainly. Of course." The duke took the sword with the delight of a mischievous boy, his eyes lighting up as he stared at the polished blade.

Isabella cringed. Her father had never hefted a blade any more menacing than a butter knife.

Her worry must have shown clearly on her face because Calum came before her and touched two fingers beneath her chin, lifting her eyes to his.

"How is my wife this morning?"

"I am already lonely, and you've not yet left. 'Tis an unhappy bride who wakes alone on her wedding morning."

He lowered his voice to a murmur. "When I return, I'll make it up to you. But until then, perhaps this will help ease your loneliness . . ."

He bent his head slowly to kiss her—

Until the quiet was shattered by the sudden clanging of steel against stone.

Calum and Isabella turned as one to see the duke shaking his head as he bent to retrieve his sword from where he'd dropped it on the floor. He looked at them and shrugged. "Whoops . . ."

Isabella looked at Calum. *"Whoops?"* She closed her eyes in utter dread. "Good God, 'tis a nightmare."

"Dinna worry, lass. I'll watch after him."

"I know that you will." She blinked. "But who will watch after you?"

He gathered her into his arms and kissed her, kissed her deeply. It was the only answer he could offer her.

Within another hour, they were readying to leave.

They were all assembled. Fergus, Lachlann, Mungo, and Hugh stood with Calum, the duke and Douglas in the hall, going over the last-minute details. The rest of the forty-man crew were standing by awaiting instruction. M'Cuick had been in the kitchen since dawn packing up the food stores and skins of fresh water they

would need. There was but one face missing amongst
the crowd.

But when Alec came into the hall, he looked neither
ready nor planning to go.

He went to Calum. "We've a complication. St. Clive
has gotten away."

"What?"

"It must have been in all the chaos of everyone running about this morning. He slipped away when no one
was watching. And he's managed to steal the stallion,
which means there's a good chance he's headed straight
for the authorities."

"Well, he'll have a difficult time of it explaining how
he came to be riding Cumberland's lost horse."

Alec's worry, however, showed on his face. "There is
a Hanoverian detachment eight miles away at Durness,
Calum. If St. Clive can manage to find his way there,
they could be here within a day's time. And if you're
gone, it will all but prove any accusations of piracy St.
Clive may make against you." Alec went on. "But I'm
thinking 'twill be difficult to charge a man with high-
seas piracy if they find him here at home, snuggled in
with his new wife."

Calum shook his head "I must go—"

Alec cut him off. "It occurs to me they've no way of
knowing which Mackay I actually am."

It was a brilliant plan.

Calum looked at him. "You would do that?"

"What was it his grace said last night? 'Family looks
after family . . .'" Alec looked at Calum. "Just come
home safe. I've no wish to try to replace you in your
wife's heart."

"Laird!"

Hamish came suddenly running into the room. "Come quick! There's a ship coming in just off Kervaig."

Calum turned to Alec. "St. Clive?"

"Nae, it cudna be. Not so soon. Even riding he would take at least a day."

Alec was right.

The ship that had appeared was a Welsh trawler. And that trawler had netted a rather exceptional catch.

"Da?" It was Fergus who first recognized Uilliam, and even he wasn't certain.

The man who sat waving weakly from the small oared skiff was a near-ghost of the burly Scot who had raised the three young men already breaking forward, crashing through the surf to meet him. His hair and beard, once a vibrant reddish blond, were now nearly white and so badly matted as to resemble the stringy, yarnlike wool of the mountain sheep. His cheeks were hollowed, and his eyes were sunk deeply into his skull. When they reached the boat and pulled it onto the shore beneath the castle cliffs, they saw, too, that he could not walk on his own. His leg had been removed below one knee, the result, no doubt, of the injuries he'd sustained on the battlefield at Culloden.

But he was home.

Fergus and Calum each took him, draping his spindly arms around their shoulders as they hefted him onto the shore.

One of the Welsh fishermen who had brought him handed him a crude crutch that had been fashioned out of a tree limb. He patted Fergus on the arm, nodded to Uilliam, and said *"Hwyl fawr!"* before climbing back inside the skiff and rowing back to the trawler that had anchored in the bay.

"What'd he say?" Lachlann asked him.

Uilliam looked at his youngest son and blinked wearily. "I dinna have the slightest notion. 'Tis been that way since we left Carlisle. Cudna understand two words they said. Nice lads though. Good ale."

Fergus asked, "How the de'il did you escape, Da?"

"I dinna have to. Haen't you heard? The Crown has issued an Act of Indemnity. They've granted amnesty to those who took part in the rebellion."

Calum stared at him. "You were freed?"

"Aye. One day I think I'm headed for the Colonies. The next they just drag us all out of that stinking hold and toss us on the jetty at Carlisle to find our way home, and me with my one leg. The local kirk took me in, fashioned me that crutch, and then found those Welsh lads who were headed for Amsterdam. They agreed to sail me home." He closed his eyes, took a deep and labored breath. "'Tis good to be home. I ne'er thought I'd smell the heather or see those hills again."

They took Uilliam to the castle and installed him in the chamber off the kitchen just as they had Kettie a handful of days earlier. M'Cuick set about immediately preparing his possets, while Fergus and Lachlann helped their da into the washtub and fresh clothes.

It was late, and the rain was falling hard against the windows as Calum, Isabella, and the others sat around the table in the hall, discussing the unexpected turn of events.

"Freed," Calum said, somehow unable to believe it.

In an apparent move to pacify those who had been outraged at the actions of the Hanoverian army across Scotland after Culloden, King George had decided to give those prisoners yet being held their freedom. Not everyone, however, was pardoned. There were names that were exempted from that amnesty—those whom the

Crown felt had had a heavier hand in inspiring the rebellion.

And one of those names was the Scot known simply as "The Adventurer."

"They do not know who you are," Isabella reminded Calum. "They only know the name of your ship."

"So then we'll rechristen her." He looked at her. "We'll call her *Maris*, maiden of the sea."

Isabella smiled. "I think that is perfect."

At the farthest end of the table, the duke was sulking, his face not the only thing making him look blue. "So it seems I'm not to have any adventure."

Bella stood, circled the table, and patted his back. "You've adventures to come, Da. You've a new grandchild coming, the first of what will hopefully be many."

"A grandfather! I'm too young to be a grandfather . . ." He shook his head. "It's all just such a disappointment. I mean I'm glad the Bain fellow is home safe and all, but I was so looking forward to an adventure." He looked up at his daughter. "It isn't every day a man gets to paint his face blue."

The duke, however, could never know that his adventure was yet to come.

It was several days later and Isabella was in the hall putting the finishing touches to a sketch she'd spent the morning creating. It had been a busy, bustling time while the men of Calum's crew, now free to return to their homes and get on with their lives, readied themselves to leave Castle Wrath. Their last task had been to repaint the hull of the *Adventurer*, giving her a sleek black coat of paint with her new name, *Maris*, emblazoned in gold across her forecastle. Mungo and Hugh had even made a figurehead carving of a dark-haired mermaid wearing a crystal stone. On the morrow, Calum and Alec would be traveling together with Isabella on her maiden voyage, sailing round Whiten Head to Durness and the home of the Mackay chief.

Isabella looked up and smiled when she saw Alec coming into the room. "Alec . . . have you seen Calum about? I was hoping to ask him if we were—"

Her words died off when a second person came into the room, looking exactly like the first.

"Calum?" She looked at one, and then the other again. "Alec?"

In order to put a final close to his time as a privateer, Calum had shaved his scruffy beard and trimmed his long hair, pulling it back in much the same manner as his brother. Now they were virtually indistinguishable. They had dressed alike, in the Mackay plaid, and even stood side to side in the same manner, watching her, and enjoying her uncertainty as to which of them was actually her husband.

She walked over to them. So they thought to play a game with her? Well, two, rather, *three* could play that game.

Isabella stopped before the first of them, stood on her toes, and kissed him, kissed him deeply and passionately, wrapping her arms around his neck and melting against him. She left him blinking when she stepped away.

Then she grinned, and took a step toward the other.

"Whoa, lass . . ." said the first, whom she already knew to be Calum from the color of his eyes. "I'm not of a mind to share quite everything with my brother."

Isabella laughed as Calum pulled her back into his arms for another kiss. She looked at him closely, rubbing her hand against the smoothness of his shaven jaw.

"Does my lady miss her pirate?"

"Nay, because he is still here." She flattened her hand against his chest, felt the pulse beat, the heat of his skin beneath the thin layer of his shirt. "You are still an adventurer in your heart, and you always will be, Calum. 'Tis one of the many things I love about you."

They turned when Fergus and Lachlann came striding into the room.

"What is it?" said Calum, already reading their dire expressions.

"We've just spotted sails. Past Faraid Head. 'Tis a man-of-war."

The English.

Isabella gasped. "Calum?"

Calum, however, had been expecting it.

"Get Mungo, Hugh, and any of the others who're still close enough to hear the call o' the pipes. Lachlann, you know where the arms are?"

"Aye, Calum."

"Good. You and Alec must go and start bringing them out, loading the muskets, priming the flintlocks. Get Hamish to help you. Druhan and Aidan can, too, but I dinna want them out here when the fighting breaks."

"Fighting?" Isabella looked at him. "Calum, do you really think it will come to that?"

"We've got to be prepared, lass. I'll do my best to talk them away, but if it comes to a fight, we will defend the castle. No' when the soldiers arrive, you must go down to the kitchens and see to Kettie and Uilliam. If it should come to a battle, I want you to promise me you will run and take them with you."

"I'll not leave you, Calum."

"Shh. Listen t' me no', lass. There's a tunnel in the back of the cooking hearth in the kitchen. It will lead you and the others to safety. Once you're away, I want you to head for Durness. Uilliam knows the way. Go to my uncle, the chief, and tell him what has happened."

Isabella was beginning to get very, very frightened. "Calum, no—"

He pulled her into his arms and held her. "'Twill be all right, lass. Trust me."

And she did. She trusted him completely. She just prayed nothing happened to him.

The next hour flew by on the wing of a lark. Isabella could do nothing more than stand pacing in the hall, watching as those sails drew nearer and nearer while men scrambled all about, setting up muskets and swords, hiding them behind doors and under tables should it become necessary to fight.

She stood at the hall window and peered through Calum's spyglass to the bay down below the castle cliffs. She could see the soldiers, having anchored their ship, cutting toward the shore in two small oared boats. They landed on the shore and started filing up the winding path toward Castle Wrath, their red coats forming a stark line against the sandy shore.

Isabella thought of Elizabeth, how she had fooled the English captain months earlier in order to help the Stuart prince escape to France. It was on that thought that Isabella suddenly hinged on a plan.

She quickly turned and went to find Calum.

Lord William Blakely truly hoped he hadn't been sent on a fool's errand.

When the young St. Clive had arrived at his headquarters, spouting nonsense about rebel pirates and Jacobites, he'd nearly refused to see him. He had, after all, received word just the day before learning of the Act of Indemnity that had been passed in London, thereby making his future policing of the area obsolete. He'd been given orders for an immediate and swift withdrawal, after which he was to return to England to await news of his next post. Lord William, for one, couldn't wait to quit the barbaric Highlands with its unhealthy climate and backward, Gaelic-spouting savages. Thus when his aide had informed him of St. Clive's sudden arrival and his wish to see him, his first inclination had been to ignore him.

It wasn't until St. Clive had threatened the involvement of his father, the Earl of Chilton, that Blakely had consented to listen to his tale. They had shared a bottle of claret and when St. Clive had finished, complete with Isabella's refusal of his proposal of marriage, Blakely had offered but two words to the young gentleman.

"Go home."

"What?"

"Just go home, my lord. Even if they were Jacobites, there's naught I can do any longer. The Crown has granted amnesty to the rebels. Unless one of them is the Young Pretender himself, I cannot touch them. So my best advice is for you to take yourself off to London, get back amongst the ladies and the balls and the gaming houses. You'll soon forget about the girl."

"But he is a pirate! There was a price upon his head of some twenty thousand pounds."

Blakely's ears had pricked at the figure. "Twenty thousand, you say?"

He could feign he hadn't heard of the amnesty in time. So Blakely had called together a small detachment of thirty men, and had headed for Cape Wrath, where he was now, climbing the steepest, most inhospitable path he'd ever seen.

When they arrived at the castle walls, there was a lad waiting outside to meet them.

"Good day to you, sir. Come along, quick. You nearly missed it, you did!"

"Missed it?" Blakely said as the lad turned and scurried through the doorway. He turned to St. Clive. "Missed what?"

They had no choice but to follow and did so, walking right into the castle courtyard. There was no one, not a soul walking about to stop them. An old saying flitted through Blakely's thoughts, something about being wary of enemies with open doors . . .

"So where are all these murderous pirates you spoke of, St. Clive?"

The young lord scowled and pushed past him. "Just follow me."

He led them across to the tower door, up the stairs, along the corridor, and straight to the great hall, where the doors were closed. The sound of voices could be heard coming from within. St. Clive turned to Blakely, smiled smugly, then stepped back to allow the commander to enter before him.

Blakely pushed through the door, shoving it open, just as the man standing at the front of the assembly said, ". . . and if there be any who know of just cause why these two should not be lawfully joined as husband and wife, let him speak it now or forever afterward hold his peace."

Every face in the room turned to look at Lord William Blakely.

"What is going on here?" he said, putting as much authority into his voice as he could muster.

A large man, with blond hair and pale blue eyes, stepped forward from the assembly to meet him. "Isna that plainly obvious, Sassenach? We're havin' a weddin'."

Blakely looked at the man and frowned. "Where is the man Calum Mackay?"

"He's standing at the front of the room, there by the hearth. He's the groom."

Blakely was getting a very bad feeling, but he'd come too far to turn back now. He marched forward, his boots clomping to the silence of the room, and came to a stop before the hearth where a man and a woman stood facing him. Another man, obviously the pastor, stood behind them. He was tall as a tree trunk and looking none too pleased at having had his service interrupted.

"You are Calum Mackay?" Blakely said to the groom.

"Aye."

"I am Lord William Blakely, commander in His Majesty's army. I've come to question you."

The man, Mackay, scanned the room around them. "I'm a wee bit occupied at the moment, my lord. I was just about to get myself wed."

The lady who stood as the bride came forward. "He sent you here, didn't he?" Her voice cracked with emotion.

"Who, miss?"

"Lord Kentigern St. Clive. He swore he would do anything, anything he possibly could to disrupt our wedding. And now"—her blue eyes began to well with big tears—"now he's done just that. Oh, Calum . . ."

She dropped her head to her groom's chest.

Blakely remembered another old saying, about the misfortunes that came to those who made a bride cry. He lowered his eyes. "I was told that you were the Scottish pirate they call the *Adventurer*." He glanced around at all the eyes staring at him in condemnation for having ruined this joyous occasion. "Apparently, I was misinformed. I beg you all to accept my deepest apologies."

He turned, and started to beat a hasty retreat for the door. Son of an earl or not, he would wring St. Clive's neck personally for this.

And then he paused having spotted something out of the corner of his eye, something that had him turning, crossing the room to the far wall.

"These paintings," he said. "Where did they come from?"

Standing by the hearth, Calum tried to maintain a sense of calm when he responded. "Paintings, my lord? Which paintings?"

"*These* paintings. They look very much like two paintings I purchased from a private collector on the Continent. They were stolen when the ship that was transporting them to England was waylaid by pirates"— he turned to face Calum—"by a particular Scottish pirate known only as 'The Adventurer.' I think, Mr. Mackay, you will need to come with me to Durness after all."

Calum slowly moved his hand toward his belt, ready to take his pistol . . .

"The paintings are mine."

Calum turned as the duke stood from the assembly to join him. He came to stand before the Hanoverian commander, his face no longer blue, but carrying an expression of haughty disapproval. "I bought them in Edinburgh. They are a wedding present for my daughter."

"And you are?" Blakely asked, clearly not convinced.

"The Duke of Sudeleigh."

Blakely's face registered his surprise, as well as his

immediate dilemma. While he might suspect that the paintings were the very ones he'd had stolen, and that Calum had been responsible for their thievery, he wasn't about to call a celebrated English duke a liar. "Well, I am apparently mistaken a second time," he said. "My apologies, your grace." He turned for the door.

He had nearly made it before St. Clive came rushing through. "What are you doing? Arrest them! All of them!"

It was then Blakely saw that St. Clive had pulled a sword.

"Put down your weapon, St. Clive."

"If you're not going to do it, then I will."

Blakely, however, had had just about enough of Kentigern St. Clive for one day. He looked at his men who stood waiting at the door. "Seize him."

Kentigern bolted, rushing toward Isabella who yet stood at the front of the room.

The soldiers pursued him, pouring into the room in a sea of red coats.

Calum's men, sensing danger, withdrew the pistols and swords they had hidden underneath the table, by their chairs, behind the hearthstone.

Isabella heard someone shout her name, and turned and stood, frozen, as Kentigern raced toward her, the blade of his sword raised, with a look of pure insanity twisting his face like the mask of a demon.

He is going to kill me, she thought as she stood there, somehow suddenly unable to move.

In the moment just before he reached her, Isabella felt herself being pushed off and away, sending her tumbling to the floor.

She lifted her head and recognized Calum. It was then

she realized he had stepped in to take the blow meant for her.

Isabella opened her mouth to scream at the very moment St. Clive's blade entered Calum's body.

"No!"

She couldn't breathe. She crawled across the floor, her fingernails scratching along the stones, clawing her way to where Calum had fallen. She reached for him, felt the wetness of his life's blood spilling onto her hands.

She watched him close his eyes against the terrible pain of the sword thrust. "Lass . . ."

Isabella lifted her head, crying out for someone, anyone to help. Her heart was pounding, choking her, her tears blurring her vision. "Please, God, no . . . don't let him die. Please!"

Already his body was trembling with shock.

No!

She saw her father through the sea of bodies that were scrambling around her. She cried out for him.

She saw at least a half dozen of Calum's men dragging a raging and screaming St. Clive out of the room.

Fergus, M'Cuick, Douglas, Lachlann, all raced forward as one.

Isabella was frantically ripping at her petticoats, trying to stem the flow of blood that was seeping from the slice in Calum's side.

"Bella . . ."

She looked up, saw Alec. "Alec, help me, please . . ."

But it wasn't Alec who was standing beside her. It was Calum, his hazel-colored eyes wide with concern. Which only meant that the man lying on the floor, bleeding from the sword wound, was Alec.

M'Cuick came with water, some cloths. He peered at

the wound, the flesh it had laid open. He sucked in a breath. " 'Tis a fearsome injury."

Isabella stood up, trembling as she watched M'Cuick tend to him.

Calum put his arm around her shoulders and held her.

"He saved my life," she whispered.

"Aye, lass. He did."

Some of the other men, familiar with such wounds, were shaking their heads, doffing their bonnets, crossing themselves as they muttered a quick prayer.

"Calum, he cannot die."

" 'Tis a terrible wound, lass. M'Cuick will do all he can for him."

"No." She refused to consider it. "We cannot let him die, Calum. Not like this. Please we must be able to do something!"

"Just pray, lass. Pray for a miracle."

A miracle.

And, suddenly, Isabella knew what to do.

She knelt beside M'Cuick and lifted the silver chain from around her neck. She held the stone of the MacAoidh up before her and looked at Calum. "You once told me this stone had been used to cure sickness by dipping it in water."

She reached for the bowl of water M'Cuick had brought, and dropped the stone into it.

The stone immediately flashed, like a spark of lightning. Isabella reached for the cloth, soaked it in the water, and pressed it against the wound to stem the flow of the blood. And as she held it there, she closed her eyes and said a silent prayer.

Epilogue

August, 1747

Isabella closed the door softly behind her.

The room that stretched before her was filled with shadows as the late-afternoon sun drifted its way off to the west.

It was a dark room, paneled in oak and lit only by the brisk fire that burned in the hearth. A basket stood beside the hearth filled with fresh peats. A worn Turkish carpet, its colors long faded, covered the floorboards beneath furnishings that were once grand, now weathered from generations of use. The room smelled of the books that lined its walls, aged and cracked along their bindings. It was a room that had seen grander times, that had been left behind by a new era just dawning.

Much the same could be said for its sole occupant, who lay quietly on the chaise that faced out onto the back garden.

"Is that you, child?" he said, and motioned to her from the shadows.

Isabella crossed the room, stopping just beside the chaise. "Good day to you, sir."

"Come." He patted the edge of the chaise beside him. "Come closer so that I might see you."

Isabella did as she was bid, smiling as the Mackay chief covered her hands with his gnarled aged ones.

"My nephew was right," he said, his rheumy eye still managing a playful twinkle. "You do have a mermaid's face."

Isabella lowered her eyes, smiled. "Calum likes to tease me . . ."

"Oh, but it wasna Calum who told it to me."

Isabella looked up. "Alec?"

"Aye. He says you must have just a wee bit of mermaid in you. You did, after all, save his life."

"As he did mine, sir," she said. "'Twas the stone's doing, not mine."

"Aye, but the stone would not have had any effect for someone who did not deserve its power. 'Tis why it ne'er brought anything but misfortune to those who sought to steal it from the clan."

Isabella simply smiled.

"Calum tells me you seek my advice in the decision of what you should do with the stone."

"I do, sir. I love them both. I cannot believe that either is the better choice over the other."

"Then the answer is clear."

"It is?"

"Aye. They shall both serve as chief when I am gone."

Isabella looked at him. "Both?"

"Aye. As you said, neither is stronger in character than the other, and together they can face any challenge that comes their way. It is how it should have been from the beginning. I should never have separated them as I did when they were born. 'Twill not be the same for their children. They will all live as one family. United. Together. And the stone . . . I think 'tis time the Mackay lasses kept it. Pass it mother to daughter instead of father to son. 'Tis better for it to be used for the healing. No longer for battling."

The chief was taken by a fit of coughing that had Isabella fetching him a glass of water from the sideboard.

When she came back to the chaise, she brought with her a small miniature portrait she had noticed hanging on the wall.

"Sir, who is this man?"

The chief took a sip of water, glanced at the miniature, and nodded. "That is my brother, Artair."

"Calum's father?"

"Aye. 'Twas painted just afore he went off to fight for King James in 'fifteen . . .'"

Isabella felt a shiver as she stared down into the suddenly recognizable face.

It was the same face of the man she had previously known as the Comte de St. Germain.

"It was him," she whispered.

"What is that, child?"

"The man who gave me the stone when I was in Paris—the man they call St. Germain. It was him. It was Calum's father."

Isabella ran to the door, pulled it open. "Calum! Alec!"

"You're certain of it, Bella?" Calum said when she told him the unbelievable news.

"Yes, Calum. Don't you see? It all makes sense now. Your father didn't die at Sheriffmuir as you believed.

Somehow he must have gotten away, and he escaped to France."

"Where he assumed the persona of the comte," Calum finished.

"But why?" wondered Alec. "Why not simply live in exile?"

"To protect you."

They all turned to the old chief.

"What do you mean, Uncle?"

"Your father knew if it was discovered that he was yet alive, this estate and all the lands of Mackay would have been forfeited to the Crown for his part in the rebellion. As it was, the only way we managed to save it was to have the chiefship assumed by me. As a supporter of the Crown, King George need ne'er fear the new Mackay chief raising an army against him."

"You just said *we*, Uncle," Calum said. "Who else made this decision to have you assume the chiefship?"

The Mackay looked at him. "Your father, of course."

"You knew he was alive, all this time . . ."

"But if you knew, why did you never tell us," asked Alec.

"That, my dear boy, is a question you must ask your father."

Calum looked at Alec and then to Isabella, who smiled and nodded in understanding.

"To Paris, lass?"

Isabella nodded and stepped into his arms. "To Paris."

And to a new adventure.

Dear Reader,
I hope you enjoyed reading The Adventurer. *As I finished*
writing, I remained enthralled with the idea of the
legendary charm stone, so much so that I began to wonder
what would have happened to it afterward, after Isabella
and Calum, after their children, generations on. I'm
thrilled to announce that I'm going to explore that idea in
my next novel, taking the Mackay charm stone into the
21st century. I hope you'll look for it in the fall of 2003.
Until then, here is a little hint of what is to come. . . .

Jaclyn

She'd been scrutinizing their most recent acquisition, a rare first edition of *The Tenth Muse* by Anne Bradstreet, when the call had rung in on the store phone.

"It's for you, Lib."

It was Rosalia, their Wednesday afternoon clerk, who spoke, poking her dark head around the doorway of the book-crammed office. She wasn't, however, her usual cheery self.

"It's . . ." She hesitated, bit her bottom lip. "Um, it sounds serious."

Libby didn't even ask who it was. She only fished for the receiver hidden beneath the nest of packing material that littered the desk beside her.

"Hello? This is Libby Hutcheson."

"Isabella . . . this is Dr. Winston."

From that moment on, and for the rest of her life, the poetry of Anne Bradstreet would be linked to her mother's death.

That had been a week ago. Libby was no longer sitting in her comfortable but cluttered office at Belvedere Books at 58th and Lexington on Manhattan's east side. Instead she was standing in the parlor of her mother's Victorian house, high above the Atlantic in Ipswich-By-The-Sea, Massachusetts. It was the same parlor where Libby had played as a child, had had tea parties with her mother on summer afternoons, and where her height every year had been chinked into the door-jamb with her mother's favorite paring knife.

Even then Libby felt her gaze unwittingly turning toward that doorjamb, giving in to a small smile as she remembered how she had always tried to lift her heels a little off the hard-wood floor to make herself taller than she really was. She re-membered, too, how her mother would always catch her and say "Flatten those feet, Isabella Elizabeth Mackay Hutcheson . . ." with the lilt in her voice that had remained with her long after she had crossed the ocean to America.

Libby had always hated the fact that she hadn't grown tall and lanky—and blond—like her friend, Fay Mills, who had become a runway model at the age of sixteen, had left high school in Ipswich to move to New York, and now had her face beaming out from the covers of a growing number of maga-zines. Instead, Libby was just *average*—average height, aver-age weight, average black hair and eyes that were more smoky than blue. She made an average salary, lived in an average stu-dio apartment on West 76th Street that needed far more work than her average salary would allow, and since she spent most of her time surrounded by musty, aging books, she wore aver-age clothes, comfortable khakis and chunky oversized sweaters that she ordered from the L.L. Bean catalog because she was too busy most of the time to go shopping.

"You'll ne'er be average to me, Isabella Elizabeth," her mother had always said. "To me you'll always be my one-of-a-kind. . . ."

The only child Matilde Mackay Hutcheson had ever had.

Feeling the now familiar sting of tears threatening to spill, Libby closed her eyes, took a deep breath, and tucked the memory back into the corner of her mind. It was then she caught the whisper of voices coming from the other side of the arched doorway.

"A shame it is, poor child."

"Yes, Libby's all alone now," agreed the second voice. "No brothers or sisters to comfort her. Not even a husband . . ."

It was Mrs. Phillips and Mrs. Fanshaw, two of her mother's neighbors who had always made it their business to comment on the business of others. Libby should have expected they would certainly have an opinion of this particular occasion.

"And how old is she now, Libby? Must be nearly thirty."

Thirty-one, Libby wanted to say, but decided to keep her presence unknown. The other one spoke again.

"Goodness, I was wed and had three children by the time I was thirty. At this rate, by the time little Libby finds herself a man, it'll be too late for her to have any children to leave this place to. And to think, all those bedrooms upstairs, empty still. Poor Matilde and Hugh never had any other children."

"I wonder if she'd be interested in selling the place. Charles Derwent had always told Matilde she need only name her price and he'd buy it from her. The view is simply the best anywhere on the north shore . . ."

Libby stiffened, a simmering outrage deafening her to whatever else her mother's neighbors and friends might have to say. Sell her mother's house? She couldn't possibly.

"What other choice will she have?" one of them persisted. "Living so far away now in that city?"

That city. As if New York was akin to Sodom and Gomorrah.

"Oh, yes," the other said. "Though she never let on, I know Matilde was simply destroyed when Libby moved away. And look how she came to visit less and less often these past few years, too. Poor Matilde. At her age a woman should have been surrounded by grandchildren, instead of sitting on that porch alone each night, staring out at the sea . . ."

Libby turned toward the front window, catching a glimpse of her mother's rocking chair, its wooden spindles bleached from years of sunlight and the sea wind. She felt an unpleasant shiver run along the back of her neck. Had her mother felt alone as they said? Abandoned by her for having moved to New York those five years ago? Libby thought back to the day she had told her mother of the position she had accepted with Belvedere Books, Manhattan's oldest and most prestigious antiquarian bookshop. It had been an opportunity she had only ever dreamed of, a chance to spend her days immersed in her love of old books.

Most of the time she wasn't even in the shop. She spent a

great deal of her time traveling to estate sales and out of the way shops, in search of only those editions that were most rare. She had an eye for it; it was the reason she'd been offered the job. And although she reasoned it was the travel that prevented her from making any real commitment to a relationship, Libby loved her job and wouldn't have it any other way.

Often her travels had brought her through New England, and she would stop and spend a long weekend with her mother, just the two of them. But truth be told, those weekends had come fewer and farther between in recent years. In fact it had been three months since Libby had last been to Ipswich.

Libby couldn't deny the fact that her mother had died alone, siting in that very parlor where she now stood, only to be found by one of the neighbors who had grown worried when Matilde hadn't shown up for the weekly meeting of the Ipswich Gardening Club. Dr. Winston, the family's doctor since Libby had been a child, had said that her heart had just quit. She'd had no symptoms, no episodes that would have warned of such a thing coming. He'd said it, Libby knew, to try to comfort her and ease the guilt obviously everyone knew she must be feeling. His kind words and gentle smile had done nothing, however, to lessen the harsh reality that Libby should have been there with her.

They were right. Matilde had had no one else.

"I'm here now, Mother," she whispered, even as she knew it was too late. Libby closed her eyes and waited out the emotions that were rushing through her like a flood wave.

Three hours later, the house was once again empty. Except for Libby, of course, who, after the last of the mourners had left, patting her hand and pitying her with their eyes, had lowered into her mother's rocking chair on the porch to sit. She'd wrapped herself in the weathered folds of the woolen throw Matilde had kept there, and watched the darkness of the night descend over the Atlantic horizon.

Sitting there while the sea wind blew in across her face, Libby pressed her nose into the scratchy blanket and breathed in her mother's soft scent. She'd never in her life felt more alone. Growing up an only child, her mother had always made certain Libby had never felt the isolation, always keeping her busy with reading or baking or repainting the kitchen, as she had done nearly every six months throughout Libby's childhood. Matilde had been more than a mother to her. She had been Libby's best friend, her closest confidante. Libby had never realized, had never once considered what her move to New York must have done to her mother.

Libby had been excited and young and ready to strike out on her own. And Matilde had never once made Libby feel guilty for having done it. She had taken whatever she had been able to get, those random weekends, those rushed phone calls whenever Libby had been particularly buried in her work, not even raising a fuss when Libby had had to cancel her last scheduled visit in order to attend an estate sale in upstate New York instead.

Libby had always intended to make it up to her mother, take her to Boston for the symphony or the ballet. Only the days had turned into weeks, and Libby just hadn't been able to get away.

Now it was too late.

Libby got up from the chair and walked the length of the wraparound porch to the screen door. She found a small sense of comfort in its familiar, strident creak as she opened it and headed for the kitchen. She made a pot of tea, taking the time to use loose leaves like her mother always had, and not her usual quickly steeped muslin bag of whatever happened to be handy. She chose her mother's favorite from the tea rack, a blend which she had sent to her from London each month, and even heated the china pot with a dash of boiling water like her mother always had before adding the leaves and filling the pot to steep.

While she waited, she opened the cupboard and started to reach for her favorite mug, a clunky oversized thing emblazoned with an image of the Statue of Liberty that she'd sent to her mother shortly after she'd moved to New York. But her fingers fell short of it, and instead reached underneath it to one of the dainty porcelain cups and saucers, painted with brightly painted flowers that her mother had always insisted upon using for tea. Libby gave into a smile as she splashed the steaming orange-brown brew into the cup, remembering how she used to badger her mother about them whenever they had tea.

"Teacups like that are for decoration, Mother. Not for drinking. They hardly hold more than a few sips."

Matilde had simply shaken her graying head. " 'Tis a far sight more proper than that basin of a thing you insist on drinking from."

Setting the saucer and cup, and its matching pot on a tray, Libby walked carefully up the curving stairs to her bedroom. But she stopped, and after a moment's hesitation, continued down the hall until she had reached the door of her mother's room.

It was not completely closed, so Libby had only to nudge the panel with her knee. It swung open easily over the gleaming hardwood floor, and Libby stood for a moment in the doorway, staring at the room that was awash with the moonlight coming in the tall windows. How many times had Libby spent the night with her mother there in that tall four-poster bed? It had been more often after her father had died when Libby had been just twelve. They would sit and Matilde would brush out Libby's dark hair, when it had been long and straight and pulled back in its usual ponytail. It was after she had moved to New York that Libby had had it cut to her shoulders—more in keeping with the style of a city girl, she'd reasoned—though she kept it simple, parted on the side and tucked behind her ear which had it flipping up a bit under her chin.

The china clinked softly as Libby crossed the room and set the tray on the bedcover. It was a high bed, made all the more so by the thick featherbed that layered the mattress on top. Libby used the small bed step and sank slowly into the down-filled covering. She was instantly enveloped by her mother's flowery scent, and lay there for several quiet moments, staring at the ornamental trim on the ceiling as the sea tide softly broke on the shore beneath the house through the open window.

Libby reached and clicked on the bedside lamp on the nightstand, took up the tea cup for a quiet sip as she eased back against the feather-filled pillows. Earlier, she had changed from her black suit into her favorite flannel lounging pants and oversized Boston College sweatshirt. She had pulled her hair up into an unruly ponytail and had removed her contacts from eyes that were red and irritated from crying, wearing her glasses instead. Somehow she could imagine her mother sitting up at some heavenly tea table, shaking her head in dismay. Libby had countless crisp linen nightgowns that her mother had given her each Christmas, but somehow they had always been too pretty, too pristine for her to wear, so instead they filled an entire drawer in her apartment, scented with a floral sachet and never, ever worn.

She finished the tea, poured another cup but found she wasn't tired, not at all. She should be exhausted, having slept little in the past week as she'd made the arrangements for her mother's funeral service and burial and met with the family lawyer, John Dugan, to discuss the details of the estate.

Even he had suggested she might sell the house. The truth was Libby didn't know what she was going to do with it. It was a big place, with some five acres of land that ran down to its own private stretch of shore. Leaving it to sit empty except for her occasional weekend visit seemed cruel somehow. But selling it went against everything Libby had ever been raised to believe. Her mother had loved the house. If she sold it, the land would likely be sold off in lots, divided up and developed. Dugan had suggested it would make a fine B&B, and Libby had considered it, but in the end, she'd decided not to jump to any decisions until she'd had time to properly grieve for her mother, and think with a clear head.

Restless now from the conflict of emotions that came with her thoughts, Libby reached for the drawer to the nightstand in search of something to read that might occupy her mind. Her mother always kept whatever book she was reading there, and Libby smiled as she recognized the weathered leather cover of one of Scott's Waverley tales tucked away inside.

It was from a set that Libby had given her mother for her birthday several years earlier, a complete Centenary edition collection that Libby had splurged on. This particular title was *Castle Dangerous*, one of her personal favorites, and Libby turned the book, looking for the usual ribbon that marked Matilde's reading place.

But it wasn't a ribbon pressed between the heavy vellum pages. Instead, it was an envelope, addressed to her, *Isabella Elizabeth*, in her mother's hand.

Libby felt her breath catch in her throat. She turned the envelope and pulled the glued flap free to read the letter contained inside.

My Dearest Isabella, if you are reading this then I am well and truly gone. Please don't despair over my passing. I have felt it coming for some time now. I have had a full and wonderful life, blessed with much happiness. My dearest happiness, my daughter, has been in having you.

With my passing, the time has come for me to tell you something of a family secret. Do not be angry that I did not choose to share this secret with you before. In time, you will understand. If you will look underneath the lamp on my nightstand, you will find a key. The box that the key will open is contained in my armoire, on the very bottom, behind my slippers. Find it. Look at what it holds, and I promise everything will become clear to you. Just know that I love you more than I ever thought it was possible to love.

It was signed simply "Mother."

Libby set the letter aside and slid off the bed. She lifted the lamp, found the key just as her mother had written waiting underneath. It was a small key, the old sort of skeleton style, the sort now only used for decoration. She walked to the tall mahogany armoire and opened its double doors. Again she was overwhelmed by her mother's scent, as if she was standing right beside her. Libby searched the bottom of the compartment where her mother's blouses and skirts hung neatly, reaching to the back, behind her row of slippers until her hands found the shape of a small wooden chest.

Libby pulled the chest out, fitted the key inside its lock and turned. Her mouth fell open and she sucked in a breath when she lifted its lid to reveal a large crystal attached to a silver chain lying inside.

It was at once beautiful and mysterious, and Libby lifted up the chain, watching the stone dangle from it in the lamplight. It sparkled and seemed to grab the moonlight, reflecting a milky blue. How odd, Libby thought, that she had never seen the stone before, for she had often raided her mother's jewelry chest to play dress-up when she'd been a girl. She would have remembered seeing this stone.

Libby slipped the chain over her head and felt the weight of the stone around her neck. It was the most spectacular thing, the way the stone seemed to capture the light and hold it deep inside.

Libby searched further inside the chest and found a set of books tucked beneath the cloth where the stone had lain. She picked up the topmost one, and recognized her mother's handwriting on the pages of what revealed itself to be a journal. It was a journal of her mother's life, a journal Libby had never known her mother kept.

As the clock ticked through to the early hours of morning, Libby sat on the floor before her mother's armoire and read, read every page, learning of her mother's childhood in Scotland, before she had come to America. It was in those pages Libby learned for the first time that her mother had not been married to her father when she had come across the ocean as she'd always believed. She had met him in Boston, had married him some two years after she had arrived. Libby had been nearly three when the man she had always known as her father had officially adopted her.

Adopted.

Libby stared down at the paperwork. Her heart was pounding. Why? Why had her mother never told her? All of her life, Libby had only known Charles Hutcheson as her father, had never once thought that he might not be. If he wasn't truly her father, then who was?

Libby sifted through the documents, soon spying the letterhead of John Dugan, Attorney at Law, lifelong family lawyer who had made the arrangements those nearly thirty years before.

And she knew just where she would begin the search.

The search for who she really was.